HEART OF A DRAGON

The DeChance Chronicles Volume One

By David Niall Wilson

The lightning flashed closer, and he tossed in his sleep, nearly slipping from his narrow cot to the dirt floor beneath. Flashes of green and gold flickered from the darkness in that instant, and then faded. Salvatore blinked, hoping the strobed image would take a more defined shape in his private darkness, but it did not. Again, all he saw were the huge, yellowed eyes, glaring down at him. He felt the thing's hot breath, and knew its rage - its thoughts.

He stepped closer still, and the sky around him exploded in a sudden burst of light. The fury of the storm washed over the beach, drenching him; the lightning flashed so suddenly, and so bright that his sight was stolen. His breath ended in the sudden wave of water, ears pounding with the twined beat of surf and storm and the roar of thunder, rippling over the sand and melting to a mind-shattering scream of rage.

Salvatore reeled under the assault. He fought to close his eyes and blank the nightmare images from his thoughts. He fell back, landed roughly on the damp sand, and he saw it. The dragon reared over him in the strobed lightning illumination, its form and rage embedding themselves in his mind and soul.

Salvatore shook his head and whispered, "No," to the howling wind and roaring dragon, but there was nothing he could do. The dragon screamed and soared into the darkness, visible now, though barely. The sky melted from image to image as only dreams and nightmares can. Salvatore screamed then, too. He knew this Dragon, recognized the pulsing heat at the center of the creature's image. He wanted to cry out, to scream a warning, but it was too late.

Dedication

This one is dedicated to the editors at the old White Wolf Publishing house, and to Stephen Mark Rainey, editor of the late and lamented *Deathrealm* magazine, where the original short story—"In His Heart Live Dragons"—was published. Also my heartfelt thanks to Bob Eggleton for the use of the amazing dragon image on the cover, Voice Talent Corey Snow, who became, and remains, the "voice" of Donovan DeChance through all the audiobook editions, and to my brothers and sisters in Tiburon, MC, where I learned what it's like to truly belong.

Special thanks/acknowledgments

I would like to thank, first and foremost, the love of my life, Patricia Lee Macomber, and my wonderful children, Stephanie, Bill, Zach, Zane, and Katie, who put up with my enthusiastic outbursts about the world of Donovan DeChance on a regular basis, and who have always loved and supported me. I'd like to thank Kurt Criscione, the keeper of the series bible for this and other works of mine, all of which seem to constantly intertwine, David Dodd, for helping me turn Crossroad Press into something more than a hobby, and Aaron Rosenberg, for not only handling most of our print books—but for teaching me how to do it myself. Last but not least, I'd like to thank the words, and the magic, for being my companions in life.

"I do not care what comes after; I have seen the dragons on the wind of morning."

—Ursula K. Le Guin, *The Farthest Shore*

Chapter One

The park was quiet. Clouds scudded across the last remnant of the sunset, obscuring the muted reds and golds that clung to the skyline. The hum of street lamps kicking to life brought dim, yellowed illumination to the night, but it did little to ease the menace of the encroaching shadows. Instead it shaped them and drew them out in elongated patterns on the rolling hills and small forested patches of Santini Park. The hint of a storm crackled in the evening air, bringing the heavy, water and ozone scent of thunderstorm and the soft flicker, far off over the ocean, of lightning fingers stretching down toward the rolling waves.

On the East side of the park, other shadows moved. They slipped from alleys, slid from between parked cars and out of the darkened doorways of decayed apartment buildings and dingy warehouses. Eyes, teeth, jewelry and blades glimmered softly in the dying light. They crossed the street stealthily, entered the park in silence, and disappeared into its depths. No words were spoken, but there was fluidity to their combined motion, and purpose. They entered like a horde of vermin and disappeared into the darkness.

Moments later the silence was shattered by the thrumming roar of a single engine. It wasn't the purr of a sports car, or the roar of V-8 power, but the steady throb of a large V-twin, powerful and throaty. The echo of that sound resonated through the park, caromed off buildings and reverberated in the depths of alleys. The sound multiplied and grew, challenging the distant voice of the thunder for dominance of the night. The first bike slid down Holley St. and into sight at the edge of the park. Its single headlight sliced through the blackness. The rider rolled to a stop, the bike's polished tank and chrome reflecting the weak light of the street lights. He pushed the kickstand down and stepped off. He left the engine running.

Black hair swept over his shoulders, tied back with a silver clasp that caught the light when he moved. The clasp was a spider, long legs twined about his pony-tail tightly. His eyes were small chips of blue ice. His chest was bare beneath a cut-sleeve denim vest, faded and crisscrossed with stains and patches, chains and memories. He was lean and strong, long muscled legs beneath tight jeans ending in scuffed engineer boots ringed by a leather strap, decorated with chipped conches. From his belt a long knife swung, slapping lightly against his thigh.

He stood for a long time, bike leaning on its stand, the engine throbbing. He swept the park with a cold gaze that seemed able to cut through the shadows. Nothing moved but leaves sliding quickly across the grass, caught in the grip of the approaching storm. There was no sound but the bike, and the whisper of wind through the trees.

Snake waited another moment. He wanted to see them, to know they were there, and where, but he also knew that wasn't going to happen. They'd drawn him here, and there was no choice but to get on with it. He reached over and killed his engine.

He raised his arm and waved it in a slow arc. The sudden silence that had fallen when the engine died was broken by the soft throb of more engines. They ground to life and then rose to a sudden roar. The darkness was crisscrossed by brilliant slices of light, dispersing as the bright headlight beams sliced through it, and reforming as each passed, single file. They parked in diagonals, lining the edge of the park. There were dozens of them, each pausing for a moment, canting to one side to catch on its kick stand, then falling to silence.

The storm crept slowly closer, just off the coast and heading inland. The lightning flashes grew in brilliance and frequency. Snake stepped forward onto the soft turf of the park common, and the others filled in behind him, row upon row, tattered jeans, dark eyes, their weapons, belts, and leather gleaming with steel and silver. Each wore a sleeveless denim vest with the club's colors, blue and green dragons, whirling in a tight 69, devouring their own tails. The top bar simply stated the obvious: "Dragons MC". The bottom rocker, lined in blue, read "San Valences, CA."

A tall, dark-skinned man stepped up beside Snake and scanned the shadows. Vasquez was leathered and worn, years of sweat and road-dust sun baked into his skin; his arms were corded with muscle born of hard labor. His eyes were deep brown, nearly black, and his hair blew free and shaggy about his shoulders.

"They're out there, Snake," he said softly. "I smell them."

Snake nodded, not speaking. He breathed slowly and gathered his energy. He sensed them too, shifting through the shadows. *Los Escorpiones*. The thought of the young, violent Latinos made his skin crawl, but he knew he could show no sign of fear or weakness. The others could spare a moment to think of how their hearts were growing chilly and empty, or how their lives were riding on the actions of a few short moments. Snake had no such freedom. If he faltered, their courage would break, and they would be finished. Leadership always came with a price.

Along the line Snake heard the shuffle of booted feet, the soft clatter of weapons, and slowly the growing murmur of nervous voices. It was time. They were charged and ready and he couldn't afford to hesitate and let that moment pass.

He threw his head back suddenly face turned to the churning clouds of the approaching storm and screamed. His fists were clenched, arms curled up and back toward his chest and the sound rose, unfettered, from deep within his soul. At that moment the lines broke and the Dragons surged forward. Pent up rage, fear, and adrenaline burst in a flood of screams, merging their voices and their hearts with the energy of Snake's bellowed challenge.

As they thundered down the sloping field, shadows melted free of darker shadows and *Los Escorpiones* were on them. The storm broke at that moment, as if the heavens sensed the coming clash and wanted their rightful share of the fight. The lightning flashes were so closely spaced that the landscape became a strobed parody of battle, like a scene from a poorly written zombie movie.

The darkness was split by cries of anger and pain. Each flash showed pale, drawn features and flashing metal. Gunshots rang out, lost in rolls of booming thunder and echoed beyond them. Warriors crashed together, weapons drawn, lips curled back in the fury of battle and the terror of death. The scent of blood and screams of anguish washed away in sudden torrents of rain; the grass soaked blood and water into its heart and the sky was striped and marbled with the anger of the Gods.

The storm grew in fury; they slid and slipped on mud and the gore of the fallen, and they fought. Blades ripped soft skin and hard tendons. Gunshots, half-wild in the heat of the battle and the clutches of the storm, ripped through hearts and heads, spattering the ground, trees, and combatants with bits and pieces of those they'd called brother.

Vasquez towered over his opponents, a mountain of flesh and bone they tried again and again to scale. They clung to his shoulders and he shook them off. His blade ripped through limbs and organs with wild, uncontrolled abandon. Bodies flew from him, tossed, reeling from heavy blows, and his dark eyes shone, alive with reflected lightning and deep-seated rage.

There were too many. For each he knocked aside, two more slid from the shadows. And they were fast. It wasn't the speed of youth; Vasquez was fast. It was inhuman speed. They shot out of the shadows and tried to climb him like a tree, swarming like rats over something dead and rotting.

Vasquez bellowed in rage, kicking and slashing, leaving a trail of *Escorpiones* strewn across the park, but it wasn't enough. Those he left broken and sliced rose again as if nothing had touched them and launched at his throat.

About ten yards away, locked in furious combat with a young, lean Latino, Snake saw Vasquez going down. He cried out, called for help from the others, but there was none to be had. Snake brought his knee up suddenly, slammed it into the boy's chin and snapped back his head. The *Escorpione* fell, but as Snake turned and leaped toward Vasquez, another rose from the shadows, and another. Too many.

He wheeled and pistoned his fist into the jaw of the first that lunged at him and sent him skidding across the muddy field. Then he reached for the second and cursed as a sharp blade raked his forearm. He pulled back and kicked instead, knocking the boy's legs from beneath him. Snake pounced, grabbed his opponent's long hair and yanked back hard. He slid his blade in between ribs, out, and back. He let the boy fall and turned. Something was wrong. They were too fast. When they fell, they didn't stay down. It was crazy, and he had no time to figure it out. He fought for his life.

The wind picked up suddenly. Rain whipped into their eyes and blurred one body to the next and each face to the shadows. Snake couldn't see Vasquez any longer, though there was a rolling, flailing pile of bodies a few feet to his right. He spun toward them, caught a form moving up on his left and swung to grip the man's throat, only to find it was a Dragon he held. They met one another's gaze for a long moment, leader and follower, and then he released and turned away.

At that moment, Vasquez roared free of the mass of flesh that held him, flinging bodies to either side and swinging his huge fists like hammers, all thought of weapons forgotten in the heat of the moment. *Escorpiones* fell away like dust, and still it wasn't enough. As Snake cried out to the huge biker, his arm outstretched toward that wild, untamed face, the night exploded once again.

It wasn't lightning. A single gunshot and Vasquez's throat erupted. Blood spurted and splashed; his huge hands gripped the hole uselessly, his eyes shocked, voice silenced. The *Escorpiones* who'd swarmed over the big man only moments before scrambled back, wild eyed, not certain at first who held the gun, or who'd been shot.

"No!" Snake screamed, he leaped for his fallen brother, just failing to catch the massive body as it crashed to the ground. Rain and mud and gore coated Snake's hands and his jeans as Vasquez slumped at his feet. In the distance, the muted wail of sirens sounded, and Snake became aware, slowly, that it wasn't over.

He leaned in quickly to check for a pulse, but the ruined mess that had been Vasquez's throat relieved him of that hope. No way was the big man alive. Lightning flashed again, and Snake looked up, caught the rising, urgent whine of the sirens and shook the tears from his eyes. The *Escorpiones* were scrambling back, the approaching police driving them even more urgently than the scent of Dragon blood. Snake knew he had only moments to act.

He leaned down, turned Vasquez quickly, dragged the denim vest from the man's shoulders, and clutched it tightly in his hand. He turned and shook it at the sky. He screamed again then, in torment, and in rage, screamed to be heard above the voice of storm and sirens. The sound echoed, endless and powerful.

The Dragons knew that sound. It began the battle, and it ended it. Already they were turning from the last remnants of their private skirmishes, dragging their tortured and injured bodies through the mud, cursing and slipping, fighting to reach their bikes and the streets before the police arrived.

Snake hesitated. He didn't want to leave Vasquez like this. He didn't want to abandon the remnant of his friend to the city and the police and the reporters who would swarm over the park come morning. He wanted to spin back the hands of time and free himself of the pain, end the guilt and the huge, empty, gut-grinding pain of the reality at his feet.

He shook his head a final time, glanced down at Vasquez's inert form, then spun and raced to his bike. It would serve no purpose to be taken in and questioned. He had a greater responsibility, and though it ate at his soul, he would stand up to it; with honor.

The bikes were sluggish in the rain. Some of them wouldn't start at all, and were pushed down side-streets, obscured by rain and darkness. Snake kicked once, twice, and his engine ground to life. He gunned it, felt the throb of the big V-Twin, and wanted to just pop the clutch and slam himself and the bike, pain and responsibility be damned, into a building. He worked the throttle, revved the engine carefully to dry the distributor, and spun it in a quick skid that nearly bounced him off the curb before the tires caught. He roared up the street and slid down thirty-eighth as the cops hit the main drag at Laurel and Thirty-Sixth. They would find what they really wanted. No one moving and nothing but another mess to clean up. They didn't want to cuff and question in the rain. They didn't give a spit in the wind for the lives of any involved. Vasquez' bike remained, canted to one side and forgotten beside those of five or six of his brothers.

Turning toward The Barrio, Snake gunned it and shot recklessly through the storm.

In his dreams, Salvatore Domingo Sanchez shook. The wind whipped against the thin outer walls of his shed mercilessly, threatening to rip the tired old structure from its foundation and send it spinning away into the storm, which loomed like the maw of some huge, malevolent beast.   That is how his nightmare started.

Then he was walking down a beach. The soft sand beneath his bare feet, sifted through his toes and the salt-spray from the ocean teased his senses. It was dark, no moon, and no stars. There was only the beach and the roar of the waves crashing on the stones further out to guide him along the shore.

Circles of glowing light loomed through the darkness, huge and imposing. They did not flicker, as torches might, or pierce the darkness in long beams, like those of flashlights, or headlights. They glowed, hoarding their illumination, using it only to draw his gaze and thoughts into their depths. They were eyes. Salvatore shuddered as the outlines became clearer, and though he wished with all his heart to turn and to run, he could do nothing but pad slowly down that unknown beach.

The sound of the wind beyond the walls of his shed became the breath of something large and sinuous, and the rain, crashing in heavy waves across the time-worn walls and tin roof the scrape of talons on stone and sand. Salvatore clutched his dirty, tattered sheet closer about his thin frame. The glowing orbs grew in size as he approached until they filled his vision, and out beyond the crashing waves, lightning crackled against a backdrop of purest ebony. Salvatore concentrated during those flashes of light and tried to make out the form of what lay beneath and around those eyes. He failed. There was an amorphous shadow against the backdrop of pure darkness that was the moonless sky, but no outline, no structure that he could apply to make the thing more real, or less terrifying.

Salvatore's heart thudded in his chest, seeming to miss every other beat in its hurry to skip from one moment to the next. He tried to breathe slowly, but could not seem to fill his lungs at all, forced to settle for small gasps or air that served only to raise his heartbeat to a thundering pulse in his head.

The lightning flashed closer, and he tossed in his sleep, nearly slipping from his narrow cot to the dirt floor beneath. Flashes of green and gold flickered from the darkness in that instant, and then faded. Salvatore blinked, hoping the strobed image would take a more defined shape in his private darkness, but it did not. Again, all he saw were the huge, yellowed eyes, glaring down at him. He felt the thing's hot breath, and knew its rage - its thoughts.

He stepped closer still, and the sky around him exploded in a sudden burst of light. The fury of the storm washed over the beach, drenching him; the lightning flashed so suddenly, and so bright that his sight was stolen. His breath ended in the sudden wave of water, ears pounding with the twined beat of surf and storm and the roar of thunder, rippling over the sand and melting to a mind-shattering scream of rage.

Salvatore reeled under the assault. He fought to close his eyes and blank the nightmare images from his thoughts. He fell back, landed roughly on the damp sand, and he saw it. The dragon reared over him in the strobed lightning illumination, its form and rage embedding themselves in his mind and soul.

Salvatore shook his head and whispered, "No," to the howling wind and roaring dragon, but there was nothing he could do. The dragon screamed and soared into the darkness, visible now, though barely. The sky melted from image to image as only dreams and nightmares can. Salvatore screamed then, too. He knew this Dragon, recognized the pulsing heat at the center of the creature's image. He wanted to cry out, to scream a warning, but it was too late.

The Dragon wheeled once, roared its defiance into the face of the storm, and flipped to its back in mid-air. It hung there for a long moment, and then plummeted toward the sand and waves. Salvatore turned and crawled toward the surf. He wanted to scream again, but the image of the falling dragon had robbed him of breath once more. He whispered, low and soft. "No."

The sudden crack of thunder too close to the shed ripped through Salvatore's dream and brought him bolt upright on the cot, shivering uncontrollably. His sheet was drenched in sweat, and wind whistled through the cracks in the walls and tore at him, dragging goose bumps up to ripple over his skin. His teeth chattered, and his eyes were open so suddenly, and so wide, that he was momentarily blinded. He saw nothing but the final image of the dream. Nothing but the dragon.

He gasped and fought to calm his heart, and his breath. The dragon released his vision, but it was trapped inside him, thrashing and raging against the storm that was his mind. He glanced toward the doorway, wanting to rush out into the night, and to find out what had happened. The visions never came to him without cause

Slowly, Salvatore rose, pulled his tattered jacket down from its hook on the wall and wrapped it around the damp sheet. He closed his eyes, but sleep was very slow to come, and not deep enough to provide rest. He dreamed of the dragon until the sun reached soft orange-red fingers over the skyline to tempt him from his bed. Finally he rose, dressed, and slipped out the door into the fresh morning air, where he walked to Old Martinez's steps and sat on the cool concrete to wait the "Prophet's" arrival. All he could expect was a warm cup of tea and a slice of bread, but at least he would not greet the morning alone.

Chapter Two

Donovan DeChance sat by his fire and stared into the flames, lost in thought. He was a tall, striking man with long dark hair that washed back over his shoulders. His eyes – at first glance - seemed black, but they flashed violet if he turned his head just the right way. At that moment, he was idly stroking Cleopatra, his Egyptian Mau, and worrying over a problem that had haunted him for years. It seemed no more likely to be solved in that moment than it had in any of the other thousands he's spent pondering it, but he persisted.

The main room of his home was a combination library, den, living room and office. The walls were lined with floor-to-ceiling bookshelves so tall that there were rolling ladders attached to each to make the uppermost shelves accessible. Along the base of the shelves were crates filled with more books, manuscripts, scrolls and documents. The contents of those crates overflowed onto the floor and spread out to cover every horizontal space in the room with the exceptions of his chair, his desk, and the altar in the corner.

On the table beside him a tumbler of whiskey waited beside the slip of paper that had sparked his mood. It was a delivery notice – three more crates to arrive within the next couple of days. He knew he could find room for them along one of the walls, or behind his couch, but that wasn't the problem. Soon, something would have to give, and he wasn't ready to abandon his bedroom, or the few hideaways remaining to him.

When the phone rang he stared at it, at first unable to draw his thoughts back into the moment. He seldom got unexpected calls. For a moment he considered letting the answering machine handle it. He glanced at the crates and stacks of books and sighed heavily.

"Soon," he said, lifting Cleopatra carefully off his lap and standing. "Soon we will figure this out, Cleo, or you will find yourself sleeping four feet in the air on papyrus scrolls."

Cleo yawned, stretched and rubbed against his leg as he stepped to his desk and reached for the phone. Even the phone was old. It was black with an elegantly curved handset, and it looked out of place beside the wide, flat-screen computer monitor and the CPU.

"Yes?" Donovan said.

"It's Cord. I have information I think you'll be interested in."

Donovan frowned. He glanced at the fire, and at his chair, then back down at the phone. He considered chancing it and trusting his security, then sighed heavily.

"Not on the phone," he said. "Club Chaos. Ten o'clock."

"You're buying," Cord said.

The line went dead, and Donovan hung up. Cord was one of a string of informants and less-than-reputable denizens of the San Valencez underground who reported to Donovan regularly. The darker half of the city rested in a delicate balance, powers vying for control on all sides, new players dropping into the game unannounced, and Donovan couldn't afford not to remain current. He dealt in information and knowledge. His life often depended on knowing just a little bit more about things than anyone else involved in them, and so, instead of sitting and sipping whiskey as he tried once more to solve the conundrum of too many books and too few shelves, he turned toward the city.

"You'll have to watch the place for me, Cleo," he said. "I'm not expecting company, but we never know, do we?"

The cat stared up at him and licked its lips. The connection between the two was a deep one. If Donovan closed his eyes, he could watch himself through Cleo's eyes. He often wondered what the cat saw in those moments, but, once again, it was a subject for another time and place.

Donovan stepped to one of the few shelves in the room

that was not completely overflowing with books and studied a small rack. Charms and pendants dangled from metal hooks. There were vials filled with powder, rags and pouches, and an array of stones lined up in careful symmetry. He never went to Club Chaos without proper preparation, particularly when Cord was involved. The man was much smarter than he let on, and Donovan wasn't naïve enough to think he was the only beneficiary of that intelligence.

He studied the pendants carefully. He settled on an equal-armed cross in deep amethyst. It was set in an intricate pattern of silver with tiny carved characters along each band. He slipped this over his neck and dropped it beneath his shirt. He took a second group of green crystals that dangled from strong, thin chains joined by a loop at one end and dropped them into his hip pocket. He studied the rest of the shelf carefully, and then turned away. It was going to be a quick trip, and there wasn't any particular threat. He had his usual protections, and on any normal day they were enough. He just liked to have something up his sleeve for emergencies.

Cleopatra hopped up onto his desk and watched him with wide, baleful eyes. He stepped over and scratched her between her ears. She arched her back and pressed into his touch. Donovan smiled.

"Keep your eyes open, Cleo," he said. "I don't want any surprises when I get back."

Donovan glanced at the phone. He considered calling Amethyst. He knew she'd probably meet him if he asked her, and he'd feel better if someone else at least knew where he was. He shook his head, frowned, and turned away from the phone. He had no idea where his sudden paranoia was coming from, but he'd learned over a long life to trust his instincts, and though he didn't sense any particular danger in meeting with Cord, something felt wrong. No reason to drag anyone else into it, whatever *it* might be.

He stepped out of his door, locked it carefully, closed his eyes and set the wards. He felt ancient forces converge as he mouthed the incantations. The ornate wooden door grew unfocused, shimmered for a moment, and as he stepped away it took on the aspect of a more mundane frame – painted dingy white and stained from too many hand prints and boot toes over the years. Donovan had stayed in those rooms a very long time, and he'd made a number of "upgrades" – he liked to keep them to himself. He owned the entire building, though it would have been difficult to trace it back to him. It allowed him to make hidden modifications, and to come and go as he pleased, while appearing to those around him to be just another tenant.

He avoided the elevators and took the stairs to the first floor. Once there, he turned toward the back of the building. There was a maintenance exit that led to an alley behind the building, and he slipped through it quietly into the muggy southern California night. He stood very still in the shadows and waited. If anyone had been watching for him to exit, they'd follow. If anyone outside was waiting for him, he wanted to know they were there before making a move.

All that stirred were scraps of paper in the breeze. The alley opened on the street at one end; at the other was a solid brick wall. Donovan turned away from the street. When he reached the rear wall, he walked along it slowly, counting bricks. He touched the thirty-third from the right, on the eighth row from the bottom. The brick shimmered. Donovan stepped back and watched as the tombstone shaped outline of a doorway formed on the surface of the wall. Three stone steps led down into the darkness beyond the doorway, and he took them quickly, running down all three, back up two, and then stepping back down and pushing on the wooden door ahead of him. It swung inward, and he stepped through, leaving the alley behind.

The door closed behind him with a click, and he stood in a corridor. Stone walls stretched out to the right and left. Along those walls doors were lined up at even intervals, trailing off beyond his sight. The air was cool and dank and there was an odd, smoky scent in the air.

Torches shone at intervals along the corridor, but there was no indication of how long they'd burned, or who might have lit them. Donovan had discovered references to the corridor in a crumbling diary written by an early Californian explorer. It matched notes in ancient European texts, and at least one carefully preserved Asian scroll. All indicated a set of corridors, a nexus providing a central entrance and exit to a series of portals. The network was vast, and if everything he'd read was correct, all of those doorways might not open onto Earth. Fortunately, all of those he'd managed to open did.

There were lesser portals known to many of the denizens of San Valencez, but to his knowledge, Donovan was the only one to discover this older route, and he kept his secrets very close. Sometimes a secret was the difference between life and death.

When he'd discovered this first entrance, he'd purchased the building closest to it. The wall and the brick were an illusion – the steps that led down to the portals each had their own wards. His opened with a simple mathematical solution contrived of climbing and descending the correct number of stairs in the proper order. Others required more intricate keys and rituals. It was a mystery he'd only begun to unravel, but it had proven very useful. He believed that there had once been keys, possibly formed of crystal, but their location was lost to time

The corridor was ancient and powerful, and he never stepped into it without a twinge of nerves. Whatever power had created the portals and the corridor that joined them had stood for centuries, perhaps longer. The thought of how far they might stretch, and of who – or what– might share that corridor at any given time was sobering. It was also possible for magic – over time – to fade, or warp. He didn't think he wanted to be in the corridor when that happened.

Donovan walked slowly away from the doorway that led to his alley. As he walked, he counted the doorways on his right. He'd found that if he tried to watch the doorways on both sides, it threw off the count in some arcane manner. Fourteen doors down he stopped, turned to his left, and crossed to the portal directly opposite. He opened the latch and stepped onto a short stone stair that led up into the alley outside Club Chaos.

Chapter Three

The sky was dark with clouds. Drizzle misted the air and dripped down the glass windows of shops and diners. Neon signs blinked, flashing their multi-colored messages to shadow people on the streets. Donovan walked to the end of the alley and glanced up and down Hawthorne before ducking back into the shadows beside Club Chaos. There were other entrances, but they wouldn't take him where he needed to go.

There are cities within cities. What we know and believe we know about places and events is based on our observations, and experiences. The alley beside Club Chaos looked like any other alley; it was dark and littered with debris blown in by the wind. One thing set it off. Near the center, there was a phone booth. There was nothing remarkable about it, and unless you really thought about it, even the most logical question might not occur. Why was it there?

There was no reason for a phone to be located in a dark alley. It was unlikely that those passing on the street would see if it they needed it. It was even less likely they would leave the safety of the street lights and rummage in their pockets for money to make a call there in the shadows, particularly in a time when everyone from school children to the elderly had a cell phone.

Donovan glanced over his shoulder toward the street and saw that he was alone. He ducked into the booth, tucked the receiver under his chin, and dialed 360.

The phone booth was the entrance to the many facets of Club Chaos. There were levels upon levels to the place, each serving a different segment of the city's population. Live music played on most levels. There was jazz, reggae, rock and even swing in one of the older sections. Donovan wasn't interested in the night life, or the parties. Not this time, anyway.

When the booth spun, he stepped into a dark room lined with candle-lit tables. A polished wooden bar ran along one wall. There were no bright lights. There were no mirrors. It was a quiet place where sound didn't carry. Donovan closed his eyes for a moment, and then opened them to acclimate his sight.

A lone figure sat at the bar. He was tall and thin with long gray hair that spread out around his head like a nimbus of dirty string. He didn't look up from the tumbler of whiskey in front of him, but Donovan recognized Cord immediately. He crossed the room and took the stool beside him.

"Whiskey," he said to the bartender, "on ice with a little water."

Cord remained silent until Donovan had his drink and the bartender retreated. It didn't take long. They called this bar "The Crossroads," lying as it did somewhere near the heart of Club Chaos, but they might as well have named it "Discretion."

"So," Donovan said at last, glancing at Cord out of the corner of his eye. "You said that you had information?"

"You brought money?" Cord asked.

Donovan frowned.

"I never pay before I know what I'm getting. You've dealt with me before."

Cord slid his gaze sideways. The man's face was angles and slits. His eyes barely seemed to be open, and his mouth was set in a grim line. The informant's skin seemed to be stretched taut over a pointed chin and high cheekbones. There was no way to read his emotions, assuming they existed. He stared at Donovan for a moment in silence, and then turned back to his drink. He spun the tumbler slowly on the damp napkin it rested on and started to talk.

"There are things happening in the Barrio."

"Martinez?" Donovan asked quickly.

"Not Martinez. Anya Cabrera."

Donovan frowned.

"Anya has always been active in the Barrio. That's hardly a great secret."

"She has expanded her operations," Cord said. He turned to meet Donovan's gaze. "She has taken up with *Los Escorpiones*. They now participate in her rituals, and they are spreading their influence, challenging for territory."

"Voodoo is a very old practice," Donovan said slowly. "While I don't claim to understand those who find comfort in it, it's not inherently dangerous, unless there's something more?"

"Oh, there's more," Cord said.

The man fell silent. Donovan waited a moment for the rest of the information, and then realized they'd reached the turning point. Nothing more would be forthcoming without payment, and the only question remaining was – how much, and would the information be worth the price? He considered what he knew about Anya Cabrera. As long as he could remember she'd held court in one or another of the dark corners of the city. She had a shop that was open by day, selling candles and amulets, hexes and wards. Most of it was pointless and powerless, but she was a shrewd woman. Enough power trickled through her door to keep clients coming and going in a steady stream.

Cord wouldn't have called him if things hadn't changed. Donovan slid his hand into his jacket and drew a fifty from an inner pocket. His jacket was probably his single greatest asset. He'd designed it, adding pockets and hidden slits in the lining over the years. It was armed with small scrolls, scraps of parchment, pendants and charms. He also kept it well stocked with a variety of money in various denominations. Some of it was very old, some of it was from places far away. Most of it was green and folding and worked just fine in Club Chaos. He laid the bill on the bar, but closer to his own drink than to Cord's. He didn't turn to watch the man, nor did he worry that the money would be snatched. He waited, and after a moment Cord began to speak.

"The *Loa* walk a fine line between this world and their own," he said. "They enter when the wards are set and the moment is right. They walk and they talk through the living, and then they depart. That is how it has always been."

Donovan said nothing. He knew all of this, and knew that Cord was only building to his point.

"Anya Cabrera is summoning the *Loa*," Cord said, "but they are not departing as they should. Some have remained days, possibly weeks. Each time she holds her ritual, the portals remain open longer; the veils have grown thin. She controls them – the living, and the spirits who inhabit them. She plans a war."

"You have seen this?" Donovan asked.

Cord nodded. "Last night in Santini Park, there was a battle. You may have heard?"

Donovan nodded. He'd known there was to be trouble – two local gangs – but it hadn't seemed of importance. There were many such groups in the city, and quite a number in the Barrio. Power was a tenuous thing, and always under contention. Donovan kept tabs on such activity, but rarely found a reason to get involved.

"Anya Cabrera was in Santini Park?" Donovan asked, at last.

"Not in person," Cord said. "But she was also not far distant, and before the battle, there was a ritual. Some of those who fought were the possessed."

Donovan thought about this for a moment. When he didn't respond, Cord continued.

"Several of The Dragons fell. One of them was Vasquez. If the storm hadn't broken when it did, it would have been worse. Anya Cabrera intends to run any power from the Barrio that is not under her control. The boundaries between the Barrio and the rest of the city are already tenuous. This could be a problem."

Donovan nodded. He withdrew a second fifty from his pocket.

"Vasquez? You're sure? The one they call El Gigante?"

Cord nodded. He didn't look up as Donovan passed over the money. "If anything changes, I'll be in contact."

Donovan remained seated as Cord slipped off his stool and faded into the shadows. There was only one exit from the room, and it led into the phone booth. There were chambers in the back, and darker alcoves where larger groups could sit and speak in silence. No matter how loudly you conversed at The Crossroads, the sound didn't carry. The bartender continued quietly polishing beer glasses and watching the door. Probably, if one looked carefully enough, there were other exits. Donovan had never questioned it; he appreciated the privacy afforded, and was pretty sure he didn't want to tangle with whoever provided it.

After giving Cord time to make his departure, Donovan rose and left the bar. The alley was as empty as it had been when he arrived. He straightened his jacket and stepped out into the street, turning uptown toward home and blending into the growing evening crowds.

During the day, Donovan avoided the streets as much as possible. His striking appearance and slightly antiquated wardrobe tended to attract too much attention with the sun high in the sky. At night, a different city emerged. Those who were out and about had their own agendas, and their own concerns. They had no time to worry about a tall, lone figure walking quickly away into the city. Donovan didn't feel like taking the portals … he wanted to think.

His knowledge of Anya Cabrera, and of voodoo, was rusty. There had been no reason to pay attention to the old woman for some time; the more active power in the Barrio was an old man named Martinez, and Martinez was content to remain within comfortable borders. San Valencez was a large, sprawling city with many levels of apartments and ghettos surrounded by outlying suburbs. The Barrio was only a small, southern quarter, home to poor Latino families and bordered by the territories of two gangs – The Dragons, and *Los Escorpiones*. The form of Voodoo practiced by Anya Cabrera had a very small following in the city, but it was concentrated in and around the Barrio.

Still, Donovan knew some things. He thought back to other times, and other places far from San Valencez and California. Donovan had come by his learning through long travels and even longer nights of study. He'd visited Jamaica, and Haiti. He'd spent time across the border in the jungles of South America and the cities of Mexico. Back in his study he had books, manuscripts, hand-scribed notes he'd taken himself, and he thought that, perhaps, it was time to review some of them and refresh his memory.

There are many channels of energy running in and through the world. Places of power rested where they crossed, and lines of magic littered their trails. Each of them was the source of mysteries and rituals, but one thing was true of each and every one – there was a balance. Nothing came without cost, and there were rules. When the rules weren't followed, the balance became skewed, and when that happened it was no longer an individual concern. Imbalance in one quarter led to a similar imbalance somewhere else – equal and opposite. Donovan had devoted much of his life to the protection of that balance.

If what Cord had told him was true, Anya Cabrera was dangerously close to upsetting it. There was a reason the *Loa* only visited during particular rituals, and there was a reason they needed to return. While controlling them on this plane might seem simple and appealing, control, like anything that required effort, wore thin over time. The thought of those dark spirits walking the streets unfettered sent a chill up his spine.

He passed Forty-Second Street and turned, glancing in the direction of Santini Park. He knew that any evidence of the night's activity would have washed away in the storm. Probably the area was cordoned off by the yellow crime-scene tape and sawhorses, shadowed and forgotten by night. He turned away and continued toward home. He had reading to do, and he needed to get word and questions out to other contacts. It was looking to be a long, interesting night.

Chapter Four

Salvatore sat cold and miserable, huddled on Martinez'ss front step. When the old man finally rose and stepped outside, he glanced down and shook his head.

"How long have you waited here?" Martinez asked.

Salvatore shrugged. "I watched the sunrise."

"Come inside," Martinez said roughly. "It is too drafty here for my old bones, and there is tea."

Salvatore stumbled to his feet, and followed the old man inside. He glanced around, as he always did, intrigued by the small home's interior. Shelves and alcoves lined the walls. Each held vials of powder, rolled strips of paper, old books bound in worn, rough leather, feathers, candles, and more. There were symbols, or letters in a language that Salvatore was unfamiliar with, painted on the walls. There were rugs and tapestries depicting strange places, and stranger creatures.

The air was scented with herbs and spices, and other aromas more difficult to place. It was impossible to say why, but the simple smell of the place calmed him, and the thought of the hot, pungent tea Martinez always served helped him order his thoughts. He knew he would have to tell Martinez about the dream, but he didn't know how to start, or how to bring it to life in words. Sometimes the old man listened with careful interest, and other times he silenced Salvatore in scorn. The latter was rare, but Salvatore had a good memory. This time, he knew, it was important that the old man listen. The image of the fallen dragon, lying prone and lifeless on the beach, flickered through his mind.

Martinez glanced over his shoulder, and Salvatore dropped

his gaze. A moment later they were seated at the battered kitchen table. To Salvatore's surprise, the old man gave him bread and butter with his tea.

"You haven't slept," Martinez said.

"I dreamed," Salvatore said simply. "It was very real."

"Tell me," Martinez said softly.

Salvatore sipped his tea to clear his throat, glanced longingly at the bread and butter, and then did as he'd been asked.

"I was in another place," he said. "There was an ocean, and there were eyes; great orbs of light that filled the sky. I was frightened, but I could not look away. Then I saw it. It was a dragon, huge and powerful. It screamed, and I wanted to run, but I could not move."

"Did it see you?" Martinez asked. The old man's voice remained calm, but when Salvatore glanced up, the old man's eyes glittered with a light Salvatore had seldom seen.

"Yes." Salvatore said. "It turned to me, but then, something happened. Very suddenly it flew into the sky."

A sudden knock on the door interrupted Salvatore's story. He fell silent, uncertain what to do.

"Wait," Martinez said. "Eat your bread and drink more tea. We aren't done here."

Martinez rose and answered the door. Salvatore shook his head slowly to clear it of visions, and reached for the bread. His fingers trembled with hunger and he fought the urge to stuff all of it into his mouth in a single bite. He spread the butter over it evenly and took a small bite from one corner.

When Martinez opened the door, a large, dark haired man stood outside. The man's arms were covered in tattoos. His hair was long, pulled back in a pony tail. He wore jeans, boots, and a denim vest covered in pins and colorful patches. A chain dangled from his hip, looping back and fixing his wallet to his belt. Salvatore had seen the man before, though he did not know his name.

"What is it, Jake?" Martinez asked.

Jake's face was drawn and pale, and much like Salvatore, he seemed to have gotten little or no sleep. He held another vest in his hands, and he twisted and wrinkled the fabric nervously as he stood, as if on the verge of some outburst, or emotion.

"It's Vasquez," he said softly. "He's dead. Last night, in Santini Park..."

"I have heard," Martinez said, cutting the man off gently. "I did not know if was truly El Gigante, but I heard many died."

Jake nodded. "It was *Los Escorpiones*, but...something was wrong."

"Come in," Martinez said, stepping aside.

The old man glanced at Salvatore, then back at Jake.

"It is okay to speak in front of the boy. He does odd jobs for me. He will be...discreet."

Jake glanced at Salvatore, frowned, and then nodded. He stepped inside and a moment later, he'd joined them at the table. Martinez poured another cup of tea. Jake took it without even glancing at it and poured a long shot down his throat, ignoring the burning heat.

"This will sound crazy," Jake said. "but it's true. I was there, and I saw it with my own eyes. If it hadn't been for the storm, I doubt I'd be here to tell the story."

Martinez sipped his tea and waited. Salvatore ate his bread slowly and kept his eyes averted, pretending not to listen.

"I've fought *Los Escorpiones* before," Jake said finally. "They are snaky bastards, but they're just men. We've had something of a truce for several years now, but lately they've spread out and gotten too bold. We heard rumors that things had changed, but Snake figured it was just talk. Last night we were supposed to put them in their place. We didn't expect to win, exactly, just to reassert ourselves. If you don't make a show of power now and then, your borders tend to shrink. No one was happy about it, and the stories didn't help. By the time we got there, with the lightning and the storm clouds gathering, everyone was spooked. Everyone but Snake.

"At first it seemed like we were the only ones in the park. Then they were there. I swear to God they were not human. They moved faster than any men I've ever seen. I cut one of them at least three times, but he wouldn't stay down. Snake said no guns, but after a few minutes a couple of the guys pulled theirs all the same. It didn't seem to matter. They couldn't get off a clean shot, and when they did it was like shooting smoke.

"We lost five men, and another ten were cut or hurt. Just before the storm broke, they took Vasquez. I wouldn't have believed it if I didn't see it. He went down under a mountain of them, and we thought he was done, then he just erupted – rose up like some sort of crazed monster in an old movie and started flinging the little bastards off him like they were rats. It didn't matter. They took him down – and that's when the sirens rose. We took the colors from those we lost, and we got the hell out of there."

Jake paused for a moment then, catching his breath. It seemed as if the big man might break down, but he got control of his voice, and he went on.

"I'm not one to run from anything, but I'll tell you. I was glad to turn my back on that fight – happy to get away with my life."

He glanced down then and saw that he'd twisted the vest in his hands into a tight roll. One of the pins had popped off – a small chrome dragon. He slowly released his hands, then picked up the pin and stared at it.

"He was a good man," Jake said. "Vasquez was a mountain. Snake depended on him, and…"

He fell silent then, and Martinez spoke at last.

"I understand. I, too, have heard the stories. I believe there is a real danger, and I will do what I can to help. That is why Snake has sent you to me, yes? For my support?"

Jake nodded. He glanced around the room dully.

"You've known me a long time, Martinez. You know I've never much believed in all of this," he swept his arm out to encompass the shelves and the walls. "I believe in what I know, and I don't' know … this. At least, that's what I thought. Now…"

He trailed off. Salvatore ate the last bite of his bread and washed it down with a sip of tea. He turned as Jake slowly unrolled the vest he'd been bending and twisting out of shape. It unfurled onto the edge of the table, and Salvatore stared. His hands shook, and a bit of the tea in his cup splashed onto the table. Jake and Martinez turned to him, and he lowered his eyes once more.

"I am sorry," he said softly. "I am very tired."

Jake only glanced at him for a moment, and then returned his attention to the vest in his hands. Salvatore felt Martinez's gaze remain on him for a moment longer, but he didn't meet it. He couldn't get the image of the vest on the table out of his mind. He'd seen it before – and he knew of the man who'd worn it. His heartbeat sped, and he did not try to drink again, fearing another spill.

Martinez broke the silence.

"Tell Snake that I will do what I can. What is happening affects us all, and we must stand together. Tell him to send word to the other clubs...the smaller ones. They will already know that something is wrong, and I believe they will offer support. Tell them all to keep their eyes, and their ears open. Anything and everything they learn about these others – *Los Escorpiones* – I need to know."

"The police took him," Jake said. It was hard to tell if he'd heard what Martinez said. He was staring at Vasquez's colors. "His body won't be released immediately – his family is trying to get control of the remains – and to arrange services. You'll come?"

Jake glanced up then, to gauge Martinez'ss reaction.

"Of course," the old man said. "I will come, and I will help with the preparations. I have contacts with the authorities as well...I will see what I can do to speed the release of his remains. I am very sorry for your loss. I have known the man you call Vasquez since his mother named him Pepe twenty years ago. I knew her mother as well."

Jake frowned, as if trying to calculate how old that would make Martinez, or whether to believe it was true. He rose slowly.

"I'll tell Snake what you've said. It will ease his mind, I think. I'm sure he will come to you – to talk."

Martinez nodded. "I am always here," he said. "I'll be waiting."

Martinez rose and saw the bigger man to the door, closing it behind him. Then he returned to the table and sat.

"What did you see?" he asked abruptly. "When you spilled your tea?"

"I know that vest," Salvatore whispered. "He is El Gigante – one of The Dragons. I saw him – I mean…" Salvatore fought for the right words. His face flushed; he knew it would sound strange – that Martinez might not believe him. "I have seen his dragon."

"Last night, you mean?" Martinez said. He wasn't asking. "You saw it in your dreams; you saw him die."

Salvatore nodded. "Yes." He glanced up. "I couldn't save him. I couldn't help him. I could only watch, and I was afraid."

"There was nothing you could have done," Martinez said. "There are powers at work – powers you know nothing about. Still, you were there – and you saw. That is something that few have ever been able to accomplish. There may yet be a way that you can help. The others like Jake – they are all Dragons. Do you understand?"

Salvatore did understand. He'd dreamed of the dragons more than once, seen them soar and heard them scream, but always at a distance. Salvatore walked the streets, at times, running errands for Martinez, or just searching for food. He saw the Barrio's Dragons roaring past on their glistening bikes, parked outside local bars, meeting in the park. He knew where their clubhouse was located, and when he saw the dragons – the real ones – he always knew which of them they were connected to. He didn't' know how he knew, or why he saw them when no one else did – but he knew Jake's dragon as well as that of the fallen giant, Vasquez.

"I have seen them," he said softly. "I have seen many dragons…but I don't know how to help."

"You still draw?" Martinez asked, changing the subject to quickly Salvatore was confused.

"Yes," he said.

"Do you paint?"

"A little," Salvatore said. He was shy about his art, uncertain what others would think. He kept it locked away most of the time. "I have little paint. I have made some canvas by cutting scraps and cleaning, but it is hard."

"I will get you the canvas, and the paint," Martinez said. "Go and draw. Draw the dragons as you've seen them. I don't understand it completely yet, but you have a part to play before this is all through."

Salvatore gulped the lukewarm remnant of his tea and rose. He started for the door, but Martinez called out to him.

"One more thing," the old man said.

Salvatore turned.

"Stay clear of Anya Cabrera and *Los Escorpiones*. If you hear anything, or see anything, come straight to me."

Salvatore nodded. He slipped out the door, already thinking of his pencils, and what he would draw. If was good to have something to concentrate on – something other than the dying dragon on the cold sand of another world.

Chapter Five

Martinez stood for a long time in his doorway, watching as Salvatore disappeared down the street. He would have taken the boy in long before and begun the long, arduous training he knew was a part of both their futures, but there were other matters that had to be dealt with first. He only hoped they both survived.

When he realized that he'd been standing alone in the doorway watching an empty street for too long, Martinez heaved a heavy sigh, stepped back inside, and closed the door. There was work to do, and he hoped that he wasn't too late for it to matter. He'd had reports for some time that Anya Cabrera had stepped over the boundaries of common sense, but this was the first actual confirmation. The descriptions of the battle, and of *Los Escorpiones* left nothing to the imagination. There were forces unleashed in the Barrio, and they needed to be returned to their rightful place before it was too late.

Martinez scanned the shelves above his table and finally pulled out a tall, oversized leather volume from between two others that were almost identical. He lifted the large tome easily, his wiry strength belying his slender, aged frame. He might be old, but there was a lot of life left in his bones. More than most would credit.

Standing only a little over five feet tall, and weighing in at only about a hundred and forty pounds, Martinez did not cut an imposing figure. His hair was long and gray, wisping about his head like a silver nimbus. He wore a white cotton shirt and ancient dungarees. His feet were encased in sandals so old they looked like they were formed by bands of dirt. On the street he blended into the background, drawing little or no attention – unless you knew him.

His eyes were the key. They were grey and bright like chips of ice. There was a power in their depths that was undeniable. If you got close enough to meet that gaze, you realized that your first impression had been very, very wrong. Whatever the old man might be, he was not weak. Among the inhabitants of the Barrio he commanded the respect due a force of nature.

The book he'd pulled from the shelf was old and brittle, and Martinez handled it with care, separating the pages with one long fingernail and sliding them open. He knew what he was looking for, but it had been a very long time since he'd needed it. So long, in fact, that he couldn't clearly recall the year. The book was written in thin, spidery script. There were incantations, recipes, symbols and wards. He hesitated over each entry; it was good to keep them all in mind, and to know where they could be found. There was too much to know for any one man to remember, so he refreshed his mind when he could.

Finally, he reached the page he was looking for. Brilliant designs were scrawled across the yellowed paper. Their color was vivid, like the illuminated script of ancient monks. Most of the pages in the book were black and white –simple script and symbol with as little decoration as possible. This page was their antithesis. Martinez traced the designs on the page and stared at the colors.

For all the intricacy of the designs, there were very few colors. Three in all. Red, Blue, and Yellow. The primary colors. The colors of all that is real. Everything else, he knew, was a shade – a variant. Three was a powerful number, and these shades – these particular colors – were powerful as well. There were things one could do to enhance their potency. Famous works of art had shared the secret – works of literature through the ages had benefited from illustrations a bit more perfect than others. The magic was not always in the hand wielding the pen. Sometimes the colors spoke for themselves.

Martinez had watched Salvatore draw. He'd watched the

boy wield over-sized bits of chalk and bring things to life on
the sidewalks of the Barrio and on the walls of local buildings.
There was innocence about him, and a power few suspected.
Martinez knew that Salvatore almost never drew just for the
joy of his art. He drew because he was compelled. He drew
to drive the images and demons of his dreams from his mind.
He had begun, even at his young age, to peer into the truths of
other worlds. He saw things that others did not, and what he
saw made no sense. Instead of going crazy from this pressure,
Salvatore had learned to draw. The art was his power – his
strength. Martinez knew he would have to serve as guide.

He worked his way around the room, gathering the items
he'd need. He took a dash of powder from one vial, some
leaves that he crushed to dust with a mortar and pestle, a few
drops of brownish liquid, and a scrap of parchment that he
scrawled a series of symbols across, and then burned to ash.
He was methodical and thorough, coming back to the book
often to check details and compare his gathered ingredients to
those listed. After some time and work he has everything he
needed, each piece of the arcane puzzle carefully packaged in
plastic wrap, or a vial. He rolled all of it together in a soft bit
of velvet.

There was a cupboard above his sink. Martinez opened it,
took out an old, cracked pitcher, and slid aside two glasses. He
stretched up and tapped three times in the center of the board
at the rear of the top shelf. The board tipped out into his hand,
and he caught it deftly. He tucked his package in behind it
and then pressed it back into place. Once it was secure, he slid
the glasses in front once more and lifted the old pitcher back
into its place. He didn't think anyone would be watching …
not yet … but it was never too soon to take precautions.

He closed the cupboard, and then traced a circular symbol
on the wooden door with one finger. When it was complete,
he blew on the spot, then turned and spoke a single word once
each to the north, east, south and west, before returning to
the table and closing the book. He dusted it carefully with
a rag from his pocket, and then placed it back on the shelf
where he'd found it, adjusting those on either side so that the

three matched perfectly. Sometimes, he knew, the best way to disguise a thing was to leave it in plain sight where it wasn't expected.

There was nothing more he could do on his own. He had everything he needed for the base color – the primary red. What he needed went beyond that into variances and shades, and for that he needed information. There was only one to whom he could go to get what he wanted, and he wasn't looking forward to asking. The man who held that information wasn't an enemy, exactly, but neither was he a friend. There was a bad memory shared between them, and even if he got past that, the man would have to be convinced. There wasn't much time; Martinez would have to be quick in the convincing.

The sun had risen nearly to the center of the sky. Stripes of light glinted through the battered shades on his windows. Considering the waves of heat rising from the street, it should have been sweltering inside, but it remained cool. The temperature, in fact, was exactly what it had been when Martinez dropped off to sleep the night before, and when he woke in the morning. Just as with Martinez himself, there was more to the old home than met the eye.

He didn't need to live in these tiny quarters – he could easily have afforded a much larger place. He could also have gotten plenty of servants from the ranks of the poor families inhabiting the Barrio. It wasn't the kind of thing that mattered to Martinez. He had other concerns, and he was as comfortable as he needed to be. The rudimentary dwelling and simple lifestyle kept him sharp.

Out on the street the throbbing roar or engines rose, and he stepped to his window. Four motorcycles rolled past slowly. Martinez saw the colors of The Dragons on their back, but he didn't recognize this group. They weren't from the Barrio, but had come from deeper in the city to pay their respects. Vasquez had been well liked – almost a legend for his strength and size. He would be missed, and the Dragons would not take his loss lightly – or without retaliation. The others would have their friends and comrades as well. The Barrio did not take death lightly. The storm clouds had passed, but the Martinez knew that he stood in the eye. There was more to come, much more, and worse.

When the sound of the passing bikes had dulled to a low rumble, he opened his door and stepped into the street. He turned toward downtown and began walking toward the home of Donovan DeChance.

Chapter Six

Tucked away behind the Four Brothers Cantina on a dead end street barely wider than an alley, a dark shop faced out from beneath colorfully painted canvas awnings. Beaded chains dangled in front of the windows. Crosses and crystals glittered in the dim light that managed to filter in through from the street. Candles softened by the warmth of the sun canted at odd angles and hid behind scraps of dark velvet and an array of odd, featureless dolls.

A visitor to Anya Cabrera's shop might have been reminded of New Orleans. All the stereotypical paraphernalia of voodoo, witchcraft, and Santeria lined the shelves. Milky glass candle holders with pictures of the Virgin Mary and the various saints stood in rows on shelves above others lined with books and small statues. The air was filled with the aroma of dozens of different types of incense. Tiny bins of crystals, spices, herbs and arcane ingredients were tucked up under the bottom shelves and covered the countertops.

There were bamboo chimes above the door that announced visitors and more beaded curtains that hid secluded, deeper alcoves from sight. If you entered through the front of the shop, that is what you saw. For tourists or those wandering blind, it was a quaint, sort of spooky attraction where you could pick up some strange incense and a voodoo doll to put on your desk at work and name after your boss. For the locals, those who believed, the candles and herbs and small spells chanted over, spat on and sealed in wax were an important part of life.

There were other ways in and out of the shop, and it wound back through a labyrinth of passageways, curtained rooms, and storerooms. No one knew how long Anya had inhabited that place, but the deeper in you got, the more it resembled a nest, or a hive.

As the sun began its slow descent toward the ocean beyond the city, a lone figure made the turn into the short street. He did not look behind him, or to either side. His dark hair was slicked back over his ears and tied with a leather thong in back. His tattooed arms jutted from the chopped off sleeves of a black denim jacket. On the back of that vest a scorpion was embroidered in brilliant green and gold. Hector Alvarez walked with a slow, confident stride, his movements fluid and graceful.

He entered the shop and turned to the counter running along one wall. There was no one seated behind it, and he stared for a moment, growing very still. He turned and scanned the shelves and the beaded passageways leading back into darkness, but nothing stirred. He didn't want to call out. There was an ancient brass bell lying on the counter, but he had no intention of ringing it. He had been invited to this meeting – he wasn't about to let that invitation be converted to a summons.

"May I help you?"

The words fell like the tinkling of a bell, soft, but clear. Hector spun back to the counter. Seated just beyond it, in clear sight, a slender woman with deep, brooding eyes watched him calmly. Her long, dark hair was woven into small braids and decorated with tiny silver caskets. They jingled when she moved her head. Hector glared at her and stepped closer.

"I'm expected," he said.

She watched him, unimpressed. She shook her head and the silver caskets jingled. At the sound one of the sets of beaded curtains parted and two men stepped through. They were nearly identical, black as if they'd been carved from twin logs of ebony, bald, with eyes that glinted like chips of obsidian. They wore armbands of gold in the shape of entwined serpents, and large gold pendants on chains dangled from their necks. They didn't speak. One stepped through and off to one side, the other held the curtain open with a massive arm.

Hector turned back to the girl behind the counter. He knew

her, or, he knew of her. She was one of several apprentices to Anya Cabrera. Her name was Kim, and she'd been working in the shop since she'd been a very young girl. No one ever saw her on the streets, except running errands in the market. No one knew where she'd come from, who her parents were, or how she'd ended up in Anya's care. The one thing Hector knew for certain – and he knew this because, on a previous visit, he'd passed the girl's rooms and seen it with his own eyes – she slept in a coffin. Her furniture was made of piled grave markers and wooden caskets of every shape and size, molded and re-designed into shelves and cabinets. Hector had caught only a short glimpse through dark curtains, but in that moment he'd seen the girl rise from her...bed. The image had burned itself into his memory, and now, trying to meet her stare – the stare of a mere girl – his blood slowed and expanded like ice in his veins.

She held his gaze a moment longer, and then nodded toward the two men, and the passage beyond.

"Raoul and Stephen will escort you," she said.

Her voice barely rose above a whisper, but it carried. He turned toward the passageway, squared his shoulders, and brushed past the two men. He wanted very much to look back and see if she was watching him, but he controlled the urge. He was afraid that if he turned back, she would not be there, disappearing as quickly as she'd appeared. Hector's face was flushed, and the blood pounded through his veins. He did not like being toyed with. He was the President of *Los Escorpiones* – a powerful man in the Barrio. The old woman was powerful as well, and she had proven an important ally, but he could not show weakness. He'd come alone, but there were others watching. They filled the streets beyond the shop, waiting for a sign, or for his call. They would descend like an avenging army at the first sign of trouble, but despite this knowledge, Hector prayed it would not be necessary.

He wasn't worried about Raoul or Stephen. Hector always packed heat, and he was no slouch in a fight. It was this place, this dark, rat-hole with all its odd turns and shadowed rooms. There was no way to know, once you'd taken the first half dozen corners, which direction you were heading. There were other ways out – he knew this because he'd been escorted out by at least two of them over the years, but he was certain if he had to find any of them on his own, he'd be lost for days. Maybe forever. Things in Anya Cabrera's den were not as they seemed, and he suspected, though it made no sense, that they were not always the same, either. Not in the way the streets of the Barrio were always the same, or the lines on his hand.

Raoul led the way down a long, narrow passage. They turned left twice and right at least once. Ahead Hector saw a light. They headed straight for it, and moments later stepped into a large room with rounded edges. The walls were covered in tapestries, and the floor was carpeted in some sort of lush, green shag that resembled grass too long denied the intimacy of a mower. The air was heavy with the scent of Sandalwood, though the smoke was mixed with other more subtle aromas and too thick to be enjoyable. On the far side of the room, seated in a large, ornate chair decorated with red satin and gold gilt, Hector saw Anya Cabrera. From where he stood it was hard to make out details, but despite this her eyes glittered as she watched him. Nothing else in the room would focus, but he saw those eyes clearly.

Hector crossed the room. His feet felt heavy, and his legs were sluggish, but he forced them into motion. He knew it was a test. Everything with Anya Cabrera was a test. He had no intention of failing it. He told himself, as he had on so many other occasions, that she was only a woman. His mind flitted briefly back to Santini Park, and the storm. He saw dark figures moving with incredible speed. He heard the screams and the cries – not those of a normal battle at all, but of something darker.

"You are punctual," Anya said, breaking the silence. "It is a good trait in a young man, and so rare."

"I do not like to waste time," Hector said. He managed to keep his voice steady. "I have the report you requested on our – encounter – with the Dragons." He fell silent for a moment, but when she didn't answer, he continued. "I also have concerns."

Anya arched one eyebrow. She smiled, but there was no

warmth or humor in the expression.

"Tell me," she said. "Then we will talk."

Hector did. He told her how the Dragons had arrived in a roar of chrome and throbbing engines. He told her that Snake had been present, and about Vasquez, the fallen giant. He also told her about his own men, moving like the shadows of bolts of lightning; rising when they should have been dead, fighting on against overwhelming odds like demons and swarming like hordes of vermin. As hard as he tried to prevent it, his voice shook when he told of the storm breaking, and their retreat. He'd gathered his men together, moving like wraiths into the alleys and darkened streets. The Dragons had left their dead and fled. *Los Escorpiones* had lost no one. Not a single casualty.

"This is a problem?" Anya asked softly.

"There are no dead," Hector replied, "but neither do they all live. Two of my men, Paulo and Bernini, have not spoken since the battle. They sit, and they stare, and they do not move. They are like empty shells. Several others stare into shadows with wild eyes, as if they sense things just out of sight, but can never quite find them. I left no men behind, but at least five of those who follow me are as good as dead – possibly worse."

"They will return," Anya said. "You will bring them to me, and leave them. When the time comes – when you need them to fight – they will be by your side. It is a promise."

Hector had a lot more on his mind. He wasn't thinking so much about the next time he needed the men to fight. Paulo was his cousin. Paulo's wife and children were sitting at home with a father who would not talk to them and could not see. Bernini was Hector's second in command. It was difficult enough to maintain control over the volatile ranks of *Los Escorpiones* without having to lose his right hand man. He said none of this because he was certain she already knew it, and because to do so would be to hand her knowledge she could use against him.

"The Barrio will be yours soon," Anya said. "Our people will overrun all opposition; none will walk the streets without our permission. Victory, in a war like this, never comes without cost. Are you unhappy with the services I have provided?"

"You know that I am not," Hector said. "I only question

the use of my men as something…less. I have stood with them, shoulder to shoulder. I have shared their pain and broken bread with their families. They follow me because they trust me to lead them well. They will not trust me if I turn them into…"

"Yes?" Anya said, her voice almost a purr. "Turn them into what?"

"Diablos." Hector spat. "When I fought last night, it was not men at my side. No one moves that fast. No one walks away from a knife in the gut as if it never happened. I do not know what you did to them, but I know that it was wrong."

Anya Cabrera unwound herself from her seat like a snake, her movements dark and sinuous. Her hair was long and streaked with gray. She wore a silk gown that draped to the floor, sliding over her hips and cut very low at the neckline, where a beaded necklace dangled an obsidian figurine between pale breasts. Her eyes were such a dark green they appeared black in the shadows, and her smile – if it was a smile at all – was thin and absolutely unreadable.

Hector stood his ground. He wanted to turn and rush for the exit, but he knew to do so would mean his death, or worse. He remembered what had happened to his men. He thought about Paulo, the man's empty eyes and limp, vacant features. He did not want to become like Paulo.

Anya stepped closer, and then she raised her right hand, palm up, and snapped the fingers of her left. The younger woman, Kim, slipped out from the shadows behind Anya's chair with a jangle of silver and placed something in Anya's hand. Kim was gone almost as soon as she'd appeared.

"I understand your concern," Anya said softly. "And I understand how you feel about those who follow you. If you trust me, I will bring you through this, and you will be stronger than you have ever been before. Those who stand with you will be rewarded. I have a gift."

She held out the object Kim had given her, and Hector saw that it was a velvet bag secured at the top by leather ties. On the surface of the bag, symbols had been stitched with brightly colored thread. He didn't recognize them, but they drew his eye. Anya opened the bag, tipped it up, and shook three small dark statuettes into her hand. They resembled the one dangling about her neck.

"Take these," She said, dropping them into Hector's hand. "Keep one for yourself. Choose two that you trust – not those who have been touched, but others. Give the other two to them. In two days time I will hold a service. You must come, and you must bring your men. All of them. We will unleash a power, you and I."

Hector turned the small statues over in his hand, examining them. They were waxy to the touch. Something passed from the soft stone into the palm of his hand, and he nearly dropped them. Instead, he closed his hand around them tightly.

Anya stepped closer. Hector swallowed, but he didn't flinch. She insinuated herself against him, brushed her long hair over his shoulders and leaned up to whisper in his ear. He felt the brush of her breasts through the soft silk of her gown.   The blood drained from his face, and he trembled with the effort of remaining still. Her scent was musky, and it stole his ability to concentrate. He knew if she came closer, she'd feel his erection, and the thought of what she might do was nearly more than he could stand. His muscles tightened and he bit down hard on his bottom lip.

"We will rule the Barrio. The *Loa* will come to us. They will walk the streets and they will leave our enemies like litter in the gutters."

Anya trailed her fingers up Hector's chest and drew her index finger up his throat to the tip of his chin. She leaned closer and licked his lip as if tasting him. Then, with a flourish, she stepped back.

Hector grabbed his courage a last time.

"My men?" he asked.

Anya met his gaze and held it, then, as if satisfied with what she'd seen, she nodded. She snapped her finger again, and one of the huge, bald black men stepped forward. It might have been Raoul or Stephen, or one of half a dozen others. Hector couldn't be certain without turning away from Anya Cabrera's gaze. His father had taught him to never look away from a snake. You might get bitten, but you would see it coming.

The big man handed Anya a small, clear bottle. She passed it to Hector.

"Give each of them a single spoonful of this."

Hector took the bottle, but he didn't look down to examine it.

"It will cure them?"

"It will test them," Anya said flatly. "If they are strong, it will bring them back to you. If they fail to meet its challenge? They will die. It is the only way."

Hector swallowed again, and then nodded. He turned and started across the room.

"Do not forget," Anya called after him. "Two nights from now ... in the yard."

The curtains at the far side of the room parted. This time it was the girl, Kim. Hector wondered vaguely how she'd gotten ahead of him and into the passageway. He hadn't seen her pass, and he hadn't heard the telltale jingle of the ornaments in her hair – yet there she was. He followed her into the gloom without looking back, the waxy, disturbing figurines clutched tightly in one fist, and the bottle in the other. As he walked, finally, his erection loosened, and he began to breathe more steadily.

Chapter Seven

The farther Martinez walked from the Barrio, the more he stood out among those he passed. They took no notice of him as he slid from aging prophet into the guise of a homeless vagrant by traveling only a few city blocks. There were cities within cities in San Valencez. The inhabitants of one seldom crossed the border into the next. It was comfortable that way. No one had to act to protect a border that wasn't threatened, and what was there in the Barrio that would tempt the well-tailored suits of downtown into the squalor of the Latin quarter?

Martinez kept one hand in his pocket, where he turned a small parchment around and around in his fingers. He had been saving it against just such a day as this. He intended it as a gift, but the gift would be more of a peace offering, and a bribe. It had been many years since he'd stepped foot in the home of Donovan DeChance There were reasons for that long absence, and he wasn't certain that even the gift in his pocket would bridge that particular gap. It didn't matter; he had to try.

DeChance collected information. There was nowhere in the world more likely to yield a lost tome, or a forgotten manuscript than the townhouse in downtown San Valencez. Martinez hadn't seen for himself, but his sources told him that much of the information had been scanned and catalogued digitally – that the arcane knowledge of the world was being organized for the first time on computer memory banks and protected more carefully than the gold in Fort Knox. Martinez had no use for telephones, or computers, pagers or stereos. He was born of a different age, and he clung to what he knew best. It didn't mean he wouldn't take advantage of sources as they presented themselves. If DeChance had what he needed, he'd have to find a way to convince the man to share.

The sun was low in the sky when he finally climbed the steps up into the building that held DeChance's townhouse. There was no doorman, just a series of buzzers in an ornamental brass panel. Martinez smiled as he pressed the number thirteen and waited. He heard a metallic buzz, and a moment later DeChance's voice grated through the small speaker.

"It has been a long time," he said.

Martinez smiled. He'd had no illusions about arriving unnoticed.

"Too long, I think," he replied. "And without the apology I should have offered long ago."

The speaker was silent, but a second and louder metallic buzz announced that the lock barring Martinez from entering had been disengaged. The old man pressed through and entered the foyer. He knew the way to the elevators, but they made him claustrophobic, and in any case they would be of no help. Most buildings in the older part of San Valencez – those that climbed higher than a dozen floors - skipped the number thirteen. The elevator in DeChance's building was no different, except that the elusive thirteenth floor actually existed. Martinez took the stairs slowly, resting often. He knew DeChance would be patient. He only hoped he would also be forgiving.

The climb gave him time to think – and to remember. The rift between himself and DeChance was entirely his own fault, and he realized that he could have fixed it any time –on any given day. He could have come here, as he was coming here tonight, and made things right. It had never been important until now, and that meant that it became important only when he needed something. Donovan would see that too...and yet, as he trudged up the stairs toward the thirteenth, Martinez found that he was suddenly and honestly sorry it had come to this.

He rested at each level. He was an old man. He'd been an old man for a very long time, and before that he was middle aged, and young for equally long times. He had seen things and known things - so many things - that he'd managed to forget which were important, and why. He waited an extra moment on the twelfth landing, and then climbed the last set of stairs and pushed through the dusty door to the thirteenth floor.

There should have been doors lining the hall, but there were not. He knew that if the doorman, or a health inspector, were to somehow make it to where he stood they would see that line of doors on either side of the hall. None of them would open onto Donovan's quarters. He wasn't exactly sure how it had been done, but it was similar to how he kept the temperature in his home at a constant level and stored far more than his simple four walls could possibly hold. There are many sets of rules governing the universe; Martinez knew more than one. Donovan DeChance had been gathering the knowledge of the ages almost as long as Martinez had been reading the future in piles of animal bones and mixing potions. They walked through two different worlds, but occasionally, their roads crossed. All roads cross; regardless of the theories of Euclid.

The door opened slowly as he approached. There was no one standing there to greet him, as he'd known there would not be. He stepped inside, and it closed behind him with a dull click. There was a fire in the next room. Martinez squared his shoulders and stepped through into Donovan's den, expecting the worst.

Donovan stood by the fire and watched as Martinez entered. The old man looked just as he remembered – like a very old, crazed hippie who'd lost his way from the seventies, or a character in a Carlos Castaneda novel. He knew Martinez had been born somewhere in South America, but there was a point in time before which all stories diverged. Donovan had never asked. It was not his business.

"Too many years have passed since you were last here," Donovan said.

He stepped across the room and held out his hand. Martinez took it without hesitation, and the old man's grip was firm. Their gazes met … just for an instant … and then Martinez glanced away, taking in the lines of boxes, the overflowing shelves, and Cleo, who sat on Donovan's desk, washing one paw and eyeing him suspiciously. Martinez laughed.

"I see you have not found a solution to your predicament," he said. "Things have become more, complicated, since my last visit."

Donovan chuckled.

"I was thinking about that only this afternoon. It seems something intrudes every time I am ready to deal with it. There is a power aligned against me; perhaps it is too ancient, and too powerful."

"Perhaps," Martinez said.

The old man smiled, and Donovan thought the expression looked genuine. This meeting was not going at all as he'd expected. He decided to drive straight through the moment to the heart of the problem.

"Have you seen Luis?" he asked.

The words were spoken softly, almost casually, but Martinez froze. His features went rigid and pale. Donovan stepped to the bar and poured two glasses of bourbon. He didn't look at Martinez. He turned and offered one glass to the old man, who took it and sipped silently.

"I have seen him," Martinez said softly, swirling his drink slowly and staring into it as if it might hold some sort of answers he couldn't find elsewhere in his memory. "Not like that, though – not since that night."

They drank in silence for a while, and Donovan's thoughts shifted back across the years. It had been more than twenty, but his memories were as vivid as if it had happened only hours before. Some memories are more powerful than others. Some never really let go.

The moon was full, and Donovan moved quietly through the streets on the border of the Barrio. He scanned the buildings, watched the rooftops and kept to the darkest shadows. He was in unfamiliar territory, and he knew there were those who would not appreciate his presence.

He had the photo in his pocket. It was of a young girl, Angela. She had smiled for the camera, twisting several strands of dark hair in the fingers of one hand. It was a smile full of potential

– a smile with a future and a family. The photograph was of a dead girl, and Donovan intended to find the one responsible. He had promised to do so, and in all the long years of his life, he could honestly say he had never broken a promise. Until now he'd never promised anything he wasn't certain of.

A shadow flitted between two of the small homes and Donovan grew still. He slowed his breath and sank back against the wall of an old warehouse. Whoever it was, whatever it was, it has passed. Donovan moved on.

He pulled a small leather case from his pocket. He opened it to reveal a round leather circle with a brass rim. A flick of his wrist and a lens swiveled into view. It was cut from green crystal, and in the dim light he could see nothing through it. Donovan turned, pressed his back to the wall, and breathed a short incantation. He held the lens up, pressed it to his right eye, and scanned the far side of the street.

The lens glittered and what had been too dark to make out seconds before took on new clarity. Streams of silver wound up toward the sky and disappeared into the clouds. Donovan checked each in turn. They moved, winding in and out of the streets of the Barrio. Each time he found one that was white, or silver, he moved on. To the left of the center of a tall building just across from him, a reddish thread moved rapidly deeper into the dark streets.

Donovan watched a moment longer, marked the track, flipped the lens closed, and returned it to its case. He slid the case into his pocket, and crossed the street. He looked both ways and then plunged down an alley. No one saw him cross that border, but his passing did not go unnoticed. There was another thread, had he continued to look. It was yellow like gold, or sunlight, and it spun down into the center of the small community. As Donovan entered the Barrio, that thread quivered, like the string of a harp that has been stroked.

There weren't many people on the street, and Donovan had taken measures to keep the majority of those who were out from noting his passing. He moved quickly, stopping from time to time to pull out the crystal and scan the skies. He wanted to be in and out as quickly as possible. He knew that he was in danger entering the Barrio unannounced, but there was nothing to be done. A girl had been killed, and the killer was getting away. The trail led into the Barrio, and Donovan believed he would find, when he had the time to look into it, that the trail led out as well. This place belonged to old Martinez, but when the borders of one place leaked death onto the streets of another, action was required.

There was a balance in the city, and sometimes it was as delicate as a single death. Donovan thought he'd caught this one quickly enough, but time was still critical, for his own safety, and for the prevention of more death.

He passed along the wall of a half-forgotten church, and at the corner, he checked the lens. He slipped it back into his pocket quickly. He was close – very close. He rounded the corner of the building and made his way through debris and piles of old garbage toward a vacant lot behind the building. Light flickered from a fire, and he heard voices speaking very low. Donovan reached the back corner of the building and peered around.

In the center of the vacant lot, a fire burned in an old barrel. Cinder blocks had been stacked around it to create a fire break. There were several shadowy figures gathered in small groups. They didn't notice Donovan, and when he got a closer look at them, he realized why. They were homeless. They had gathered to share what small rations they'd gathered that day, and the huddle together by the fire, sharing the dim light and the warmth.

He saw a young couple with a smaller shadow clinging to the woman's leg. There was an old man, and a younger man – maybe in his twenties – with eyes so white and wild they glimmered in the firelight. He looked as if he hadn't eaten in a week, but he paced rapidly back and forth, glared into the shadows, and then spun back and away to pace again. Donovan knew the signs of addiction well enough, and wondered briefly why the others allowed him to stay. He would not help them, or feed them, or protect them. The man would take what he could get; he had no choice.

Donovan was about to turn away, disappointed, when a

cry broke the silence that froze his blood to ice. It rose from low tones to a high, baying howl. Donovan saw those in the clearing draw closer to the fire. The father grabbed his child up in his arms, and then drew his small family together in a tight, protective embrace.

Something flashed past on the far side of the lot. It moved so quickly that Donovan could not bring it into focus. He reached into the inner pocket of his jacket and drew out a pocket watch. He held it up, gripped one of four protruding stems, and turned the knob. He closed his eyes as he did this, and when he opened them, things had slowed. The group around the fire stood like statues. Donovan remained where he was, and was rewarded by a second cry. It rose very slowly this time. The sound was like a horrified scream screeching from the needle of a record player on too-slow a speed. The watch in his hand ticked slowly. It was counting down from 60.

Donovan moved. He pressed off the wall and hurtled into the vacant lot. He slipped past the immobile vagrants and the fire … which had also slowed to the point it seemed to move in stop frames. On the far side of the lot Donovan saw a shadowed figure, still moving, but slowly. He ran, and as he ran, he drew a long, silver cord from his pocket. As he approached the fleeing creature, the clock continued its relentless countdown.

The thing stood erect, its body covered with dark, glistening fur. The face, though vaguely human, was elongated. The ears were too long, and the jaws were open wide, revealing a long, lolling tongue and sharp, canine teeth. The eyes were yellow and jaundiced, wide with fear and crazed. Donovan unrolled the cord and ran round the creature in a tight circle. He bound it with three tight turns, and just as the last seconds ticked away on the face of the pocket watch, he spoke a short incantation, released the cord, and stepped away.

The world rushed back into focus. The sound of the fire crackling slammed into him and nearly deafened him. The others in the lot still hadn't seen Donovan, who stood watching as the thing trying to hurtle itself forward and out of sight tumbled suddenly forward and writhed on the ground. It howled, and Donovan stepped back. No one else moved. They turned and they stared at the creature struggling on the ground, and the dark, unfamiliar man standing over it.

Donovan moved first. He stepped toward the fire, holding up his hands.

"I am not here to hurt anyone," he said. "I need to make sure that no one else is harmed by this one," he turned and gestured to the creature. It seemed unaware of his presence, or of anything else but the cord that bound it. Its frenzy only increased as it continued to struggle, and the harder it fought for its freedom, the tighter the bonds became.

"Who are you?" the young father asked. "Why are you here? And that...what is that?"

Donovan started to answer, but fell silent as another figure melted from the darkness. Tall and thin with his gray hair waving about his face like the mane of some deranged lion, Old Martinez stepped into view. His expression was caught somewhere between anger and pain. He stepped toward the creature, and Donovan moved to come between them. Martinez ignored him. With a sweep of one hand, Martinez sent a small cloud of dust out to settle over the thing. What followed was a sizzling, popping, gut-wrenching sight. The body on the ground twisted and jerked. The features became malleable, shifting from the creature Donovan had captured to the face of a young man, and then back again. It took only moments, but seemed like hours. When it was all done, the young man lay, loose in the now pointless silver binding, in a fetal curl on the dirt.

Martinez knelt at the boy's side and laid a hand on his shoulder.

"Louis?" he said. "Louis, can you hear me?"

"He killed a girl," Donovan said, stepping closer. "In the city. I left her mother in mourning; I promised to see that there was justice."

"This is not your concern," Martinez said, rising to face him. "The Barrio is mine...Louis is mine. I will deal with this."

"How long have you known?" Donovan asked. He didn't turn, or back down. "How long have you known, and how did he get out into the city?"

Martinez frowned, and it seemed he would ignore the question completely. Then his features softened, just for an instant.

"I have known his family since his father was a boy," Martinez said. "This happened one, maybe two years ago. The one responsible has been dealt with."

"Why was Louis not dealt with as well?" Donovan asked. He knew the words sounded harsh, but there were times when sentiment could not be taken into account.

"Lycanthrope is a disease," Martinez replied. "It does not require a sentence of death if it is controlled. Surely you know others – in the city beyond – who have lived much longer with this curse."

"They do not kill young girls," Donovan replied. "They have learned control, and have agreed to the proper restraints. I can do the same for your young friend. He will be well cared for – protected from himself, even as others are protected. You know it is the way. You should have brought him to the city when it happened."

"As I said," Martinez replied, "I will deal with this. The Barrio cares for its own."

"You know I can't let that happen," Donovan said. "If you let me take him, and you can provide adequate detainment – have it tested – he can be returned. It's the best I can offer."

"You dare to threaten me?" Martinez said. "Even here? Even in the Barrio, so far from your books and your precious friends, you dare to act as if you can walk in and take something without my consent? You should not even be here."

Donovan's heart raced, but he kept his mind clear and controlled the tremble that tried to slip out his arm to his fingers.

"I followed him here. I crossed your border in pursuit of a killer. In the past, that has never been considered a breach of etiquette, or trust…"

"This is…different." Martinez said.

The boy began to stir, and Martinez turned back to him. Donovan watched, and that momentary distraction was his undoing. In that moment, something small and covered in tan fur leapt from the shadows. It gave a growl and latched onto

Donovan's heel. He spun, kicked out, and sent the small creature flying, but that moment was all that Martinez required. He cried out in a language Donovan vaguely recognized as originating in South America – very old – and the air grew suddenly black with a dark, cloying mist. Donovan cursed and lunged toward where the boy had lain on the ground, but he found nothing but bare ground. There was no sound. Not even the crackling of the fire broke the silence. Whatever Martinez had conjured, it dulled sight and sound, scent and sensation. Donovan closed his eyes and waited.

When he opened them, he stood alone. The lot was empty, and the fire was out. There was no sign that anyone else had been there, and no sign of where they might have gone. He considered pulling out the green lens and following. He knew he could track Martinez easily enough, but he wasn't sure he was prepared for such a confrontation. He'd hoped to get in and out undetected. The situation now required more than he could bring to the table alone.

He turned, slowly, and left the Barrio the way he'd entered. He stepped into the shadowed streets beyond, turned into an alley, and a moment later he was gone. He wondered what he would tell the girl's mother. He only hoped that he was right, and that the girl was dead. If she lived…

Donovan shook his head. So many years.

"He was my son," Martinez said softly. "I should have told you, but I was afraid that he'd be taken anyway. I was afraid you, and others, would use the knowledge to find him more easily and lock him away."

"I would have helped you," Donovan said. "I had no answer for that girl's mother. When we sent word to you, asking how you had resolved the situation, you never responded."

"I should have told you," Martinez sighed. "I should have trusted you, but I did not know you – I'm not sure that I know you now. I did not want to lose him."

"And did you?"

Martinez smiled. "No. In fact, you may be interested in the solution that I found. He was difficult, as you may imagine, but he did not escape. Not again. His family helped...and others. We kept him well protected at the proper times, and then I found what I had been looking for. It's a collar, cast silver and inscribed with the proper symbols at the proper time. As long as he wears it, the moon has no effect. He has been living a normal life ... giving me grandchildren. I should have come to you...told you... there are always things we regret."

Donovan nodded. He took a sip of his bourbon.

"You have the instructions?" he asked softly. "There are others that I know of, men and women who have been too-long imprisoned..."

"Of course," Martinez replied. "I have them with me, and more. I've brought you something – not that a gift can make up for years of silence – but I've also come to ask for your help. I have another boy under my care now and a war on my doorstep."

"I tend to stay out of wars," Donovan said, "particularly in the Barrio. I've heard rumors, though, disturbing rumors. I'm told that Anya Cabrera is walking a very fine line."

"She has long since crossed that line," Martinez said. He caught himself before he spat, realizing he was not on the street. He sipped his drink in an effort to cover the motion.

"You have information?" Donovan asked?

"I ... believe that I can handle it," Martinez said. It didn't sound as though he believed the words himself.

"This is too big," Donovan said. "The stakes are too high. It won't be just the Barrio in danger if she goes too far, and my information says that is exactly what she intends. I need to know that I can trust you this time, Martinez. I'm going to look into this...it would be a great help to me If I knew that I didn't have to worry about you blocking my efforts."

Martinez studied his drink. He took another, longer sip, and then, very slowly, he nodded.

"There are things that I must do," he said. "I have protected those in the Barrio for a very long time. They have come to me already – and they are frightened. I must do what I can."

"And I will help you, if I can," Donovan replied. "I have my own methods, though, and I believe we'll work better apart than together. A truce, then?"

Martinez glanced up and smiled. It was a crooked expression, and difficult to read, but Donovan had seen it before, and he returned it.

"What is it you have come for?" he asked.

"There is a boy, Salvatore Domingo Sanchez. He lives in a shack near my home, and he is an artist. The boy is truly brilliant – what he can do with chalk, or pencils, or paint ... it is powerful. He has formed connections in the Barrio, but he is not ready for the challenge. He needs an edge. I need to make paints for him – special paints – born of the prime colors. There is only one thing I need. In all my years, I've never been able to find the formula for Rojo Fuego."

Donovan stared at the old man. He hadn't heard those words in decades. Fire Red. The color of dragon's fire. The formula in question was very old. There couldn't have been more than four or five copies of it in existence. One of them resided in an encrypted file in a folder on Donovan's hard drive. He'd destroyed the original.

"That is a very powerful formula," he said.

Martinez eyed him, taking a drink, but not dropping his gaze. "I know what it is...young man."

They stood like that in silence for several breaths, and then, very suddenly, Donovan laughed.

"I cannot tell you how long it has been since someone called me that – and it was true. Okay, you have a deal. I will trust you with this formula, and you will trust me within your Barrio."

Martinez smiled again. "That is fair."

Donovan stepped around his desk and started tapping keys on the computer terminal. A moment later the printer in the corner beeped, and a single sheet of paper rolled slowly out. Martinez waited respectfully until Donovan walked to the machine and retrieved the paper.

"You mentioned a gift..." Donovan said.

Martinez grinned. He reached into his pocket and pulled out a very old, tightly folded sheet of parchment.

"It is brittle," he said. "Have a care with it."

"What is it?" Donovan asked.

"It is the instructions for creating the collar," Martinez said softly. "The cure for lycanthrope, such as it is. I didn't know for certain that you would ask about Louis. I did not know, for sure, that I would tell you the story if you did. I knew you would find this of value."

Donovan reached out and took the ancient paper carefully from Martinez'ss grip. In its place, he handed off the freshly printed formula.

"Be careful," he said. "You know what you hold, and I will not ask you why you need it, but there are a great number of others depending on the two of us. We must tread carefully."

Martinez tucked the paper into his pocket and held out his hand. Donovan took it, and they shook warmly.

"When this is over," Martinez said, "You must come to the Barrio. I will introduce you to Louis...and we will share another drink."

"I will look forward to it," Donovan said.

They both emptied their glasses, and Martinez turned toward the door.

"I haven't much time," he said.

Donovan nodded and stepped past him, opening the door.

"Be safe," he said.

Martinez turned, and one last time, he smiled.

"And you, my friend. And you...go with all the Gods at your back."

Martinez disappeared into the hall, and Donovan closed the door. He turned to his desk with the parchment still unopened in his hand. He knew there was a chance that when he opened it, there would be nothing there – or that whatever was written on it would be a fabrication. He didn't believe it. What he believed was that a burned bridge had been brought back from the ashes. He placed the folded paper on his desk. He wasn't quite ready to test his intuition, and he had a lot of work to do.

As if understanding, Cleo walked over and plopped down on top of the parchment, pinning it to the desk. She began washing her paw again, and Donovan laughed. He poured bourbon and scratched Cleo's ears. He raised his drink in a silent toast to Martinez, and to Louis. It was shaping up to be an interesting night.

Chapter Eight

After Martinez was gone, Donovan reached for the phone. Even though he now had a somewhat safer time ahead of him in regard to the Barrio, he thought it might be best to bring in an ally. Martinez had seemed sincere, and if it proved genuine, the gift he'd brought would do a great deal of good, but Donovan wasn't quite ready to invest his complete confidence. The old man had his own agenda, now and always, and it was best not to assume that it ran parallel to his own.

On the second ring a bright, cheerful voice answered.

"Hello?"

"Amethyst?" he asked.

"Who else would I be, love?" was the quick reply. "You did dial my number."

Donovan chuckled. "Some things have come up – some rather odd things. I was wondering if you might be free for dinner? While we eat, we could talk…"

"It sounds wonderful," she said, "but you come here. I've been out twice this week, and from the tone of your voice you aren't coming over to talk about old times or plan that vacation you keep promising me."

"You're going to cook, or should I bring something?"

"I'll cook. I'll surprise you."

"You never fail to do that," he said. "I'll be over about eight, then. I've had an interesting visitor, someone you know. There's trouble brewing in the Barrio. Cord came to me yesterday with reports."

"Anya Cabrera?" she asked.

"You've heard then?"

"I heard some disturbing things, but none that I've been able to cobble together into anything coherent."

"We'll compare notes then, and put together a battle plan."

"You expect a battle, do you?" she asked

Donovan smiled. He could almost see her impish grin as her words shifted up in tone.

"I do. It is best to always expect a battle. That way, when you find peace, you enjoy it all the more. I'll see you this evening."

"Bring wine."

The phone went dead and Donovan hung his up more slowly, staring at it and shaking his head. He turned and stroked Cleo, who rubbed eagerly up into his hand.

"More and more interesting," he said. "What do you think, Cleo? Is that paper what he says it is?"

The cat actually seemed to think about it before turning, folding in half, and washing her back foot. Donovan picked up the folded parchment, fingered it gently, and then carried it to his shelves. He tucked it carefully into the front cover of a large leather volume on the end of the shelf.

"There will be time enough to test it later," he said.

Cleo paid no attention to him at all. Donovan strode to the door, opened it and stepped into the hallway beyond. A moment later, he was gone.

When Donovan reached Amethyst's door, he held a paper bag with a bottle of wine in one hand, and a single rose in the other. He was there on business, but he never visited empty handed. They'd known one another a very long time, but he still liked to surprise her.

The door opened, and Donovan stepped inside. It closed behind him with a soft click. The hallway was dimly lit. The air was scented with Jasmine. Everything was deep earth tones, soft satin and dark velvet. Amethyst stepped in from her den and smiled at him.

She was a tall woman with flame-red hair. Currently, that hair was adorned with cascades of dark, smoky crystals that winked at him with soft glimmers of light. She wore a floor length gown, slit up the side, and he could not help glancing at the flash of leg it revealed as he stepped closer.

"You dressed for the occasion?" he said.

"No," she laughed. "I had business earlier. I haven't had a chance to change. You like it?"

Donovan took the invitation to inspect her and smiled his appreciation.

"Very much so."

He handed her the rose, and then slid the wine out of its bag. Amethyst smelled the rose and then trailed it down her cheek and under her chin, obviously enjoying to the soft petals against her skin.

"I love roses," she said. "But you knew that."

"The wine is from Spain," he said. "Marques de Riscal."

"Red wine and red roses," she said, laughing. "If I didn't already know better, I'd think you had something in mind other than strange visitors and the Barrio."

"I wish that were true," he said. "Today Old Martinez came to visit. He brought me a gift."

"What did he want?" she asked, suddenly interested. "The two of you haven't spoken since..."

"That is done, too, I think," Donovan cut her off. "The lycanthrope was Martinez's son. His name is Louis. If what I'm led to believe is true, the gift Martinez brought me contains the instructions for creating a collar that prevents the change."

"A cure? He brought you a cure? What's he been doing with that all these years? Do you trust him?"

"I don't know. He seemed sincere, and there is no doubt that there is trouble in the Barrio. It wouldn't serve his interests to start trouble on a new front if he already has a war brewing on his doorstep. He came in search of the formula for a particular pigment of paint – Rojo Fuego."

Amethyst took a deep breath.

"You'd better pour that wine, then," she said, "because Martinez was here too. He didn't tell me any interesting tales of his son. He brought me a particularly powerful pair of "Apache Tears" from the desert. It's why I'm wearing these now." She brushed her fingers through her hair and the obsidian crystals tinkled. "I was celebrating."

"I take it that he needed something from you as well, then?" Donovan asked. "Something he didn't bother mentioning to me. He must have known I'd find out."

"I traded him three crystals," she said. "Prime crystals… red, blue, and yellow. They were concentrators."

"And he asked for all three?" Donovan frowned.

"No, he only asked for the red. I keep them in sets – I don't break them up. The other two alone would be of no use to me, and the one in imbalance would have been too powerful for any normal use. I explained that to him, and he was as patient as he was condescending."

"He doesn't have a normal use in mind," Donovan said.

He told her quickly about the young artist, Salvatore Domingo Sanchez.

"I don't know what Martinez is planning, but it involves the boy. There is something about the 'Fire Red' that is important to him…important enough that he doesn't trust the formula alone. I can't think of another reason he'd want your concentrator. He intends to use it to enhance the mixture."

"But why?" Amethyst asked. "If he's making paint for this boy…"

"We'll have to figure that out," Donovan said, "and soon. There's a more immediate problem, though. According to what I heard from Cord, and from comments that Martinez made, Anya Cabrera is meddling with powers that she will not long be able to control. She is trying to run Martinez, and anyone else who stands against her, out of the Barrio. Unfortunately, what she is unleashing will not stay bottled up for long. If she isn't stopped, we're going to have a problem leaking out into the city that we might not be able to solve."

"I heard that she was spending time with one of the local gangs," Amethyst said. "They're called *Los Escorpiones*, and even before Anya Cabrera, they were trouble."

"There is a gang near Martinez, as well," Donovan said thoughtfully. "If my memory serves me, they are called 'The Dragons.'"

"Dragon Red," Amethyst said. "Coincidence?"

"Never," Donovan replied. He stepped past her to her bar

and grabbed a corkscrew. "There's no such thing as coincidence
– only controlled bursts of fate. We need to gather more
information."

"Not tonight, I hope?" she asked.

"No," Donovan replied. "There's nothing we can do until
morning. Well, almost nothing."

They both laughed, and he poured the wine. As Donovan
swirled his before the first taste, it caught the light, deep and
red. Like blood – or paint. Something was bothering him, but
he couldn't put a finger on it.

Then Amethyst stepped closer and wound her arms around
him, licking the rich red wine from his lips, and whatever
thought he'd been about to have melted away.

Chapter Nine

Salvatore sat on the sidewalk outside of his shack. Much of the surface was covered in brightly colored drawings, soaring eagles and ocean waves breaking against stones on the beach. Where he sat there was a plain, white square of concrete, and in the center of that square, Salvatore drew.

He started with a black piece of charcoal, rough and sharpened to a point on one corner. He didn't see concrete, or even a blank slate. His mind was trapped in the dream that had driven him from sleep. The morning breeze riffled his hair, but sweat trickled down his neck and under his dirty t-shirt. He'd slept only a couple of hours, spent the rest of the night huddled on the corner of his bed, shivering and waiting for the light.

Now he worked. He struggled to force the images from his mind. He thought that maybe, if he recreated the dream, he could be free of it. Barring that, he could share it, and maybe someone could help him find his way through to a place where he could rest again. The moment the sun had broken across the city skyline, Salvatore had stumbled out into the light.

In the night, he'd dreamed. He'd walked again on that beach, a beach that could not exist. The dragons hadn't seen him – they had soared against the dark backdrop of the sky, winding and whirling around one another and screaming their defiance. Salvatore had found a place on an outcropping of stone to sit. The dragons were beautiful. He sat and watched them for hours, powerful and free. In the distance there was darkness deeper than anything he'd ever experienced. It didn't move closer, but it loomed like storm clouds on the horizon.

He felt a pressure between the two – the screaming,

powerful serpents and the billowing, gathering darkness. Neither advanced, but both were aware of the tension. Every time one of the dragons launched into a dive toward the waves below, his heart sang, and every time the darkness moved – sentient and malevolent – he wanted to scream. He knew that the dragons would not hear him, but he wanted to scream to them – to tell them about the danger, to warn them and protect them. He didn't know how.

Now he sat in the morning sun in the world where he'd been born and raised, but that other place would not let him go. He couldn't erase the dragons from his mind, and worse – he knew them. He knew almost every one of those magnificent creatures, but not as he'd dreamed them. He drew a long, sinuous back and extended claws. The wings swept back and up, and the tail wound down and into a spiral. He saw the colors as well, but he needed to get the outline in place.

Next he grabbed his orange chalk, and his yellow. He fought with the colors, blending, erasing, and blending again, trying to get the perfect gold-sheen tint. The wings were a coppery brown, and the eyes blazed gold. He drew, erased, drew again, and erased again, fighting frantically to get the colors of the chalk to match his memory. It was difficult. He had to guess, and if he guessed wrong, he had to start over, unless the color came out too light and he could darken it. The color was important. The drawing was important. He didn't know why.

Slowly, it came to life. Salvatore didn't see the waves breaking against the shore, but he heard them. He felt the sand beneath his feet, but he concentrated his thoughts on the movement of his hand, the sensation of chalk dust pressing through the pores of his skin. It was as though the colors melted into his bloodstream, and after a while, he no longer thought about it when he picked up the red, or the green. He worked steadily and the world dropped away.

Sound insinuated itself, and he thought – just for a moment – that it was the cry of the dragon, floating to him on the breeze. Then something touched his shoulder, very lightly, and that other place receded. Salvatore jerked his hand back, afraid he'd make a stray mark, or smudge his work. Groggily, he sat back and shook his head, glancing around for the source of the interruption.

He looked up, and the anger melted to terror in the span of a second. The man who stood over him was tall, over six feet and weighing more than two hundred pounds, if an ounce. Next to Salvatore's slight form, he seemed like a monster. Salvatore recognized the man from the meeting at Martinez's home; It was Jake, the Dragon.

"I said," the bearded stranger growled, "it's awesome. You don't talk?"

Salvatore stared up at the man. He took in the broad shoulders, the dirty jeans and hair so long it was braided in back, like Salvatore's mother had worn hers. None of this had the impact of the man's vest.

It was denim, sleeves cut away, faded with dirty fringe around the edges. Salvatore could not see the back of the jacket, but even so he knew what he would see. He had seen it many times before. Jake was a Dragon, and in the Barrio, that meant Jake was a man to be avoided, or feared. If Salvatore had not seen him with Martinez, he'd never have found the courage to speak.

"I...thank you, Sir," Salvatore said at last. His eyes turned to the sidewalk once more, focusing on the nearly completed image of the dragon, his face flushed.

"No reason to be scared," the big man said softly. "I like dragons." The chuckle that followed should have sent chills down Salvatore's spine, but for some reason it did not. "Where did you find this one?"

"It ... is something I have seen," Salvatore said softly, his blush spreading down his throat.

Jake leaned closer, his eyes sweeping up and down the image on the sidewalk. He reached down, tracing the design with his finger. "You did more than draw a picture here, kid. I can feel flames; feel the heat, the warrior behind the dragon."

"He is old," Salvatore blurted. "I . . . I have seen this one many times. I had to draw him, to get him out of my head."

Jake looked at him then, eyes dark. "What do you see when you look at me, kid?"

Salvatore watched the big man's eyes, concentrating. He stared, face flushing as he knew he'd stared too long, but unable to look away. Then he closed his eyes, sat back, and rocked gently.

The image was very clear. Greens and golds, magnificent, slender and sinuous like a serpent. The dragon leapt to the forefront of Salvatore's mind, and he nearly gasped at the sudden clarity. None had ever asked him to see, to understand.

"Salvatore," he said softly.

"Huh? You see what?"

"My name," the boy repeated, is Salvatore, Senor Jake, and I see your dragon."

Jake leaned back, rocking on his heels. He did not look at Salvatore, his gaze was fixated on the dragon that sprawled, nearly complete, across the dirty sidewalk. He reached out once again, as if to touch the design, and then pulled away.

"It's funny," he said. "I look at your picture, Sally, and I see things too, familiar things. I see a man, someone I've known. You drew this dragon, but I see Vasquez. Don't know if you've heard about Vasquez - Tony wasn't anyone special, not to anyone but the Dragons. He died just the other night. Your picture brought him back to me."

Salvatore's eyes shifted quickly to meet the big man's gaze. "He was a tall man, Senor Jake? Tall with long, dark hair and a scar high up on one cheek?"

Jake stared at Salvatore for a long moment before nodding slowly. "He was. He was also my brother."

Salvatore lowered his eyes to the dragon, thinking. "It is a magnificent dragon," he said at last. "It is Senor Vasquez's dragon. I saw him many times in the Barrio, parked near the market, or the park. It was there I first saw the dragon."

"Why did you draw it?" Jake asked softly.

"I have no choice, Senor. The dragons, they call to me. I see them, and I brush them aside. They do not leave me alone. I see them again, and again, in my dreams, in the soft glow that surrounds the streetlights at night, in the flashing lights of the policia. Always I see them - until I set them free."

"That is a gift," Jake breathed softly.

"I wish that the gift were less painful," Salvatore blurted. "I wish that I could sleep, and that they did not wander through my dreams."

Jake was silent for a long moment, then he spoke. "Set mine free, Sally. I want you to set my dragon free now. You won't be haunted by it then, and I will see it, as you do. I want you to paint my dragon."

Salvatore's heart nearly stopped. The dragon had already formed in his mind. The moment he'd glanced up and felt Jake's shadow fall over him, he'd seen it and known it. He'd expected to carry that image with him, holding it and sleeping with it, sharing it with Old Martinez and waiting. The Dragons were a fearsome lot, but they had a habit of disappearing, one after another. It was never until one of the Dragons died, or had been taken away, that Salvatore released the images.

"I..." He said softly, "I do not paint. I have my chalk, the sidewalks and the walls of the Barrio. I work where I can and when I can. I have no paint, Senor Jake."

"I think I can help with that."

Martinez had come up on the far side of Salvatore's drawing silently. Salvatore turned, startled. Jake glanced up as well, apparently just as surprised to see the old man.

"I can make paints," Martinez said. "I have been working on them and gathering what I need. This," he waved a hand at the sidewalk, "deserves so much more. The wind and the rain will find it...it will fade."

Jake knelt down and brushed his finger very gently along the edge of the dragon, not really touching it.

"He will never fade." He said. "This drawing...this is a drawing of something that has already passed. I never saw him –not like this – but Sally did. He saw it, and he remembered it," Jake turned to stare at Salvatore. "And he honored it. This is..."

Jake stopped talking then. There was a tremor in his voice, and Salvatore saw a tear glistening in the corner of his eye. Salvatore looked away. It was a private moment, and he knew that if Jake was to share it with anyone, it would be the dragon. It would be his friend...his brother. Vasquez.

"You never answered the question," Martinez said softly,

laying a hand on Salvatore's shoulder. "Will you paint Jake's dragon? Will you set it free? I will provide the paint."

"I have nothing to paint it on," Salvatore said.

It wasn't a denial that he could, or would do the painting, only a statement of fact. Salvatore owned very little. He had his home, which had been abandoned by a family who moved on. He ate because of Martinez and a few others, generous people who brought him things and let him do menial jobs. He had no money for supplies. His chalk had been gathered, donated, found in strange places. He had charcoal that had been drawn from the remnants of fires in old oil barrels. He had pencils, but they were very short – discarded and found on the streets.

"I know where you can paint it," Jake said. He rose from the sidewalk, where he'd been staring at the drawing.

Martinez turned to him, and Salvatore stood, finally, though he kept his eyes downcast. He was confused, and excited, and absolutely uncertain what to say.

Jake faced them, tears streaming openly down his cheeks.

"This vest," he said, "has the colors of The Dragons on it. I would give it to you, but I can't. It's...I just can't. But I have a jacket. It's leather. I wear it to protect me. I wear it like armor. I'll bring that jacket to you, if you'll paint my dragon on it. If you have seen ..."

Jake waved at the dragon on the sidewalk. He didn't look, because he was beginning to regain control of his emotions, and he didn't want to break down. They all knew it, but no one said anything. They let him talk.

"We're in the middle of something big," Jake said. "I don't know how it will end. We know how it ended for Vasquez. I may have to go into the next battle and find that same ending; I would be honored," his voice broke, but he pressed on, "if I could wear my dragon. I want to see it before I die."

Salvatore's vision blurred. He felt his knees grow weak. He started to speak, but the words swam in his mind, and he couldn't reach them. Then everything was dark.

Chapter Ten

The world whirled slowly back into focus. Salvatore stared at the ceiling over his head. It was not his own, but at first he couldn't place it. There were sounds, too, but he couldn't separate them from the rushing in his ears. Finally, after closing his eyes and lying very still, he was able to think. It was Martinez's home. He was lying on the floor on a thin pad. His head rested on some sort of pillow and he was covered in an old blanket.

He heard footsteps and turned toward the sound. Martinez was walking slowly about the room. Salvatore glanced up and saw that there were a number of items arranged on the table. Martinez steadily added to the pile, first going to one shelf, and then to another. Salvatore sat up slowly. He must have groaned, or made some sound, because Martinez turned and smiled.

"Back in the world of the living, I see," the old man said.

Salvatore opened his mouth to speak, but it was dry. His lips were gummy and stuck together. Martinez saw and was at his side in a moment with a small cup of water.

"Drink this," he said. "You've been sleeping for several hours."

"I am sorry," Salvatore managed after a second sip of the cool water.

"No reason to apologize. You've not been sleeping well lately, and what you are doing – the dragons you are drawing – that effort is draining your energy as well. We are going to have to find you some food before you start your painting. Jake will be dropping by your home this evening with his jacket. I told him I'd get you back on your feet and ready to work. He's very excited."

"Will it be okay?" Salvatore asked. "The painting – the dragon. I see them, but I don't understand. I have never drawn one until ..."

"Until after the man was dead." Martinez finished. "I know. This will be different. This jacket will be very special to Jake, and it will help to protect him. It is a good thing you are doing, and soon I will complete the paints that you need for the job."

There was a soft knock on the door, and Martinez opened the door. On the step a young girl curtsied shyly. She held a covered bowl in her hand.

"Evangeline," Martinez said. He leaned and took the bowl from her hand. "Where is your mother?"

"She could not come, sir," the girl said. "She is serving at the church tonight. They are making soup."

Martinez slid a hand into one pocket and pulled out a folded bill. He handed it to the girl.

"You make sure to give her my thanks. Tell her she has been a help to me, and that I will not forget. Can you remember that?"

The girl nodded. Salvatore knew her – he'd seen her playing in the park on sunny days and running errands for her mother in the streets. They seldom spoke. Most inhabitants of the Barrio ignored Salvatore. They though he was odd, and they knew of his connection to Martinez. Salvatore watched her, and when she caught him gazing, he blushed and smiled. He wished at times that he had more friends near his own age – those he could share his dreams with and not worry that he sounded foolish.

The girl, returned his smile, tilted her head prettily to one side, and then turned. With a quick flash of white cotton and tan legs she was off down the steps and into the street. Martinez turned back to Salvatore.

"Her mother, Maria Santiago, is a very fine cook. I have helped her when her children were sick, and I looked after her husband when he was injured in an accident several years ago. She sometimes sends me food. I asked her to send me something for you. I believe it is bean soup. I have some bread, and a bit of cheese. I want you to eat all of it, and have some milk. Then you must rest. When I am done here, we will carry the paints to your home, and wait for Jake."

Salvatore sat very still. He was unused to anyone looking after him. He was also, he realized, starving. He couldn't say when the last time he'd had anything that resembled a real meal, or anything to drink other than tepid water. His eyes pooled with tears, but he blinked them back. He did not want to humiliate himself in front of Martinez.

"What you are doing will help us all," Martinez said. The man's voice had softened slightly. "Eat. I have much to do before we will be ready."

Salvatore rose and took a seat at the table. Martinez placed the soup before him with a large spoon, a chunk of bread, and a moment later followed it all up with some cheese and a cup of milk. Salvatore didn't know where to start. It smelled delicious.

Martinez went back to his preparations. As he ate, Salvatore tried to pay attention. There were three simple earthenware bowls on the far side of the table. Between each and the window there were metal stands from which colored crystals dangled on chains. Martinez worked slowly and carefully. He mixed ingredients first in one bowl, and then the next. The first two were flanked by blue and yellow crystals. The last had a red crystal, and it was on this bowl that most of Martinez'ss attention was spent. The old man consulted often with a printed sheet of paper.

Salvatore was fascinated. He'd seen paints before. He'd even used them once or twice when the church gathered young people in the summer. They allowed him to attend, even though he had no parents to vouch or sign for him. Salvatore enjoyed those times very much, interacting with other young people, working on the crafts and hearing the stories of the priests. He listened carefully and never forgot a tale. The others, the children from better homes, and those who attended school regularly, seemed to take the words for granted, but for Salvatore stories were magic – almost as appealing as the images he created, day in and day out, to fill his ours and free his mind.

Martinez worked at the three bowls with a pestle, grinding the ingredients into a paste. He added oils and some water, and worked at each again. The old man was patient, and though he could not hear the words, Salvatore saw Martinez was speaking constantly as he worked. The mumble that was discernable was rhythmic, like a chant, or some sort of incantation. Salvatore very much wished he could hear it, but there was the cheese, and the cup of milk to consider, and he was afraid that if he spoke, or moved closer, he would interrupt the old man's concentration.

Finally the mixtures met Martinez's approval. He checked the sheet of paper a final time, then folded it and slipped it between the pages of one of his books. Next he walked to the window and opened the shade. The late afternoon sunlight streamed in at an angle. The old man returned to the table and examined the small stands. The crystals were just out of the sunbeam's reach. He adjusted them so that the light glinted through, bent, and sent colored shimmers over the table. Martinez moved the bowls next, so that the line of light breaking through each crystal found the far rim of one bowl. Salvatore saw that as the sun continued to set, the light would slice across the center of each bowl. One yellow, one blue, and one brilliant red.

Martinez turned to Salvatore and smiled.

"Now," he said, "we wait. These will be special paints, the kind of paints that can make a difference. When you paint Jake's dragon, they will give you strength. When your vision clouds they will provide clarity. It is important that you make the connection within yourself – that you see both man and dragon as one. Do you understand?"

Salvatore wanted to tell Martinez that, though he always saw the man and dragon as one, and he was certain that he could paint the dragon– particularly with such wonderful paints– that he did not understand. He did not understand why he was now the center of so much attention. He did not understand how he could see what others could not, or why it was so important that he do this particular painting now. He wanted to thank the old man for the food and the drink, and for not leaving him passed out in the street where he'd fallen.

Instead he just nodded and sipped the last of the milk. He

was very full, and a little sleepy. He wanted to stand and walk around to look into the bowls, but he could see no way to do so without blocking the sunlight, and he understood somehow that the light was important.

"What are they?" he said at last. He pointed at the crystals.

"They concentrate the color," Martinez explained. "The light through each contains the purest hue of one of the primary colors, yellow, blue, and Red. All other colors are shades of these, dilutions, or complex mixtures. The power in a painting–the power in any image–is focused on a foundation of the three. I have one more thing to do. Do you want to watch?"

Salvatore nodded. Martinez stepped to the sink and small counter that served as his kitchen. He grabbed a long, slender knife from the rack on the wall and turned toward the door. Salvatore rose and followed. The old man stepped out into the dying sunlight and walked around the side of his home. There was a bench there, pressed up against the wall. Martinez climbed nimbly up onto this, and Salvatore stood below, watching.

Martinez balanced on the bench and stared up toward the eaves intently. There was nothing there to see, and Salvatore frowned, screening the last of the day's light with his hand so he would miss nothing. There were deeper shadows just under at the edge where the roof met the wall, and thought he couldn't see into them, he knew that Martinez could.

Something small and quick darted across the white stucco of the wall. Martinez struck like a snake. A small lizard with brilliant blue and black stripes was pinioned to the wall by the striking blade. Salvatore cried out, but Martinez let out a grunt of satisfaction, spun, and pressed the squirming creature deeper onto the blade.

He didn't glance at Salvatore as he passed; he hurried inside. Then, as Salvatore's stomach grew queasy, the old man leaned in from the side, careful not to break the beam of light from the crystal, and held the gecko over the red bowl. A single drop of blood dropped into the mixture, and Martinez pulled back. He strode to the door and flipped his wrist, sending the dying lizard flying into the street.

Salvatore still stood, staring into the bowl where the drop of blood had spread, slowly, and then– as if the paint hungered– was swallowed and disappeared. He stretched out a hand toward the bowl, and then pulled it back as if afraid he'd be burned at the touch.

Martinez returned, placed the knife in his sink, and stepped up beside Salvatore, watching as the light moved slowly toward the far edge of the bowls.

"There is no red closer to prime," the old man said. "We have no dragons here, but it is close enough, I think. When you blend these colors, you will find every hue of your dragons in their joining. The more powerful your prime colors, the more complete the spectrum of your work.

Salvatore thought about this for a moment. He closed his eyes, and saw the subtle blends that created his purple, his green, and his orange. He thought of the dragon he'd drawn with the chalk on the sidewalk and how difficult it had been to get the colors right. He'd had to force them, trying again and again. This would be different. A very small amount of the paint could be blended, and then more added to change the hue. When he opened his eyes, he smiled.

"You understand," Martinez said. "It is good. You must be very careful with these paints. I will not be able to make more in time. I do not believe Jake's will be the last dragon you are called on to paint, and we must be ready. I will show you how to store and preserve the paint. You must listen carefully and do exactly as I say. A great deal depends on it."

"I will be careful," Salvatore said softly.

Martinez nodded, but he was already moving again. He pulled three sheets of white plastic from a drawer. He grabbed the blue paint bowl and very slowly, very carefully poured the paint onto the plastic. It was thick, and it didn't run toward the edges as Salvatore feared it might. Martinez deftly rolled the plastic, tying it off at one end with a bit of cord. He worked the paint down toward that tied end, and then rolled the empty end so that it came to a cone-shaped tip, which he also tied off.

"You'll be able to loosen this," Martinez said. You can squeeze some of the paint out the tip, and then seal it again. We must keep it moist, and cool. I will help you to find the proper place– perhaps we will dig a small pit in one corner of your floor."

Salvatore nodded. He was already thinking of the perfect place, the twisting, helpless body of the lizard impaled on Martinez's blade fading as the image of Jake's dragon struggled to the surface.

Martinez repeated the process, sealing the other two colors. Again, Salvatore saw that there was extra care taken on the red. He couldn't understand this, under the circumstances. There was very little of the red in Jake's dragon. It was gold and green, scales gleaming brightly. He felt it reaching out to him and heard its call.

"We'd better get going," Martinez said, after bundling the paints carefully. He held the door for Salvatore, who stepped out into the dying light of the day. Together they disappeared into the Barrio, heading for Salvatore's small shack. Jake would be there soon, and it would be time to paint.

Chapter Eleven

Donovan and Amethyst stepped into Club Chaos from the entrance on Forty-Second Street. They didn't have an appointment, so The Crossroads wasn't the right destination. They needed to get into the more crowded areas of the club and see who they could shake out of the rafters. They were dressed for a night on the town. Amethyst wore a long, dark gown, open down her back an slit at the sides. Donovan sported his customary trench coat, and had grabbed a black fedora to complete the ensemble. They didn't want to stand out, and dressing too conservatively would have done that as quickly, possibly more quickly, than taking their appearance too far. Club Chaos served a particular crowd...those who didn't belong were usually not hard to spot, and each inner den had its regulars.

"Where to first?" Amethyst asked.

"I think the pool room," Donovan said. "I know a guy who might be in there, and if not there are a few regulars that hail from the Barrio. Last time I was there I even saw one of Anya Cabrera's goons."

"The bald ones?"

"The same," Donovan said. "It was one of the only times I've ever seen one of them out of her sight, or out of the Barrio. He must have been on an errand. I didn't bother to try and talk with him."

Amethyst nodded. "Probably wise. Either he'd have gone for your throat, or just clammed up and reported your curiosity."

Donovan nodded. They ducked past the doormen, and entered a long hallway. To either side, shorter passageways led to a variety of inner bars. Music pounded through the speakers in the hallway, and as they passed the entrances to the various clubs, they pulsed with sound – a different variety and volume from each. Rock, Industrial, Swing – even Country. There was something for everyone at Club Chaos, assuming one knew where to look. Donovan knew that the acoustics had been enhanced by other-than-mundane methods. There was no other place like it on Earth...or, at least not in San Valencez.

They made their way to the back of the main passage and followed the hallway to the left. As they continued, the sound of balls being racked and slamming into one another echoed off the walls.

"Busy." Amethyst said.

"Better for us. The more people there are, the better chance we'll find someone who knows what's going on. We probably don't have that much time. If Martinez is desperate enough to hit us both up on the same day and risk our finding out, then something bad is happening, and soon."

"There's a small Voodoo contingent in the city, as well as in the Barrio," Amethyst said. "There are plenty who go in just for what Anya has for sale. If we're lucky, we'll find one of them here, playing dark priest for the local girls."

They entered the pool hall slowly and scanned the tables. There was a booth near the first table, and they headed for it. Most of the seats were full, and all of the pool tables were doing a brisk business. Even the stools at the bar were occupied.

"You get the booth, I'll get the drinks," Donovan said.

Amethyst wound her way to the empty booth and took a seat, taking in her surroundings as she went. Donovan rounded the four small pool tables toward the bar. There were a lot of faces to process, and it was a rough crowd. He recognized several of them, but no one he thought would be of any help. At the bar, he ordered two draft beers and turned back toward the table.

A tall young man had stepped up to the end of their booth. Amethyst stared up at him, and Donovan smiled. He hoped she left enough of the boy in one piece to keep the rest of the club's patrons from either turning on them en masse or clearing out. He hurried his steps.

The young man slid into the booth beside Amethyst, and

Donovan cursed under his breath. As he stepped closer he heard the boy give out a short yelp. Donovan slid in and was about to speak, then stopped. Amethyst had her unwanted visitor by the collar. In her other hand she held a jewel encrusted mirror so that he was forced to look into it.

"Let me go," the boy said. "I didn't mean nothin'..."

"You didn't mean anything," Donovan cut in helpfully. "Anything. If you didn't mean *nothin'* then it would mean that you did mean something, you see?"

The boy tried to turn and stare at Donovan, but he couldn't pull free.

"Just look into the mirror," Amethyst said softly. "Take a look at what you see, and then I'll let you go."

The boy should've fought. He should have yanked back and tried to drag her out, or hoped that his collar tore and he got free, but instead, he looked straight into the small mirror. He started to scream, but Amethyst dropped the mirror neatly into her lap, slammed her other hand over his mouth and held him. She leaned close then, brushed her lips close to his ear, and whispered something Donovan couldn't quite make out. Then she let the boy go and gave him a little push that sent him staggering back through the tables.

He bumped into one table, sloshed beer over the top of a full pitcher and brought a string of curses and blows from those he disturbed. Then he turned toward the door. The boy ran out of the club so quickly that the room fell momentarily silent, watching his retreat. After a moment, the sound of someone breaking a rack shattered the silence. The room came back to life like a slow turning movie reel coming back up to speed.

"What did you say?" Donovan asked.

"I told him to get a good look at what women see when he smiles at them." She said smugly. She tucked the mirror back into her handbag.

"What did he see?" Donovan asked.

She shrugged.

"That depends," she said. "Whatever frightens him the most. That's what the mirror does. I keep it close to me most of the time. There's a perfect stone chip of every birthstone around the edge. I've been experimenting with mirrors – new hobby. One day, I'm going to look in there and find out what it is that scares me. We always think that we know what it will be, you know? I keep that mirror because one day I'll want to know. I'll face something, and I'll look into the mirror, and I'll know if the thing I'm facing is it. If it's the worst thing ever – the one thing I have to overcome to overcome myself."

"Pretty deep," Donovan said. "I think I'll pass on taking a look, though. There's always something worse, and there's always something better. All we can do is concentrate on the here, and the now, and right now I need to find someone who knows what's going on out in the Barrio.

"Chicken," she said. Then she chuckled.

They both sipped their beer and scanned the room. Finally, Donovan saw what he was after.

"There," he said, nodding toward the corner. "It's Julio."

Amethyst followed his gaze. At the corner of the bar closest to the restrooms and the payphone, a skinny man in a dark shirt and jeans leaned on the counter. He held a drink between his hands, turning it nervously. He glanced alternately at the phones and the door.

"How fortunate, Amethyst said. "Do you want me to go and talk with him, or …?"

"You wait here," Donovan said, "and try to stay out of trouble. I'll … convince Julio that he wants to join us."

Donovan rose and slipped around the far side of the pool tables. He came up on the spot where Julio stood from behind and laid a hand suddenly on the smaller man's shoulder. Julio gave a yelp and tried to twist free, but Donovan held him tightly.

"If you keep on like that," he said, "I'm going to think you aren't happy to see me."

Julio was just less than six feet tall with a long, slender nose, greasy black hair, and furtive, darting eyes. He wore a pendant with an Egyptian Ankh dangling from it, rings on almost every finger, and the buttons on his shirt were inverted pewter crosses. Donovan suspected that if the man had more money, the crosses would be silver.

"What you want man?" Julio said. His voice was high and

whiny. "I got no problem with you."

"Never said you did," Donovan said. "Can't two old friends just talk?"

"You ain't my friend," Julio said.

"You better hope I am," Donovan said, dropping his voice. "You'd better hope you know what I need to know. It would go better for you if you were my friend."

Donovan turned Julio toward the pool tables and gave a light shove. He steered the man to the booth where Amethyst waited, and pushed him in.

"Hello, Julio," Amethyst said with a bright smile. "It's been too long."

Julio turned then and tried to bolt. He was slippery, and he almost slid past Donovan, but he telegraphed the move, and before he got a foot, Amethyst shot out a long leg and tripped him up. Donovan caught him by the back of his shirt and tossed him into the booth, sliding in beside him.

"What's got you so riled up," he asked. "We just have a few questions, and you know we'll pay. What's got you spooked?"

"Nothing," Julio said. "I just don't like being pushed around."

"Nobody's pushing," Amethyst said. "Yet. What have you heard about Anya Cabrera?"

"That crazy old hag?" Julio said. He puffed out his chest, but not before Donovan noticed the quick, furtive glance he sent back in the direction of the phone.

"You waiting on a call, Julio?" he asked.

"Maybe. What business is that of yours?"

"You wouldn't be reporting in to someone would you?" Donovan asked. "I mean, I could go over there, maybe catch the call for you. I bet I could tell them just about everything they wanted to know. Of course, not coming from you, it might slant things. You know what I mean? They probably expect you to answer the phone."

Julio had started to sweat. His hand shook, and he stared down at the table.

"Okay," he said. "Okay. What do you want to know?"

"I already told you that," Donovan said patiently. "We know

that Anya Cabrera is up to something. We've heard she's playing with powers better left alone. You know a little about the *Loa* don't you, Julio? How would you like to be visited by Papa Legba and have him take up residence...stay a while. Maybe forever."

"That would be crazy," Julio said. He tried to smile, but it came out as a grimace. He glanced at the phones again.

"Look," he said. "There *is* something going on. She's got a big ritual planned, tomorrow night. She's hooked up with one of the gangs – *Los Escorpiones*. They've been putting out the word that something is going down in the old junkyard on the south-side of the Barrio. Anya has a place there; back in among the junked cars. It's like some weird Aztec temple or something. I don't know what she's planning on doing other than the standard ritual, but I've heard...stories."

"We heard some of those," Amethyst said. "There was a gang war in Santini Park the other night. Seems it was a little one sided."

"That's what I heard," Julio agreed. "*Los Escorpiones* were there. They didn't die right, man. They fell down, got shot, got stabbed, and kept on fighting. They took out Vasquez. You know Vasquez?"

Donovan nodded. He remembered the gigantic biker, and he'd heard stories of the man's prowess in a fight.

"Did they shoot him?" he asked.

"They did, but it didn't matter," Julio said. "They took him down. He was breaking bones, tossing those boys around like they was dolls, and they just came back. And they were way too fast. At least, that's what my sources tell me. I didn't see it for myself. I've done business with *Los Escorpiones*...their Presidente – Hector? He was solid once. I do business with The Dragons, too – and Martinez. I don't get involved in what the gangs do, and I'm not much in a fight."

"Really?" Amethyst said sweetly. "A big strong guy like you?"

"That's all I know, man," Julio said. He glanced at the phone again. "Seriously, I got to go. I have something coming in tonight – from Haiti. If I miss out on it, someone else will get it. It's important."

"Nothing illegal, I hope," Donovan smiled. There was no humor in it.

"Are you done, man?"

Donovan waited a moment, then slipped out of the booth and stood aside.

"Nice talking with you, Julio," he said. "Wouldn't want to keep your friends waiting."

"You said you'd pay." Julio said, sliding slowly out of the booth.

Donovan started to reach for his wallet, but just at that moment, the phone across the room started to ring. Julio watched. Donovan moved very, very slowly. With a curse, the man slipped out of the booth and away, almost diving for the phone when he reached the back wall.

"I think we have everything we need," Donovan said. "If there are any real answers to be had, they'll be in that junkyard tomorrow night."

"You have an invitation I don't know about?" Amethyst asked. She slid out of the booth and stood at his side. "I don't know Anya very well, but it's my impression that she's not just going to let us wander in there...or if she did, she'd be doing her best to make sure we never get out again."

"We'll have to have a plan," Donovan said. "I don't think I'm ready to bust in on her ritual just yet, but I want to get close enough to see what's going on. I also want to know what Martinez will do. If we know this, he certainly knows as well. I want to know what he's doing with that paint."

"I can't help you with that," Amethyst said, "but I might have an idea how we can get close enough to find that answer. I've recently acquired some new...toys. Let's get back to my place – I'll show you whatt I mean."

"If I didn't know better," Donovan said with a grin, "I'd think you were trying to seduce me. Again."

She smacked him on the shoulder with a laugh, and they left the pool hall, and Club Chaos behind.

"We'll have to make a stop," Donovan said. "Cleo isn't jealous, but she does like to be fed now and then."

They disappeared into the streets. It had rained while they

were inside, just a light misting, and the neon of the club's lights flashed and glittered in off the wet walls and pavement.

Chapter Twelve

The old junkyard bordering the Barrio and the southern end of the city proper crawled with activity. The yard, owned by a used auto dealer on the edge of town, was run-down and forgotten and piled to the height of a small house with decades of automotive history. There were trucks, semi trailers, sports cars and city buses. A few had been smashed to small, efficient metal cubes, but that had happened in an earlier time, when the yard's heavy equipment still operated and the owner's men still regularly combed the fallen vehicles for useful parts and recyclable salvage.

Now it was an auto graveyard, and Anya Cabrera had claimed it for her own. Moving in slowly from the Barrio side, she'd taken first one small area, working the old cars into new shapes and piles, creating passageways deeper into the heart of the warped metal jungle. Initially, there was resistance. There were laws, and ordinances. There were safety concerns. Inspectors had come, and gone. The police had hung around the edges of the yard, even tried to enter and serve warrants on a couple of occasions. None of those officers who entered the yard ever came back a second time.

Some said that Anya paid them off. Others said she'd frightened them so badly that the thought of being in that dark place by night was more than they could stand. By day, Anya and her people kept to her shop, and the deeper halls and chambers of her domain. The night was a different matter altogether.

This day her people were out in force. A passageway had been pushed through to the center of the yard, where over time a large circular area had been cleared. To one side there was a small building, a place unlike any other structure in the city. It was formed of the hulking, rotting frames of cars. A few had been cut and welded, joined to create windows, doors and walls. At first glance, it blended with the mountains of wasted metal around it, but if you stared at it long enough, it evoked images of fairy tale castles, or steampunk nightmares. That small, squat bungalow faced onto the inner courtyard. Before it a wooden table rested on short, stout legs.

Lanterns hung all around the makeshift courtyard. They weren't electric – they were the old kind with doors that opened to allow a wick to be lit, the light dispersed by a brightly polished reflector. A few feet from the circular inner wall, braziers jutted from the hard, oil-packed earth. The center of the clearing was prepared for a fire, ringed in stones covered in whitewashed symbols. The pit was filled with charcoal, deep enough to burn and smolder for hours.

Anya's assistant, Kim, came down the passageway with a wooden case. There were two others with her, tall and silent. They carried their bundles to the oddly formed room of car bodies and stopped. Kim carried hers inside, the silver caskets in her hair jingling brightly. She disappeared with a flash of light. The two others placed their loads on the ground. They turned toward the entrance to the inner circle, crossed their arms, and watched in silence.

Others brought powdered incense and quietly prepared the braziers. They worked quickly and carefully, measuring their amounts as exactly as possible. Inside, Kim unpacked the supplies she'd carried in. Shelves lined the walls, and she filled them slowly. She had candles, dark bottles with faded labels, vials and herbs. One of the boxes that she eventually carried in was filled with bottles of dark rum. Another held tequila. She had at least one more trip to make –there were jars of dried mushrooms and peyote buttons still to come.

Most of it would not be used. Anya Cabrera had a very particular ceremony in mind, and there was not likely to be any deviation, but there were other considerations. There were those who would be present, but would not participate directly. They

had to be satisfied, entertained, and paid. Anya would service
them separately. Kim would help in this – it was her duty to
handle things when Anya was too busy, or too distracted, to
handle them herself.

Over the years, though she was young, the others had
come to accept her, and to acknowledge her authority. It was
significant that she was handling the preparations for the
night's ceremony. No other would have been entrusted with it;
on all earlier occasions, it had been Anya herself.

When she finished, she stepped out into the courtyard. The
two guarding her turned, hefted the empty crates she'd left on
the front doorstep, and started back toward the street. The sun
was dropping lower in the sky, and they had at least one more
trip to make before they had everything they needed. As they
wound their way down the trail between the old wrecks, they
passed young men and women hanging more lanterns. When
it grew fully dark, the lanterns would light the only way into
the center court. There were small alcoves to either side, easily
spotted now, but that would be dark pits of shadow later on.
They would house the guards.

Los Escorpiones would provide most of the sentries. Only
those chosen by Hector would be allowed into the central court
– the rest, those guarding the way in, would be boys and men
who either were afraid, or too young for the coming battle, or too
new to the gang to be fully trusted. Some of Anya's men would
guard them too. No one would be fully trusted with any single
part of this evening – it was too important, and potentially too
dangerous.

Back at the shop, the two guards waited by the counter in the
main room as Kim disappeared inside. What she needed was
already packed, but she wanted to report in before returning to
the clearing for the final time. She made her way deeper and
deeper into the labyrinth of halls and doorways. She passed her
own quarters without a glance, and at last the reached the inner
sanctum – the room where Hector had come for his audience.

The room was empty, but there were more beaded curtains
at the back, and Kim headed for them without hesitation. She
brushed through and into a final hallway. It branched right and

left. She turned in a circle twice, spat on her hand and pressed it to her forehead. She closed her eyes and turned again. When she opened her eyes once more, she faced the left fork and – again – she plunged ahead without hesitation. A moment later she came to a wooden door. She knocked lightly and waited.

"Enter," Anya called.

Kim pressed the door open and stepped inside.

"It is ready?" Anya asked. She was seated before a small vanity. It wasn't covered with makeup, or jewelry, but with small canisters, vials, and tubes. There were three small piles of powder on the surface before Anya, and she did not look up from her work. She held a razor blade, and with it she chopped the powders finer, and finer.

"I have one final trip to make. When you arrive, all will be in readiness."

"Hector?" Anya asked.

"There has been no sign of him, but it is still very early. He will come. They will all come. It will be glorious."

Anya nodded; it was a very slight movement. Her dark hair glistened in the dim light of a single bulb burning over the vanity. The rest of the room dripped with dark shadows. It was impossible to tell where the room ended – or if it ended. The sensation was like that of standing in a deep, empty cavern.

"I will be there shortly after the sun sets. Do not let me down."

Kim turned without a word. There was no purpose to a response. She would succeed, or she would not. Talking about it changed nothing, and promises were like etching paths to failure for the mind to walk. She knew what had to be done.

She closed the door behind herself, crossed back to the main passageway, and into the shop. She picked up the last case of supplies, nodded to the two guards, and they followed her out. As they passed, one of them flipped the sign on the window to "Cerrado".

The darkness fell suddenly and completely. Kim had returned to the small room in the center of the yard and stored the last of the supplies. She'd checked the braziers, and when she found them loaded to her satisfaction, she moved on to the lanterns, and the guard posts. She stationed men at alternating positions, leaving the rest to be filled by Hector's men. Just before the last of the daylight dropped from the world, Anya entered the circle. She moved slowly, flanked on either side by one of the tall, dark, bald guardians. Another walked behind her, and when she entered, he turned at the door, just as those who'd followed Kim had done earlier that day, barring the way to any who might follow.

Anya circled the clearing slowly. As Kim had done, she checked the braziers. She stepped up to the fire pit and traced a long, dark-painted fingernail over the symbols and letters painted there. At last, she came to where Kim stood watching, turned back to the center, and nodded.

"You have done well. Place the circle. Leave it open here," she waved at the ground before the small room, "and at the entrance. Once Hector and his men are in , seal that side. When we enter, we will close the circle and begin."

"As you wish," Kim said. She turned away.

To the right of the doorway, there was a canvas pouch. She raised it from the nail where it hung, opened the flap on top, and stepped into the clearing. There was a furrow etched in the ground, circling the fire. She started slowly, dribbling the white powder from the pouch into the cut in the earth. It glimmered in the dim light of the lamps. She muttered to herself as she moved down the line, and her feet moved in an odd, shuffling dance. Her concentration was absolute.

Anya watched as Kim worked. She took note of the grace of the girl's movements, and the surety and confidence of her actions. It was good. There would be no mistakes. She turned with a flourish and disappeared into the small room, out of site. She would not exit that room until all of the others had arrived and were in place. Soon, it would begin.

Chapter Thirteen

After a quick stop at Donovan's townhouse, where he restocked the many pockets of his jacket and fed Cleo, they hurried back to Amethyst's place. She hadn't said what it was that she wanted to get, but she'd made it clear that in the face of what they were up against, it was going to be important. Donovan settled onto a heavy leather chair in her den, and she brought in a bottle of wine and two glasses.

"This is going to take a quick explanation," she said. "It's not the sort of thing I usually deal with, but when I heard it was available, I couldn't resist. If I was one of those people that believed nothing happens without a reason, I'd have to think it was some odd twist of fate."

"I've always believed we make our own fate," Donovan said. "Of course, it's about the time I say something like that when I get a strange sign, or find just the right old manuscript. Sometimes you can almost feel something – or someone – watching over you."

"It's exactly like that."

Amethyst filled their glasses and sat the bottle on the table. Before she took her seat she crossed the room to a bookshelf. Where Donovan's shelves were cluttered and overflowing, hers were ordered and neat. She pulled out a dark book with gold gilt lettering on the spine, reached around behind it, and tugged on a latch. The base of the shelves appeared to be a solid wooden cabinet, but as the latch released, the front dropped gently down to reveal a wide drawer.

She opened the drawer, removed a dark leather bag, and then slid the drawer shut. She closed the cabinet and returned the book to its place. Donovan smiled as he watched her. He knew she must cringe every time she entered his den, and he was always afraid she'd snap and start arranging and organizing things. If she did he might lose the tenuous hold he still had on his chaos.

When she'd returned to her seat, she laid the bag on the coffee table between them. Donovan reached for it, but she laid her hand on his to stop him.

"Let me tell you about it first," she said.

Donovan leaned back and reached for his wine.

"It's not a long story," she said. "It is strange though. Do you remember a guy named Chance?"

"Of course," Donovan said. "I've bought a lot of things from him. He's not always around – seems to travel a lot. It's always worth talking to him. I didn't know he was around."

"I think he only lets you know if he has something that might interest you. This time he called me, and even *he* didn't seem certain I'd want what he had. Like I said, it's not my usual thing. My collection is among the most complete in the world – I have minerals, matched sets of crystals, gemstones, elements, and just about every alchemical text still in existence. Those I don't have, I can access."

She smiled at him then, and he laughed. "That you can," he said.

"What Chance brought in is dark. I'd heard of these things, but never actually seen one, and really never had the desire. He had an order for several, but when the deal was done he had two left over. He said he could probably have sold them to the first buyer if he'd mentioned it, but he was already a little leery of that deal, and just wanted to get away as quickly as possible and in one piece. He also didn't like the idea of them falling into the wrong hands, or just disappearing into the streets.

"That left him with two, and he thought of me. He's been traveling again – Haiti this time. You might recall that he isn't really the talkative type. He told me very little of where he acquired these items; he told me their use, and he told me his price. I've never doubted the quality of his stock. Still, at first

I wasn't sure I'd take them. I told him to bring them around, and we'd see."

"Apparently they were more interesting than you initially thought?" Donovan asked. He nodded at the bag on the table. "You seem to have added them to your collection."

"I had a similar reaction to his," Amethyst said. "When I'd seen these, and held them, I worried about who might take them if I didn't. I don't know who all in San Valencez Chance does business with, but I was able to think of a few right off the bat that don't need items this powerful to get into trouble with. Anyway...they are also compelling. I have been considering getting rid of them, just because they fascinate me. I don't like things that distract me unless I've chosen to let that happen."

"So are you going to tell me what they are, or wait until I snap from the curiosity and open them myself."

"For someone as old as you are, you are very impatient."

"Ouch."

"They're pendants. It's hard for me to admit this, but I'm not absolutely certain what they are made of. It's not any known stone or gem. It's not wood, or bone, either. They are very black and a little oily to the touch. He claimed to have gotten them straight from a *Bocor* – carved by hand. He didn't know what the material was either, and didn't seem at all interested in finding out."

"But he told you what they are used for?"

Amethyst nodded. She reached out and grabbed the leather bag. She untied the cords that held it closed and reached inside. What she drew out made Donovan sit up quickly with interest. The hairs on the back of his neck stood up before he'd even brought the things into focus. Each dangled from a rough metal chain, and Amethyst held them by these, avoiding contact with the small figurines.

"They are spirit stones," she said. "They have many purposes, but there are a couple in particular that I believe may prove useful. When worn, they serve the dual purpose of obscuring your identity and presence from the living – making people overlook you, thickening shadows and encouraging others to look somewhere else, though they don't know why, and more importantly, they render the wearer absolutely undetectable to spirits."

Donovan reached out and took one in his hand. He rubbed his thumb over the surface. It was waxy, like soap, and where he touched it, it felt as if it left a sheen of … something … on his skin. He wanted to drop it like a snake that was about to strike, but when he went to do so his fingers tightened around it.

"You feel it too," Amethyst said. "It's calling to you."

Donovan pulled his hand back, and Amethyst dropped the two pendants back into the leather bag. There was an immediate release of tension as she did so.

"There is something trapped in those stones," Donovan said softly. "Whatever it is might have the ability to do the things you've said, but what it seeks is escape. It wants to be released, and I wonder – is that spirit less dangerous than those we may face?"

"I can't answer that," Amethyst said. "Without knowing who did the trapping, or how it was accomplished, it's impossible to be certain, I think. Perhaps, when this is done, and we have the time, we can look into it? If someone, or something, has been trapped against its will, we should release it."

Donovan nodded. "I am sure we can find a reference to these in my library…when there is time. For now, we have to concentrate on figuring out what Anya Cabrera is up to, and just what kind of danger we're facing in the Barrio. I have the feeling Martinez could tell us more, but I don't think he trusts us to handle it. He let me know things were wrong, so he has to know I'll go there, but he didn't tell me everything, and that makes me believe he's planning something on his own. I wish I had time to find out what it is, because I'd hate to get trapped between the two of them."

"Anya holds a lot of local rituals," Amethyst said. "She summons the *Loa*, makes sacrifices, and does minor conjuring for locals. She's been growing slowly more influential, but she has never seemed powerful enough to be any kind of real threat. What changed?"

"If Martinez and Cord are right, she's playing with very dangerous toys," Donovan said. "The *Loa* inhabit those who honor them by excessive behavior – crazed dancing, drinking the right things, sometimes drugs – Peyote or Mushrooms. Sometimes it's no more than hallucination on the part of the believer, but there are also times when the spirits they seek take over their bodies. I've seen very young children drink entire bottles of rum while smoking a cigar and cursing. That should kill them, but when it's over they fall into a deep sleep, and they are fine. The *Loa* have a great sense of humor, and they love to visit. What Anya is doing is taking advantage. She's not letting them leave."

"How is that possible?" Amethyst asked. "I thought they came and went as they pleased, within the bounds of the ritual."

"They do, but only when the ritual is completed properly. There are patterns in everything, as you know. There is a beginning, and an end to ritual, and Anya has found – somewhere – a way to twist or prolong the ending of the summoning ritual. The *Loa* are trapped in their host's body, unable to take over and enjoy their moments of freedom in this world, as they intended, and unable to escape back to their own. What is left is worse than a zombie. It's a shadow creature, half human, half spirit. They are apparently incredibly strong and fast, and from the descriptions of how they were cut down by bullets and knives, and then rose to fight as if nothing had happened, they share the ability to heal that allows hosts to drink and cut themselves without dying."

"Surely she can't keep them here indefinitely?"

"I don't know," Donovan said. "No one in my memory has been foolish enough to try. My best guess is that it's like a steam boiler. If she tries to keep them in a vulnerable human host for too long, something will burst. If the spirits are freed on this plane, I doubt anything she can do will control them. She's playing with fire."

"We'll have to get in there and see if we can't put it out then," Amethyst laughed. "But that's tomorrow. For now, this is good wine, and we will both need some...rest."

She raised one eyebrow and smiled at him, and Donovan laughed, taking a deep drink of his wine.

"A woman after my own heart."

He glanced down at the table.

"Let's put those away first, though. If we have to use them, let's put it off as long as possible. They make my skin crawl."

Amethyst did as he asked, and as she tucked them back into the hidden drawer, Donovan felt as if they still called to him. He shivered and took another drink. He wondered if they were playing with their own fire…and he wondered if they would be too late.

Chapter Fourteen

Salvatore stared at the back of Jake's jacket. The leather was black and supple, worn from decades of use. It felt like years of wind and weather, and the scent of it permeated the small shack, leather, beer, cigarette smoke, cologne. Like the dragon in his dreams the scent was uniquely Jake, and just for a moment Salvatore stood, his hand flat on the back of the jacket and his eyes closed, making the connection.

The big man had dropped it off shortly after Salvatore returned to his home. Martinez had stayed long enough to be certain that the paints were stored properly and that Salvatore knew how to mix and care for them properly. There were other materials, as well. Martinez had bought a small wooden palette, several brushes much nicer than any Salvatore had ever seen, and a bottle of spirits for cleaning them.

The jacket was draped over the back of a wooden chair. Salvatore had fastened the snaps in front, and found that if he stuffed the chest with his pillow, the leather stretched smooth in back. Jake had a broad back, and the surface he had to work on was both tall and wide.

There wasn't a lot of time. Jake had said he would return the next morning, and Salvatore intended to be finished by then. It was inconceivable that he might leave the work unfinished. He laid out the paints on his table, arranged the brushes and poured a small amount of the spirits into an old glass. When he turned to the jacket, he had a bit of white chalk in his hand.

Salvatore closed his eyes and drifted back into the land of his dreams. He reached out to the skyline of that dark, distant city. He sought the scent of the beach, the wet sand and the salt spray. He heard – very faintly – the cries of the dragons as they soared, far above the waves. A flash of green and gold passed before his eyes, and he smiled. Opening his eyes, he began to sketch.

He worked quickly. Salvatore sometimes spent hours thinking about what he would draw, but once his hand began to move it was always the same. It felt as if the images were trying to claw their way out of him. The chalk flew over the black leather canvas, his touch light and exact. He didn't want it to leave any mark that would remain when the paint was applied, but he wanted his outlines – his curves and motion – the essence of the dragon – to be perfect and preserved before he began filling in the colors and the shadows.

Finally he set aside his chalk and turned to the paints. He took the blue, and the yellow and, using the improvised squeeze tubes Martinez had provided, he laid a small line of each on the palette. He started with the dark colors, the green so deep it was almost black. The tail of the dragon swirled like a giant serpent, curling up and back down toward the floor. The wings were strong and powerful and ended in huge, pointed talons.

Salvatore had sketched the face turned so that it glanced back over one shoulder as the creature rose, tipping back into a long roll. He didn't just paint the dragon. He painted the motion of its body. He painted the light of that alien moon glistening off the scales of its back and the glimmering reflection of the waves and surf in the pools of its vast, glaring eyes.

There was beauty in the dragon, and incredible power. He felt it, and his mind recreated the colors and hues, shadows and motion that had conveyed that power when he'd seen them. For a long time he stood, working on the shadowed outline of one wing, unaware of the room around him, or the jacket itself, only seeing the dragon – the one in his mind.

And then, he was no longer aware of anything but that sandy beach. He held a stick, and he swirled the end of it in the sand. He raised his eyes and saw that the dark city was closer than it had ever been. Towers rose far above him, turrets and peaked guard shacks loomed like giant monoliths. There were no lights burning in that place. The only illumination came from the moon, far above, and from a strange glow that rose from the white froth on the waves. He was alone, and he knew that he should feel frightened, terrified even, but he did not. He climbed over damp dunes and wet stones, moving steadily upward toward the city walls.

He heard the screaming cries of the dragons far off, but there was no sign of them. The sky was clear, and the only sounds close by came from the crashing waves. Salvatore did not know why he headed for the city. He sensed that there was something there he should find, something important, but he had no idea what it might be, or how he could locate it. Judging from the height and obvious thickness of the walls, it was doubtful if he could even get inside unless some gate stood open.

He heard a roaring sound, but could not place it. He turned, afraid that some huge wave was preparing to pound down on him, but the ocean was as smooth as glass. He turned back to the wall of the city, and in that instant, the dragon screamed. Salvatore reeled back and nearly fell from the stone he'd been climbing. The creature glided up over the wall, from the interior of the city. It was huge, and it's body blocked the light from the moon and left him stumbling backward in shadow.

It was magnificent. Green and gold scales rippled along the underbelly and down the sides of the tail. The wings were dark, but they caught glimmers of light and flickered with barely contained energy.

The dragon soared over the waves, climbing impossibly high, and then turned, just as he had seen it – just as he had known it would. In that instance Salvatore locked his gaze to that of the creature and felt a snap of power and strength binding them. He turned and held out his arms, and the beast dove. It plunged so rapidly there was nothing to see but a blur of green and gold. As it drew near, Salvatore felt the rush of wind and heard the thunderous flapping of its wings. He stood, still as stone, waiting, knowing it would come for him – knowing that he would fly.

He toppled backward but made no attempt to halt his fall. He trusted the dragon to catch him, trusted his instincts. He never struck the ground, but neither did he fly. He fell away to a soft darkness, the last sound he heard the triumphant scream of Jake's dragon.

When Martinez opened the door to Salvatore's shack, he nearly stopped in shock. Only quick reflexes allowed him to rush across the room and grab the boy's shoulders from behind, easing him to the floor and preventing a nasty fall. Salvatore still held one of the brushes in his hand. Martinez took it gently and stepped to the table. He did not look at the jacket. Not yet.

Working quickly, the old man cleaned the brushes. He sealed off the tubes of color and wrapped them carefully as he had shown the boy to do the day before. It was early still, not quite four o'clock in the morning. The streetlights would soon flicker out – what few of them actually operated properly in the Barrio. Before long the sun would begin to tickle at the skyline, and not long after that, Jake would arrive.

Before that happened, there was work to be done. He needed to get the boy into his bed, and covered up so that he could rest. He needed to find food, and drink. He was certain Salvatore would be famished. Whether the boy actually understood the magnitude of the power he wielded or not, there was no way to escape the way such an encounter with the supernatural drained strength and stamina. Salvatore was already too thin – too weak.

Martinez tucked the paints away carefully, then turned and lifted Salvatore from where he still lay on the floor. The boy was light, but Martinez could easily have lifted twice his weight. He was old, but much less fragile than he appeared. There are a great number of ways to conceal one's self, and Martinez was familiar with them all.

When Salvatore was as comfortable as possible, the old man leaned in and rubbed a spot of green paint off of his pale cheek. Then he turned, and at last, he confronted the dragon. The moment he cast his eyes on it the image etched itself into his mind, and he knew he would never forget. His breath caught in his throat, and he took an involuntary step back.

The creature's eyes were deep, yellow-gold pools. They shimmered, so real he sensed the liquid at their center, and so powerful he felt their scrutiny across veils and dimensions. He was certain that, in some way, the thing saw him as well. Maybe it was just a momentary connection – a thread between worlds. It snapped, and he stepped closer.

There was no doubt that this dragon was Jake's. Every line in the creature's body traced a weathered crease in the man's face. The power of the beast was undeniable, but there was something more – an intelligence, and the sensation that – despite the sword-like talons and glistening teeth, it could be trusted. You could turn your back on it, and it would cover you in a fight. You could call out to it – and it would answer. It had answered.

Martinez glanced sharply at Salvatore. He wondered in that moment what the boy had been doing – what he had seen – when he let himself fall back. What had he expected to happen, and where had he been?

Martinez stepped onto the porch and whistled. A young man slipped from the shadows, where he'd been waiting.

"Go," Martinez said. "Bring food and drink. I will wait with him until he wakes. We must both be gone before the dragon arrives."

The boy disappeared into the shadows, and Martinez seated himself on the step. He didn't want to face the painting again. Not yet – and not alone. He sat, and he watched the sunrise. When the young man returned with the food, Martinez took it and disappeared inside.

Salvatore woke to Martinez shaking his arm gently. He sat up quickly, blinking, and stared around the room as if he had no idea where he was.

"Easy," Martinez said. "I woke you because you need to eat. Jake will be here soon – he will want to see his dragon."

Salvatore spun, saw the jacket, and rose, all in one motion. He stood, and he stared at what he had created. He traced each line carefully, his gaze critical, and amazed. He stepped first to one side, and then to the other. He could find no flaw. He turned to see how Martinez was reacting, but to his shock, he found that he was alone. Without sound, or warning, the old man was just…gone.

There was bread and cheese on the table, and a small jug of milk. Suddenly, Salvatore was hungrier than he'd ever been in his life. He turned from the dragon almost apologetically, but the food drew him. He devoured every scrap in a matter of moments and washed it down with the milk. He'd intended to break it into portions, save some for later, but it wasn't possible. He could have – and would have – eaten twice as much. When he was done, he sat on the edge of his bed and stared at the dragon. There was nothing left to do but to wait for Jake.

Chapter Fifteen

Salvatore heard Jake's voice out on the street, and suddenly he felt shy. It was one thing to know he had captured the dragon exactly as he'd seen it, and to know that it was the perfect representation of how he knew Jake in that other place – that other world. It was very much another thing to wait, vulnerable and uncertain, to see if the big man would react the same way – if he would see it as Salvatore did. If he would be pleased.

There was no going back. What had been the slick black leather of the jacket was alive with color. The paint, which Salvatore had secretly feared might not dry properly or adhere to the jacket's surface, had hardened and sealed as if it were dye instead of paint. Where there should have been rough brush strokes, the color was smooth and seamless. Salvatore assumed that this was Martinez'ss doing, and he asked no questions. For better or worse, the jacket and the dragon were one. Heavy footsteps pounded just outside, and Jake's knock shook the frame of the door.

"Hey, Sally," he said. "You in there? You awake?"

For a moment, Salvatore stood still in confusion. He'd never had a nick name before, and he wasn't certain who Jake was talking to. Then the fog lifted and he hurried to the door. He couldn't find his voice, so he pulled it open and stood, staring. Jake grinned.

"Mind if I come in?" he said.

Salvatore blushed and stepped aside. Behind Jake a tall, thin blonde woman followed. She glanced around herself, as if she didn't trust the street, or the small shack she was entering. She glanced at Salvatore, and when she saw how nervous he was, she smiled. It changed her face completely, and Salvatore couldn't help smiling back.

"So, Sally" Jake said. "Is it finished?"

Before Salvatore could answer that yes, it was finished, and that – if Jake did not mind – his name was not Sally, Jake rounded the table and he saw it. He stopped and stood very still, staring. The woman caught the expression on his face.

"Jake," she said. "Jake honey, what…"

She stepped around to stand beside him, turned toward the jacket and let out a soft gasp.

"Oh my God," she said. She stepped back, and then again, bumping up against the edge of Salvatore's cot. She didn't trip, but she dropped back onto the simple mattress and brought a hand up to cover her mouth.

Jake reached out slowly and ran his finger over the leather. He didn't touch the dragon at first. He traced its lines, rolled along its sinuous curves. Salvatore stood and watched. He didn't yet know if Jake's reaction was positive. The woman was even harder to read. Salvatore watched her, not wanting to interrupt Jake, but desperate to know if he'd done the right thing – if his work would serve.

She was an attractive woman, slender with several silver bracelets on each wrist. Pendants hung from chains around her neck and her hair was pulled back in long braid. She wore blue jeans, a tight fitting T-shirt, and black boots. Salvatore had liked her since the moment she'd smiled at him, but now that smile had been wiped away by another expression. The shock on her face had drained all her color. He noticed that she had a tiny tattoo around her wrist. It was a bracelet made of tiny twined serpents. Dragons. In the center, on top, was a single word.

Jake.

Finally, shaking his head like he was rising up out of deep water, Jake stepped back, but not far. Half a step, maybe, as if he didn't want to be too far from the jacket. As he turned, Salvatore saw that the man's eyes streamed tears. His expression asked a question, and at the same time barely contained some deep emotion.

"How?" he asked. "How could you have done this? In one night? You..."

The woman rose shakily to her feet and stepped forward, laying a hand on Jake's shoulder.

"It's beautiful," she said. Her voice was as choked with emotion as his, and Salvatore had a sudden intuition. She loved this man, Jake, and she'd seen every bit of what Salvatore saw in the dragon. She loved it too. It was an awkward, yet wonderful moment of revelation.

"It is your dragon, Senor Jake," Salvatore said. "I have only painted what I've seen."

"Is it dry? Can I..."

Salvatore nodded. He didn't know how it was possible, but he'd checked carefully. The paint was dry and sealed, as set as if it had been painted years before. Something told Salvatore it would take something truly powerful to remove the design, now that it existed.

Jake pulled the jacket off of the chair almost reverently. He held it at arm's length and stared at it. He held it up for the woman to see more clearly. She reached out slowly and stroked the dragon's back. When she did so, Jake arched his back and gasped. The two stood there a long moment, their gazes locked.

"Helen," Jake said, "would you do the honors?"

Salvatore tucked the name away carefully. Helen only nodded, but she took the jacket from Jake's hands and when he turned and held out his arms, she slid it on, first one side, and then the other. Jake shook once so that it settled onto his shoulders, and turned slowly. He could no longer see the dragon, but Salvatore thought he felt it. The man stood straighter. The jacket – Salvatore had seen it when Jake wore it in the day before, fit more perfectly, like a dark second skin. The room crackled with energy, and Jake, who was a big, burly man, seemed to move with a grace and strength that he had previously lacked.

"Sally," he said, turning to face Salvatore. "I ... I don't know what to say. I saw what you did the other day on the sidewalk, and I thought – yeah – that would be cool on my leather. I expected – something else. I didn't know. I don't know what to say about this – what to think. It's...fucking amazing."

Salvatore flushed with pride.

"I have only painted what I have seen," he repeated. "The dragon – it is beautiful."

"It is," Helen said, moving up to stand beside Jake. She seemed unwilling to let him move far from her side, She wrapped her arm in his, leaning against him so that the painted tail of the dragon brushed her ribs.

"How old are you?" she asked suddenly, turning back to Salvatore.

"I am fourteen, Senora Helen," he said softly, glad he'd been able to remember her name. He tried to stand taller and held his shoulders back, but he was not tall for his age, and he was very thin. He didn't really know her, but he suddenly wanted this woman, this woman who so clearly loved his new friend Jake, to like him.

"And your name is Sally?" Helen asked.

"Salvatore," he said softly. "I am Salvatore Domingo Sanchez."

She took this in, then slid reluctantly away from Jake and walked over and laid her hand on his shoulder. She looked him up and down, then scanned the small, shabby shack he called home, and shook her head in amazement.

"Well, Salvatore Domingo Sanchez," she said. 'That," she pointed at Jake's Jacket, but didn't look away from his eyes, "is fucking amazing. I don't mean amazing like some kid with a can of spray paint who decorates the walls of buildings, or like some guy who drew the picture in the magazine and got the mail-order artist course. I mean...I've been to museums. I've seen things that are so incredible you can only stand and stare at them and wonder what kind of person could create them. Do you understand the kind of art that I mean?"

Salvatore nodded. He'd seen books, and the few times he'd been privileged to visit schools he'd learned about men with names like Leonardo da Vinci and Michelangelo. He had loved those paintings.

"This dragon," Helen went on, "is that kind of art. This dragon is very likely the finest..." her voice broke then, and she shook her head angrily, fighting for control. "...the finest single work of art that I have ever seen."

"We are still talking about the jacket, right?" Jake asked softly.

She spun on him, and Salvatore thought she might take a swing, she was so angry. Then, when she saw his face, the anger broke like waves on a beach and she burst into almost hysterical laughter.

Jake stepped forward then and squatted down so that he and Salvatore were eye to eye.

"I don't say things like this very often," he said, "so listen up, and don't forget. Right?"

Salvatore nodded again. He wished he could get his voice to obey him, but he found that the moment sucked the air from his lungs. His heart pounded, and he sensed that something important was about to happen. Something that would change his life.

"There is no way I can pay this back," he said. "There is nothing that I have or expect to have that could make this – gift – square. You need something, anything, any time, you call me. This is as serious as it gets. This is the magic. When you grow up, when you meet guys like I've met – a woman like Helen, you'll know. You'll feel it, and you'll know. Until then, little bro, you've got me."

Salvatore felt a huge lump in his throat and he pinched back the tears that threatened to pour down his cheeks. Helen saw it and knelt beside him, wrapping both Salvatore and Jake in a hug.

Very suddenly, Jake started laughing again.

"This," he said, "is just getting freaking weird." He stood and held out his hand. Salvatore took it in his own smaller hand. Jake's grip was firm, but not painfully so. There was a warmth in it – and a charge of energy.

"I got to go," Jake said. "I have to show this to Snake, and the others. There are things coming – bad things – that I have to be a part of. There may be others who will come to you. You do right by them – they'll be behind you forever. You understand? Any of them gives you any crap, you tell them Jake has your back. If that doesn't work, you come get me and I'll tell them myself."

Salvatore nodded. Jake turned to the door, and Helen followed. She smiled back over her shoulder at Salvatore, who watched them go in silence. When the door had closed, and their footsteps had died away in the distance, he finally allowed himself to breathe.

Sunlight poured in through the battered slats of his window, and he stepped out onto the sidewalk, letting the warm rays wash down over him. It was a glorious day to be alive, and he thought, in just a bit, that he would draw. Already his mind was filled with another image – another dragon. Soon, he would set it free.

Chapter Sixteen

Salvatore sat on the sidewalk, about half a block from his home, drawing. He was surrounded by bits of brightly colored chalk. The spot he'd chosen fronted a vacant lot. The builder had begun the walkway up toward a home that had never been built. Salvatore had chosen this spot so that he could work just off of the main thoroughfare. He didn't mind that people would walk on his creations – he did, after all, draw on sidewalks – but he didn't want to be disturbed *while* he worked, and after the events of the night before, something had changed. There was an urgency to the drawings. Almost the moment Jake left him, another dragon had invaded his mind, as if filling a suddenly vacated void.

This time the serpent was a bright, ice blue. Salvatore had worn his large chunk of white chalk down to a nub filling in highlights. The blue was subtle, and there were only hints of shadows and lines for the legs, arms and scales. It was like drawing a creature of glass, or ice – much more difficult than the solid gold and green of Jake's dragon. Salvatore found himself itching for the paints and the brushes, for the simplicity of mixing colors on the palette. He still caught the scent of salt spray, but it was faint. The Barrio intruded, and he wanted to brush it aside like a veil and step through to the threshold of that dark city.

Several people passed him as he worked, but he paid them no attention. He was lost in the dragon's world – in its power and color. When one set of footsteps didn't pass by, but stopped a few feet away, it took a while for Salvatore to notice. Finally, when something cut off the sunlight on a portion of sidewalk he was about to draw on, he glanced up and stopped.

A tall Hispanic man stood over him, watching intently. He was dressed almost identically to Jake, but the two could not have been more different. Where Jake was large and powerful like a truck driver, this man was slender. He gave the impression of speed and agility, no less powerful, but more distant. Salvatore had seen him many times.

"Salvatore?" the man said. "Sally?"

Salvatore nodded. He found that he did not have the strength to rise, and despite the intrusion, and the sudden rushing of his heartbeat, the dragon was not yet complete. He didn't want to move until it had been completed.

"I'm Enrique," the man said. "I saw Jake's dragon this morning. It was...amazing."

His words trailed off, and Salvatore saw he was mesmerized by the picture on the sidewalk. Enrique squatted down beside Salvatore, not crowding him, and studied the drawing. His face was a mask of wonder and concentration.

"It's mine," he said at last, turning to Salvatore. Enrique's eyes were a bright, ice blue, and there was no room for question, or denial in his expression. He had seen what Salvatore already knew. "You have to paint it," he said. "You have to paint my dragon."

"I would be honored," Salvatore said. "When..."

"Now," Enrique said. He stood and turned in one fluid motion, unwinding like a coiled snake and moving before Salvatore could utter a sound. "I know your place. I'll be there in twenty minutes with my leather. Get your paint ready."

Salvatore knew that he should speak with Martinez first. He knew that he should resent this man walking up out of nowhere and ordering him to paint. He did not. He felt an exhilaration like nothing he'd ever experienced, and a rush of energy – and strength. He rose, his chalk and the dragon on the sidewalk forgotten. He would finish it – but he would do it right – with the paints. He would join this man, Enrique, with his dragon , and he would set it free.

~ * ~

Enrique arrived as he said he would, closer to fifteen minutes after leaving Salvatore than twenty. He carried his leather jacket over one arm, and when he entered Salvatore's home, he handed it over almost reverently. Some of the confidence had left him now, and his new attitude nearly unnerved Salvatore. It was as if he, Salvatore, was held in reverence, as if something holy was imminent, a miracle, or a visitation. Salvatore had liked it better when the man ordered him about.

"You can do this?" Enrique asked.

Salvatore took the jacket and draped it over the back of the chair, as Jake's had been. He zipped it up on the far side and tucked the arms around out of the way. Enrique's back was not quite as broad. The leather on his jacket was not as aged, and presented a smoother, more uniform black surface. Salvatore ran his fingers over it lightly, and then he turned.

"I will paint your dragon," he said. "I will show you what I have seen. It is all I can do."

"Paint then," Enrique said. "I will be outside. I will not watch you work, because I don't want to distract you, but I will make certain that no other disturbs you until you have finished."

Salvatore didn't know what to say. He could have told Enrique that no one had interrupted his life for fourteen years until the last two days. He was grateful that he would be alone with the work – with the dragon – but he thought, in this case, it would not matter. If someone else entered, that might be bad, but if this man – if Enrique – was to be a part of this creation it would disturb nothing. He would, after all, wear it when it was complete. Like a second skin. Like a second identity.

Without another word, Enrique stepped back out onto the front steps, and Salvatore turned to the table. He'd already laid out the paints, carefully squeezing some of the blue onto the palette. He had been forced to dig into his own meager supplies for an old, cracked tube of white paint that he'd found in the trash out in back of the local high school. He'd been saving it, hoping he'd be able to add other colors in time. He left the red and the yellow paints Martinez had mixed for him carefully wrapped.

He didn't hesitate. He dipped into the blue paint and began the outline. The blue that he'd used the night before to mix his greens had seemed brighter. Tonight, the paint had somehow left the tube in exactly the hue he needed for the darkest of the outline, for the shadows within the ice. It was much deeper, much closer to black, then he remembered. Salvatore did not think about it. He turned to the jacket, and he painted.

Somehow the experience was more intense than it had been the night before. The fact that Enrique stood just beyond the door might have been responsible. Salvatore thought, perhaps, that it was because this dragon was so different. It didn't matter. Somewhere after the first mix of white and blue to create the sheen of ice, the leather faded. He heard an unearthly cry, and before that other place even came into focus, the dragon dropped from the sky and soared directly over him. It flew so low that the wind from its passing nearly knocked Salvatore from his feet.

He dropped to his knees and held on, gripping wet, slimy stone. He was very close to the city now. A short walk would take him to the walls. As he gazed upward he saw that they seemed to rise forever, so far into the sky that, from his vantage point, he could not see where they ended in the lower limits of the clouds.

He rose and scrambled over the last rocky outcropping. The wall was smooth and black, and it stretched off to the right, and to the left, winding out of sight without a weakness or a break. He glanced to his left. That way lay the sea, and he thought it was unlikely there would be a gate so close to the water. He turned to his right, and began walking. He scanned the skies, but after that one, brilliant flash of sound and motion, the dragon had fallen silent. In the distance, lightning struck. Salvatore shivered.

The air was damp; a light drizzle fell from the cloudy sky. Thunder rumbled several moments after the lightning strike, out over the ocean. As he walked, Salvatore brushed the tips of his fingers over the dark stone of the immense wall. He tried to sense those who could have created such a thing – to connect with that place – but he felt nothing.

He walked for what seemed a very long time, and there was no change in the wall. He knew there could not be such an immense city without gates, but considering the height of the wall– the monstrous scale of the structure– it could be miles away. Days. He kept on walking.

He heard the flap of gigantic wings before the shadow fell over him, but it was not as it had been when Jake's dragon descended. It was fast – so fast that he had no time to turn, or cry out. There was nothing, and then there was wind, and sound. He was grasped in huge talons, gripped gently, but firmly and yanked from the ground so swiftly all breath left his lungs. He rose, but even as the ground fell away and the dragon screamed, stunning him with the power of its voice, the walls of the city came into view.

They were immense. The city glittered and glowed with light – a prismatic, multi-colored shimmer - the first illumination Salvatore had seen in that place beyond the moon and the odd glow of the froth on the waves.

Then it was gone. The dragon rose with wild abandon, cut through the clouds, and rolled. Salvatore found himself facing an endless, starless sky. He closed his eyes, and they dropped. It was the last thing that he remembered.

When Salvatore woke he was in his bed. Martinez sat on the edge of the mattress, watching him. The old man looked concerned. Salvatore smiled, though his head pounded and his throat was dry and parched. He blinked away the fog and concentrated, trying to get his bearings.

"Take it easy," Martinez said. "You have lost a lot of strength. It was too soon, Salvatore. You should have waited."

"I...I could not," Salvatore said. "This dragon, it came to me the moment Senor Jake's departed. Then ..."

"Yes, I know," Martinez said. "I should have expected it. What you have done is remarkable."

Salvatore raised himself up on his elbows, and Martinez snaked a hand around his back, supporting him as he rose to a sitting position. When Salvatore was upright, he stared in confusion. Enrique knelt on the floor across from him, facing the jacket. Salvatore could not see the dragon, but he felt it. Enrique's head was bent. After a moment's time, Salvatore realized that the man was praying.

Finally Enrique raised his head, and turned. He saw that Salvatore was awake, and he nodded. He didn't smile – every line on the man's face was taut, as though his skin had been stretched too tightly over his face. He rose, and he came to Salvatore slowly, holding out his hand. For the second time that day, Salvatore relinquished his hand to a grip he was certain could crush it. For the second time he felt a flash of electricity – a power and a bond.

"Thank you," Enrique said. "I..."

He shook his head. He could not speak, and he didn't try again. He turned and went to the chair. Very gently, he lifted the jacket free.

"It is okay," Salvatore said, his voice shaky. "The paint...it dries very quickly."

Enrique nodded. He slipped his arm into one sleeve, and then the other. As he turned, the jacket molded itself to his back. He closed his eyes, just for a moment, and then, when he turned, his face was alive with energy. His expression shifted dramatically from the intense, frowning concentration Salvatore had seen from the moment they'd met to an almost feral smile. His eyes flashed like chips of blue ice. He turned once, showing off the jacket, and then he laughed out loud.

"I feel incredible," he said. "I can't explain it. I ..."

"It is a powerful dragon," Martinez said, rising. "And you wear it well. I have a message for you, though. You must go, and quickly. Snake has called for all of the Dragons to meet. There is something happening tonight, in the old junkyard. Anya Cabrera and *Los Escorpiones* are involved. I was asked to spread the word to any I saw."

Enrique stood quietly and took this in. He nodded, then he turned and squatted down so that he met Salvatore's gaze.

"I will not call you Sally," he said. "You are Salvatore, and from this moment on, you are my brother. If you need me, you will know how to find me. Somehow – I know this. Call, and I will come. I have nothing else I can offer."

Salvatore nodded gravely.

"Take care of the dragon, senor Enrique," he said. "I believe it will protect you, as well."

Enrique held that gaze a moment longer, and then laughed again.

"You know, Salvatore, I believe you are right. I have never felt this way. Never. I have to go."

He turned, and he was gone.

Martinez glanced at Salvatore.

"I must go too. I have offered to do what I can in this conflict, and they will be expecting me. There will be food, and drink. I will have it brought to you. You must rest. No drawing. No painting. Eat, drink, and sleep. I will see you soon. There is more work for you and I before this is finished. There are a great number of others counting on you. Do you understand."

"No," Salvatore said quickly, "but I will do as you ask. This day has been … amazing. When you need me, I will be ready."

Martinez nodded, rose, and a moment later he was gone. Salvatore sat for a moment, staring after him, and then he glanced at the empty chair. The paints had already been stored, and he knew that Martinez must have done it. After a few moments his eyelids grew heavy, and he lay back on his cot. He pulled the old sheet up around his chin, closed his eyes, and willed himself to dream. This time he found only darkness.

Chapter Seventeen

Night had fallen over the Barrio. Flickering lights dotted the junkyard, marking the trail in from the outside world, and outlining the inner courtyard where Anya Cabrera and her followers waited. It was nearly time to begin the ceremony. Everything was in place, and the only participants missing were *Los Escorpiones* themselves.

The inner circle was complete except for a small opening by the front entrance to the room Kim had stocked earlier. There Anya Cabrera sat, flanked by two of her tall, ebon-skinned guardians. There was an equally narrow break in the circle across from her where the passageway opened onto the labyrinthine trail leading back out to the street. Torches flickered and trailed off into that shadowy tunnel.

There was a small cage near the fire pit. It was divided in two by a screen. On either side of that screen, a rooster strutted. One was white, dappled with black spots. The other was dark red with a brown mask. They scratched at the rough earth and circled their tiny prisons, heads bobbing and darting and eyes fierce. On either side of the cage, daggers were embedded in the earth. Only the hilts showed, one white, and the other black. Both bore small symbols etched into their frames.

Then something changed. A shadowy, obscure shape slipped through into the circle, followed by two more. They stood for just a moment, and then slid around the central fire pit. It was difficult to bring them into focus and impossible to make out any features. The three shadows rounded the circle and stood, two to the left and one to the right of Anya's entrance. She stepped up and joined them. As she did, Kim, glided out behind her and carefully joined the broken halves of the circle.

More of *Los Escorpiones* entered. When all was said and done, there were fifteen present. There were the three wraith-like figures shimmering beside Anya, falling in and out of focus, and there were thirteen others. Kim rounded the circle and closed it at the far entrance. Two of Anya's followers stepped in front of the tunnel, facing back down its length, and crossed their arms in front of their chests.

Kim began a mincing, prancing dance around the inner clearing. As she moved, she sang out in a language native to a place and time far distant. She held a torch, lit from one of the lanterns. At each of the braziers surrounding the circle, she danced in place and held the flame to the incense powder until thick smoke billowed up and out like fog. Each time she lit another brazier, the air thickened in that outer ring. Within the circle, where Anya advanced on the central brazier, the air was clear and clean.

Anya pulled out a long wooden match from a deep fold of her many layered robes. She struck it casually on the circle of stones with their white-washed symbol decorations. She held it first to one side, then to the other of the charcoal in the brazier. The coals had been pre-soaked with pungent oil, and flames immediately began licking at the edges, sliding in and around each small briquette.

"Welcome!" Anya cried. Her voice rang out, strong and powerful. She was a small woman, slender and dark. Her form and features were cloaked in many layers of gauze and silk and lace, festooned with charms, bones, silver trinkets and gold chains. As the central fire rose, she glittered and shimmered; each motion of her arms sent trails of light following after it and drawing half-lit symbols in the air.

"It is a glorious night," she said. "The spirits will rise and walk among us. Gods will visit, and we will become stronger. They will share with us, and we with them, and when we are done, none shall stand before us."

Kim had completed her circuit of the circle, and the band of scented smoke divided them from the world. Anyone standing outside the circle would see little or nothing – perhaps a back-lit shadow in the mist, or a will-o-the-wisp of light. The guards just inside the door were obscured, as well, though they could see well enough, staring out the passage leading in among the dead and forgotten automobiles and the flickering torches.

Anya stepped forward and circled the fire. As she moved, she traced her fingers over the white symbols. She spoke as she walked, and her feet began a shuffling, skipping dance.

"They are here," she cried. "They walk among us. They touch us and breathe through us and flow in and out and through our veins. They are dark, and light; they are weak, and strong. They live in the shadows, and are bound by daylight."

She whirled away from the fire, and as she did so she cast off the first layer of her garments. They were scarves, and as she passed the men who circled her fire, she stepped in closer, danced between them, wrapped the soft material around them and let it go, moving to the next. Once more around the fire, and she danced in little more than wisps of silk. Her skin was smooth, oiled and glittering in the firelight. As her garments disappeared, she was revealed, the muscled perfection of her legs and the haughty thrust of her breasts. One moment she stalked them, and the next she wound around and through their ranks seductively.

Her words, which had been clear and simple, dropped slowly into a chant that matched her dance. *Los Escorpiones* trembled slightly, but stood their ground as she leaned in and whispered words in their ears that they would never understand, brushing her hands over their flesh. She leaned suddenly to the cage in front of the fire, and with a sudden yank of her wrist, she removed the screen that separated the strutting cocks inside.

She laughed, spat on the ground before the cage, picked up the dirt where her spittle had landed and ground it between the palms of her hands. She leaned in to the fire and dropped the contents of her hands into the flames. The blaze roared and licked up into the sky.

The birds dove at one another as if possessed. They circled and struck, sharp spurs and beaks slashing like lightning. Anya laughed, and the sound of that laughter blended with the whipping, snapping voice of the fire. The birds screamed, and Anya leaned close to the fire once again. She grabbed the first of the bottles, lifted it, and smashed the top against the stone rimming the fire. Some of the contents sloshed into the pit, where they caused bursts of brighter flame and a loud hiss.

Anya stood before the cage, squatted, and watched. She continued to sing and chant. She swayed to the motion of the battle raging in that small cage. She held the bottle out before her and waved it hypnotically.

"Join us!" she screamed. "Come to us. We welcome you with mind, body and spirit. We claim the right!"

At that moment, the dark bird struck. It dipped it's head as if going for the lighter colored rooster's breast. When its opponent reacted, the red rooster dropped to the side and lashed out with the spur on one leg. It caught the white bird directly across the throat. Blood spurted, and Anya yanked open the cage. Before the fallen bird struck the ground she plucked it out. She bore it aloft, the bottle held tightly in her other hand.

The dead rooster flopped in her grip. She spun away and began a third circle of the ring. This time she reached out as she passed each of *Los Escorpiones* , marking them once on each cheek, and once on the forehead with the bloody feathered neck of the fallen bird. A few tried to pull back, or to spin away, but she was fast – far too fast – and her words held them, her dance mesmerized them. As she moved to the second in line she held out the bottle to the first. He hesitated only a second, and then he drank.

As she moved, the bottle trailed after her. By the time she reached the end of the line – the spot where the blurred, wispy forms wavered, the bottle was empty. She tossed the remnant of the bird onto the pyre and it burst suddenly into brilliant red flame. It faded back to the glow of the coals, but there was no sign of the sacrifice.

Anya grabbed another bottle then. She laughed, broke the top and threw it toward the men in line. One staggered forward, as if too drunk to remain upright, but at the last second he snagged the bottle out of the air easily. He bowed to Anya, and winked, then upended the bottle and chugged half of it in a single swallow.

"Welcome!" Anya cried.

She continued, opening and tossing the bottles, watching them caught, some almost daintily, one in a sudden and very unexpected flip, a young man flying through the air, bringing the sharp, broken tip of the bottle's neck to his lips in mid-air and landing lightly on his feet, still drinking.

As they drank, they danced. Anya led them in a circle around the fire. Somewhere along the way, the last of her clothing disappeared. She stroked herself over strong young bodies as they danced. Some grabbed her and held her close, others kissed her and then spun her away, laughing uproariously. As they moved, music rose. There were no musicians in site, but the wild chords of deep, resonant guitars, the syncopated patter of hands on bongos, and the soft lilting voices of recorders, or flutes, permeated the air.

Within moments what had seemed an organized, ritualistic experience degenerated into wild abandon. *Los Escorpiones*, the thirteen, danced and drank. Some smoked thick, green cigars tucked away behind the bottles. The dancers reeked of strong, dark rum and mescal. Voices rose in tongues that none present understood, and the flames danced merrily. Beyond the misting incense smoke, Kim watched, her eyes dark. She paced like a caged cat, just beyond the magical barrier.

It had begun.

Chapter Eighteen

Donovan and Amethyst exited the doorway into an alley across from the Barrio just after sunset. There was still movement on the street, but the two paid no attention to it. As they stepped out and scanned the area, they barely registered as light shadows on the walls of the building s behind them. They were like fuzzy, warped spots in the air, and though they passed very close to several passersby, no one noticed them.

"It seems as if at least the first half of the amulet's power isn't exaggerated," Donovan said. "Let's hope it works as well on the eyes of spirits – *Loa* in particular."

The dark, soapy stone figurine rested against his skin, and he felt the urge to squirm away from it. It was warm to the touch, and he was fairly certain that on more than one occasion, it moved. He didn't want to think about what that motion might mean. He had known that such talismans existed, but they came from a branch of study he'd avoided. Not black arts, exactly, but not "clean". The amulets fell somewhere in the in-between and Donovan knew that, particularly in realms of power, gray areas could prove the most dangerous.

They stood in the doorway of an abandoned bookstore and watched Anya Cabrera's guards at the entrance to the junkyard. Now and then one would move in, or out of the passageway. There were never less than two in sight and in the shadows a bit further down the street they could make out the forms of two young men – no doubt *Escorpiones*. Torches flickered throughout the tangled piles of broken and twisted metal. The cloying scent of incense flavored the air, and music rose from the shadows.

"Is that guitar?" Amethyst asked.

Donovan listened closely, and then nodded.

"Guitar, some sort of flute, drums … Anya has pulled out all the stops. I recognized the music – it's powerful. I knew there were those in the city who still played it, but I wasn't aware that they could be bought. They may prove a new sort of problem before we're finished."

"That's what I needed to hear," Amethyst said. "As we sneak into the heavily guarded voodoo *Loa* infested junkyard to spy on a madwoman, what I really needed was something else to worry about."

Donovan laughed.

"I don't think we're getting in through the front door," he said.

They might have slipped past the first round of guards with the help of the amulets, but if they entered that passageway, and were detected, there'd be no way out. Donovan reached into one of the pockets of his jacket and pulled out a long slender crystal on a chain. He breathed on it – causing it to fog up – spoke a small incantation, and then held it out so that it dangled freely.

The crystal swung in slow circles. Amethyst watched in amusement.

"You still have that?"

"I never get rid of anything useful," Donovan said. "Besides, it was the first gift you ever gave me."

"That would have sounded more romantic if you'd skipped the part about being useful."

Donovan concentrated. The crystal swung a final time and then, as if it had been gripped by invisible fingers, twisted up and away to the right, pointing along the side of the junkyard into the shadowed streets. Donovan turned in the direction of the pull, and Amethyst fell in behind him. They crossed the street and moved quickly along the front fence of the junkyard. There were other gates – or had been – but Anya Cabrera's people had re-arranged things inside to prevent unwanted entrance to their court. What they needed was to find something that had been overlooked. Though there were shopkeepers shutting up for the night, and pedestrians passing nearby, no one glanced at the two or acknowledged them in any way. They moved like ghosts.

They turned onto Delaporte and followed it for several blocks. As they moved in deeper, the street grew darker. The streetlights on that particular avenue were in disrepair, and though the city was well aware of the problem, workers were reluctant to enter, even in large groups. It was the home of *Los Escorpiones*, and each time the city spent the money to repair the lights, they were broken again before they'd burned a single night. It is one thing to sit back in a comfortable office and talk about taking care of the gang-related problems, and entirely another to be out on the streets trying to make it happen.

The junkyard bordered Delaporte for four blocks. Just before it turned again on Forty-Eighth, a large wooden gate rested on heavy metal hinges. It was closed, and there were chains across the opening. The homes across from that gate were low-slung and dark. There were no lights, and boards covered many of the windows. Broken and abandoned toys littered the lawns, and the sidewalks were awash in colored paintings and slogans. People lived there, but when the light drained from the sky, they melted away, huddling close in their rooms and waiting for the uncertain safety of daylight to draw them out.

Donovan studied the street carefully, but detected no movement. It seemed that *Los Escorpiones* were all involved in the night's activities. Normally there would be guards and sentries. If Anya Cabrera had her way, they would no longer be necessary.

He turned back to the gate. The chains and the lock that held it closed were rusty. The fence itself rose up to about seven feet. On this side it was built of aged, warped wood. The paint had long since peeled away, and knots had fallen free. It was cracked in a few places, but the wood still appeared strong.

"Feel like a climb?" Donovan asked quietly.

Amethyst frowned at him and stepped up to the gate. She looked up and down the street, but there was no one in sight. *Los Escorpiones* were busy, but even in their absence no one braved Delaporte. Satisfied, Anya reached up and pulled a thin blue crystal from her hair. She gripped the lock in one hand

and inserted the crystal into the keyhole. When it was in as far as she could get it without releasing the base, she closed her eyes.

The crystal let off a dim blue glow. The lock grew almost transparent, just for an instant, and then, with a click, it fell open. Amethyst held the two halves of the chain in one hand and slipped the crystal back into her hair. She hooked the lock over one end of the chain and pulled on the gate. It opened about a foot with a creaking groan.

"Nice," Donovan said with a chuckle. "You always carry lock picks in your hair?"

"You'd be surprised what can double as a fashion accessory."

She lowered the chain gently to prevent any more unwanted sound, pressed the gate open wide enough to allow them both access, and slipped inside. Donovan followed, and then pulled the gate closed behind them. If they weren't out by daylight, someone was going to see that open lock, and the chain on the ground, but for the moment they were safe enough. He turned and studied the piles of rotting vehicles for a moment, then pulled out the pendulum again. After only a moment it swung at an angle to the left.

"Shall we?" Donovan said.

Amethyst only nodded. Now that they'd entered the junkyard the music was much louder, almost hypnotic. The incense smoke was thick, and it seemed to seep from every crack and pore of the place, as if seeking to escape.

Donovan slipped between a smashed Ford Mustang chassis and the remnant of an ancient Cadillac. Amethyst followed. There was a narrow crack buried in deep shadows, and they followed it inward. Cars were piled so high on either side that the light of the moon would only penetrate when it had finally risen to the center of the sky. Donovan moved with sure-footed grace, stopping every few feet to draw out the pendulum and test their direction. Within moments the gate was lost to site.

They moved very slowly, and very carefully. For one thing, many of the trails through the yard were narrow and lined with jagged bits of metal. In the darkness it was easy to snag clothing or cut an arm by coming too close to one side or the other. The music was eerie and had grown steadily in volume as they progressed.

"The guitar is getting louder," Amethyst said softly, "but not the flute, or the drums."

"I noticed," Donovan replied. "We must be near one of the musicians. If so, we're in no immediate danger – they aren't violent. We don't want him to see us though, if we can help it. He'd be able to pinpoint our location for Anya's people without even breaking rhythm."

"That shouldn't be a problem. We're still wearing the amulets."

Donovan nodded, but didn't look convinced. He followed the pendulum around the corner of a Jeep so buried under and forgotten that it had begun to compress downward, windshield broken away, tires flattened. The scent of rotting rubber mixed with that of the soil and the rust; entropy was making a meal of the junk, wearing away at it slowly and steadily.

Their way became suddenly easier. The path ahead had been used more recently – there were signs of footprints. There was also another trail winding off directly across from where they entered the wider path.

"We're going to have to be more careful from here," Donovan whispered. "I don't think they will be patrolling this far out, but they've been through here recently. They may just be working on expanding their operations. If they bring *Los Escorpiones* fully on board, and for good, then the gate onto Delaporte will probably not remain closed much longer."

Amethyst nodded. "Which way?"

The pendulum wavered. It began to swing to the right and then faltered. The chain swung that direction, but the crystal dangled at the end, as if something had dampened the energy allowing it to defy the call of gravity. The chain pointed right, but the crystal itself pointed straight down.

They looked at one another. Donovan shrugged. He put the pendulum back in his pocket and slipped around the corner to the right, moving slowly. They made better time, but at the same time, moved with greater care. The music was much louder, and they heard voices raised in loud raucous laughter. The air around them was charged with a strange energy that made it difficult not to get caught up in the rhythm; the syncopated heartbeat of the ritual.

"They're in full swing," Donovan said. "We'd better hurry, or we're going to miss anything important that happens."

They stepped into a cleared space and stopped cold. Seated before them in the driver's seat of a long-abandoned school bus was a young man with very long hair and coal-black eyes. He held a very large-bodied acoustic guitar across his knees. His fingers flew over the strings, and the sound they produced pounded through the night to blend with the other instruments.

Donovan stood very still. Amethyst stepped up beside him. The musician had not acknowledged their presence. Still, they waited. Donovan took a step forward, and then another. A path led between a group of heavy machinery carcasses, and he stepped toward it gingerly. Amethyst mimicked his movements. They slipped wraith-silent through the clearing, and up to the entrance to that new passage, all the while keeping their eyes locked on the guitarist.

Just as they thought they had made it through unseen, the man turned. He winked at them, and there was a very subtle change in the sound from his instrument. It didn't disrupt the rhythm, or the song, but Donovan knew in that instant that some message had been sent.

"He sees us," Amethyst said. She didn't sound frightened, but she did sound confused.

"It's the music," Donovan said. "I don't think he knows who, or even what we are for certain. He's so in tune with the sound, so connected to the notes and the rhythm that he felt us pass. He's informed the others of it, too. Whatever comes next, I think we have to assume that Anya Cabrera is now aware that someone is here."

They ducked onto the path and hurried off toward the center of the yard. They were very close. Donovan spotted an old front loader. It had been parked with its shovel up in the air, high enough that it peeked over the top of most of the stacked vehicles.

"There," he said. "We should be able to see what's going

on from there and still remain out of site. She won't be any more able to see us than before. Knowing someone is here and finding them are two different things entirely, and Anya Cabrera has other things on her mind."

They scrambled up the old, yellow hulk and climbed into the deep, rusted shovel. Once inside they peered out over the toothed lip. Smoke billowed and wisped from the central square of the junkyard. They could make out whirling, dancing shapes. They saw Anya Cabrera, wearing nothing but a thin scarf around her neck, sliding sinuously in and out among the other dancers.

"Showtime," Donovan whispered.

Chapter Nineteen

Jake and Enrique came down from Santini Park toward the junkyard at a slow trot. They paid no attention to those they passed, and any who happened to be between the two and their goal stepped aside. There was something different about them, something it wasn't easy to put a finger on. They moved quickly and silently. Both men were dressed in jeans, leather jackets, and heavy boots, but it was the jackets that caught at the attention of passersby and stuck with them for years after.

As they passed, the dragons on the backs of those jackets came clearly into view. The colors were vivid, so bright they gave off an illumination all their own. Even those watching from a distance saw the details clearly. As they left the safe bounds of their own territory and entered the darker parts of the Barrio, they dropped out of sight, shifting into the shadows. The dragons left colored trails that lingered in the dusky air.

Whispered questions followed them. Everyone knew who they were, but none could answer why two of the dragons would enter the territory of their enemies alone. The news of the battle in the park, and Vasquez's fall was fresh, and the junkyard was viewed with a mixture of fear and loathing. Now the jackets started rumors of their own.

On a street corner with a clear view of the entrance to the junkyard, Martinez stood and watched them pass. He saw the dragons on their backs more clearly than any of the others watching. He had examined each at close range. He had mixed the sealant into the paint, a special oil that bound the designs to the leather. His was the charm of binding. He alone knew that there was a great deal more to Jake and Enrique now than there had been. They possessed the potential for greatness – what remained was to see how they fulfilled that potential.

The two slowed as they reached the street that opened onto the junkyard. Martinez watched a moment longer, and then slipped back into the shadows. He had a great deal to accomplish and not all that much time in which to accomplish it. From this point on, the two were on their own

Jake stopped and held out an arm to slow Enrique. The streets were clearing quickly as those still lingering noticed the two intruders. No one wanted to get caught between The Dragons and *Los Escorpiones*. They didn't mind gossiping about it, but they didn't want to be part. Besides, with the lights, the music, and the smoke rising from the junkyard, it was a good night to be somewhere else.

"You see 'em?" Jake asked. He nodded toward the entrance to the junkyard, where two of Anya's guardians stood, glaring at them. The big men were bald, dark, and seriously muscled. Jake had seen them from a distance, but he'd never interacted with them.

"I was kind of hoping for *Escorpiones*," Enrique muttered. "Those guys creep me out."

They continued slowly, walking up the gate as if they'd been invited. Jake kept a big grin on his face and made no sudden moves. He figured that the closer they got before trouble started, the better chance they had of making their crazy-assed plan work. He wasn't big on their chances for survival, but they had a few tricks up their sleeves, and there was more. He felt the dragon through the leather of his jacket. He felt stronger than he'd ever felt in his long, rough life. He thought if he got a good run he could leap right over the two guards, though he knew the thought was crazy. He imagined what the yard would look like from the air.

"You ready?" Enrique asked.

The sound broke Jake's reverie, and he nodded again. "Let's do this."

They stepped up to the gate, brought their hands out of their pockets simultaneously, and tossed handfuls of white powder into the face of the two startled guards. The action caught the big men completely off guard, and the powder struck them full in the face. With twin gurgling cries of pain and dismay they dropped to their knees. Jake didn't hesitate. He stepped forward and planted the steel toe of his boot in the first guard's forehead, driving him back. Enrique grabbed the second by the throat, lifted him like a child and drove him back so his head struck a wooden post on the fence.

"We're in," Jake said. "Move!"

They plunged through the gate and rushed down the path toward the first set of torches.

"I don't see anyone," Enrique said.

"They're here," Jake grated. "Count on it. They aren't leaving just those two on guard."

Almost before the words cleared his lips, a figure slid out of the shadows. This time it was one of *Los Escorpiones*, a thin, dark eyed young man with a chain wrapped around one forearm and a knife in his other hand. Behind him, a second peeled loose from the deeper darkness. This one was big. He had what looked like a snapped off car antenna in his hand, probably improvised from their surroundings.

About ten yards farther in, Jake saw the flicker of lanterns. These two were meant to ambush anyone getting close to that next checkpoint, catching them unaware in the darkness. It should have worked, too, except, the darkness suddenly didn't bother him. He had no idea how, but he saw clearly, even into the deeper shadows, and when the first of their attackers sprang, he dodged the man's blade easily. The boy grunted with exertion and swung the heavy chain in an arc toward Jake's head, but it might as well have been in slow motion.

Jake reached up and grabbed the chain, dragged it in the same direction his attacker had swung it, and sent the man into a spin that landed him on his back in the dirt. He moved as soon as he hit, rolling to his feet, but Jake was there, one hand on the wrist beneath the gripped knife and the other on his throat. Jake threw back his head, let loose a howl of rage, and slammed the smaller man into the wall of broken automobiles so hard that it shivered. For an instant it looked as if the wall might topple in on them, and then it steadied. Jake dropped the Escorpione and spun.

Enrique had closed with the second, bigger man, who was also older and wiser. He stepped back, urging Enrique forward, and then swung the antenna so hard it made a sizzling sound in the air. Enrique turned just enough that the blow glanced off his shoulder and drove forward. His opponent hadn't expected such a direct attack. Enrique lowered his head, bent his knees and drove up beneath the man's chin. With a bellow the Escorpione went down. Enrique tried to roll right on over him, but the big man was hurt – not beaten. He lashed out with the antenna again and caught Enrique in the back of the wrist.

That blow should have shattered bone. Jake saw it clearly. He lurched forward, reaching to block it, but he was too late. He heard the smack of metal on flesh, saw Enrique stumble, but only for an instant. There was a ripple of blue light across the afflicted wrist. Sparks flew. Enrique growled and spun back. He swiped his boot across his downed opponent's jaw so fast and hard the man's head spun, and the neck snapped wickedly to the side. Enrique dropped, ready to do more, and Jake saw he gripped the Escorpione with both hands. There was no apparent damage to his wrist.

Jake grabbed Enrique by the shoulder.

"Not now," he said. "Let's go!"

Enrique spun on him, and for just a second, Jake thought the younger man might swing. There was a brilliant blue light in his eyes, and his lips had curled back in a snarl. Then it faded and Enrique nodded. As they hurried on deeper into the junkyard, Jake glanced back over his shoulder. Neither of the two they'd fought had moved. He shivered.

The air thickened. Incense smoke wafted out toward them, and the sound of strange music engulfed them. He'd never heard anything quite like it, but at the same time it felt familiar, like a memory he couldn't wrap his mind around. They heard laughter and screams. They didn't sound like screams of pain, but Jake couldn't be sure. They were barely human. The cloying smoke stole his concentration, and the rhythm of the odd music sifted through his senses. He fought it. He thought of clear air.

The sensation was like something he remembered from dreams he'd had as a child. In those dreams he'd been able to take a run into a strong breeze, leap from the ground, and fly on thick, heavy air. He'd seen the city from the sky, swooped down through forests and parks, and come close enough to feel the salt spray of the ocean, but each time he'd awakened to find it was only a fantasy.

He felt that way now. He felt as light as a feather, as if he could take one step to kick off the crumbling Detroit steel walls of this place into the sky and be gone. He held that thought. It blocked the music, and helped him keep his breathing steady. He knew there would be more guards between them and their goal, and he also knew it was likely that by now they knew he was coming.

He smiled. Let them be ready. Let them all be ready.

"Here we come, you motherfuckers," he growled. "Ready or not."

Enrique heard him, even over the pounding drums and the screams. He turned, and he grinned. The two threw back their heads in unison and let loose a scream of their own. It wasn't a human sound, and it cut through the night like a razor. In that heartbeat-long moment, all other sound ceased. Nothing existed but the two of them, racing through the shadows past flickering lanterns. Then it all crashed back in around them, as they charged.

Chapter Twenty

Donovan and Amethyst settled in as well as they could. The old top loader was stable, but not designed for comfort. The rusty teeth rimming the front of the shovel were difficult to balance on and treacherous. Donovan pulled out a very small pair of brass binoculars and trained them on the clearing. He began at the entrance to the circular court and worked his way slowly to the right.

Amethyst only glanced down for a moment to fix the scene in her mind, then turned and slid down to sit in the old shovel, her back to the clearing. She pulled a pouch from an inner pocket and untied the straps. Donovan glanced down at her, and then returned to his study of the clearing.

"I take it you have something in mind other than watching the show?" he said.

"I want to be certain that we know what we're up against," she replied. "I'm going to take a reading. If they are aware of us, I'll know. If something out of the ordinary happens, I'll be able to warn you – probably. We're outside the circle, so there are limits."

Donovan nodded. He'd caught sight of the woman he knew only as Kim, working her way around the outside of the ring. She was doing something with the circle, bending down every few feet. He couldn't quite tell what she was up to, whether she was picking something up, repairing the circle, or placing something new.

Those inside circled the fire pit, leaping and whirling, some of them jumping impossibly high in the air, others, drinking from one of a seemingly endless supply of bottles. Anya Cabrera moved in and out of the group. More than once Donovan saw her caught in the grip of one or another of the mostly naked men surrounding her. Each time she danced, moved with them, and wound her way free before the moment could become more than what it was – part of the dance.

He thought, once or twice, that he saw something move in the smoke rising from the braziers, or in the hot coals of the fire pit. Each time, when he turned to focus on the motion, it was gone. Even so, there was nothing odd about the ritual. He'd witnessed several voodoo ceremonies over the years, once in Jamaica, twice in Haiti, and he'd even attended one here in the city, though not with Anya Cabrera running the show. He could detect nothing strange or different.

Anya's ways were westernized. The magic circle was a precaution that spoke of ritual magic, or the Kabbalah, not Voodoo, or Santeria. It was impossible for different disciplines to remain separate in the city. Things leaked. Those with power interacted, and they learned. If they didn't, they lost that power and someone else stepped up.

Amethyst had pulled a small ball of pure quartz from her pocket. It was flawless, and rare, and she held it cupped in the warmth of her palms. Softly, she blew on the smooth surface. While it was fogged, and while that fog slowly evaporated and cleared, she spoke a single word.

"Anya."

When the fog cleared, the crystal was no longer clear. Tiny flames flickered in its depths. Figures whirled and leaped. Amethyst leaned close and repeated the name.

"Anya."

Like a microscope zooming in on a drop of water, the image in the crystal focused on a single, smoothly gliding figure. Anya Cabrera was not young, but in the firelight, her hair dancing around her and her skin glowing and bare, she had a dark beauty that was undeniable. Those around her felt it and tried to catch her, to hold her. She evaded them easily, never missing a step. As she whirled, she faced in the direction of the old top-loader. In that instant, the image zoomed in again, and only the woman's face was clear. She winked once, and then, laughing, whirled away. There was no sound accompanying the image, but for just a second, Amethyst was certain she heard the woman's laughter through the music.

"She knows," Amethyst said. "She knows we're here, and she doesn't care."

"There has to be something we're missing," Donovan said. "*Los Escorpiones* are a lot of things, but I have never heard that they were particularly devout. All of those in the circle, with the exception of Anya, are *Escorpiones*. And…"

He hesitated, focused the glasses, and frowned.

"What?" Amethyst asked.

"I'm not sure. There's something – or someone – near one side of the circle. Whoever it is, they are standing very still, and I can't bring them into focus."

"I think you just found the other figurines," Amethyst said. "Someone else is in that circle. You can't quite see them, and the spirits? The *Loa* that Anya has summoned?"

"They act as if that portion of the circle doesn't exist," Donovan said. "They are paying no attention to them at all."

"That's not normal," Amethyst said. "They have no respect for anything when they come through to this world. They are seeking release, abandon, passion – they would not let anyone stand idly by and not participate in the moment."

"There's more," Donovan said. "The girl – Kim – Anya's apprentice. She's outside the circle. I can't quite make out what she's doing, but she hasn't been still since I started watching. She's been following the outer edge of the circle, bending down, rising up and moving on. Do you think she could possibly be sabotaging the circle?"

"There would be no point," Amethyst said. "You know they don't really need a circle for such a ritual. I'm not clear why Anya used it, unless she thought that drawing the symbols and setting up braziers, would impress *Los Escorpiones*. It could all be just smoke and mirrors, or a way of making what she does seem more dangerous than it really is."

"I need to get a closer look," Donovan said.

Amethyst tucked her crystal away and stood, peering over the edge of the shovel's blade.

"I don't think I'd go wandering down there," she said. "Particularly now that she knows we're watching. They're bound to be waiting for us."

"I don't have any intention of going down there," Donovan said. "I only meant that I need something better than these to see what I need to see."

"I may be able to help with that," she said. "Can I see those for a minute?"

Donovan handed over the binoculars and watched as Anna examined them. She checked the lenses carefully. After a moment, she smiled.

"It's a good thing you like old things," she said.

"What do you mean?"

"The lenses – they're leaded glass."

She held the glasses out in front of her and glanced up at him.

"You get one chance, I think. I'm feeling a little drained. Pick one thing, or one person, that you want to see. Tell me what you need."

Donovan thought about it for a moment, and then nodded.

"The girl," he said. "I need to know what the girl is doing. What is happening inside that circle is not out of the ordinary. Nothing there is worth Martinez getting up in arms, and it couldn't cause what we've been told has happened to *Los Escorpiones*. The only thing that is out of sync down there is that girl, and whatever it is she's doing. Either we learn that now, or we get the hell out of here, and take our chances with whatever comes next."

Amethyst turned to the binoculars. She closed her eyes and concentrated, and then, very quickly, she breathed on each of the two lenses. Before that fog could clear, just as she'd done with the quartz, she whispered a single word.

"Kim."

She handed them quickly to Donovan, and he didn't hesitate. He leaned up over the edge of the shovel and aimed the glasses at the circle. Kim came into focus instantly, and clearly. He could no longer see the greater circle, but only the ground beneath the whirling mass of smoke, and the girl Kim, kneeling at the outer edge of the circle. He watched as she pulled a long, slender wand from her robes and drew it across the ground. There was a second circle outside the first. It was narrower and shallower, but there were symbols between the concentric rings, and she was on the verge of closing the second, merging one line with the next.

Donovan studied the symbols and frowned. Once again, they had nothing at all to do with Voodoo, or the *Loa*. The outer circle was a ring of binding, the type that might be used if one was summoning a demon – or an angel. Anya Cabrera had none of the implements within the circle to perform such a ritual, and yet.

It hit him very suddenly, and he dropped the glasses, turning back to Amethyst, who was watching him patiently.

"Damn her," he said. "She's formed a ring of binding. The spirits were summoned while there was only the single ring, and the ritual itself – there's nothing different about it. If there had been, the *Loa* would have known. They would not have come. Now they will be trapped. She is doing exactly what we were told – she will bind them into the bodies they've inhabited. They will try to break free, but they will not be able to return to their own realm. The longer they are here, the more tenuous their own control of their power will become, and she will have them. They will be forced to do as she bids on the promise of one day being returned."

"That is a very dangerous game," Amethyst said. "These are not weak spirits one can bend to   simple tasks – they are very nearly gods. If there is any flaw in her spell – any weakness in her binding."

"I know," Donovan said. "I know. They will be free, and they will be here, and there will be nothing to control them."

He was about to say something more when a loud cry rang out from the clearing below. It was a scream of rage, a battle cry, barely human and loud enough to shake the walls and send cross-currents through the music. Everything stopped, just for an instant, and then there were screams and cries all over.

Donovan brought the glasses up again – just binoculars again. The circle remained intact. Nothing had changed within that ring. Outside, he saw that there was a skirmish of some sort near the gate to the small courtyard. Two large figures in black jackets had burst into the outer ring. They fought like demons, and any who tried to stand against them fell.

"What in the names of the Gods?" Donovan said.

"Martinez," Amethyst breathed. "Donovan...those two are dragons."

They stared down, passing the glasses back and forth, as Jake and Enrique fought their way toward the circle.

"We'd better get down there," Donovan sighed. "Things are about to get very, very ugly."

"You sure know how to show a girl a good time," Amethyst said.

They climbed down from the shovel and dropped to the ground. Donovan didn't bother with the pendulum, they'd seen the way from above. He only hoped they wouldn't be too late.

Chapter Twenty-One

Kim leaned down, drew the stout, oak wand she held across the dirt a final time, and stood. The last of the symbols had been carefully completed, and now the final seal had been set. The entire ceremony was double ringed, once for protection from outside forces, and once...this last...to keep other forces in. She stood back and contemplated her work.

She didn't try to penetrate the smoky haze and see what was taking place within the circle. It wasn't her concern. She had duties, and she had fulfilled them. Now all that remained for her was to see to those remaining outside the circle, like herself, and to watch for the culmination of the ritual. She didn't know if Anya Cabrera would exit that circle alive; she didn't know if what they were attempting was possible. Soon, she would know. If they failed, she would remain, and there would still be work to do. If Anya were to suddenly disappear, someone would have to tend the business. She had always known it would be her.

As she turned away, the silver caskets dangling from her hair jingled and the sound blended with the music. That blending made her smile, and she danced as she made her way around the circle, past the braziers, and back toward the small storage room.

She'd only gone a few feet when a sound like the tearing of the very veils between worlds erupted behind her. She spun and pressed herself into the outer wall, obscured by the smoke and watched the entrance to the small courtyard, her eyes wide.

Jake and Enrique reached the end of the entrance tunnel

very suddenly. With the smoke swirling about their feet and obscuring even the shadows, it took a moment to realize that the walls to either side had dropped away, and they were in the outer ring of the central court. The middle area was completely obscured by smoke, and the music, which had been loud before, was overwhelming here near the source of whatever dark power was afoot.

With a scream of rage intended to catch their enemies by surprise and fuel their own courage, the two hurled themselves into the mist. They didn't see Kim huddled against the wall, and they were unaware of the two guards rushing around the perimeter of the circle. Their goal stood directly ahead, and that's where they launched.

Jake struck first. He hit what seemed to be a solid, shimmering wall. Sparks shot up in all directions, green and gold sparks, and he struck with a solid crash into what had looked like nothing more than smoke. He bounced back hard and reeled into the outer wall of stacked cars. Enrique struck that same barrier a second later, reacted to Jake's motion and, instead of slamming head-on, he managed to jump andget his feet in front of him. He was moving so quickly he literally ran up the wall of smoke, kicked off, and flipped, landing back on his feet.

Jake, who'd seen this from where he stood rubbing his shoulder, gaped in amazement. It was like something out of a science fiction movie, or a bad Kung Fu flick.

"Jesus," he said.

Footsteps pounded toward him through the mist, and he had no more time to wonder how his friend had pulled off that particular stunt. One of Anya's tall, bald servants came around the circle with a short club raised over his head. Jake leaped to meet the charge, dropped, and whipped his leg across the other man's ankles. The big man went sprawling, and Jake rose, grabbed the man's head and pounded it hard on the ground once, twice, and a third time, before he turned back to Enrique.

A second tall bald man had squared off with Enrique, but this one was more cautious. Maybe he'd seen what happened to his friend, or maybe it had finally occurred to someone that the two couldn't be standing where they were without plowing through a small army of guards. Whatever the reason, the big servant turned and took a fighting stance, his gaze locked on Enrique and wary. Enrique didn't hesitate. He screamed again and ran at the bigger guard. Jake cursed and followed, watching as the huge bald man pulled a blade from his belt that had not been visible a moment before and lashed out.

Enrique turned, but that's not how it looked. To Jake it seemed more like his companion's body rippled, like the blade passed right through flesh, bone, clothing, and out the other side without leaving a mark. Enrique stepped under his opponent's guard, drove his hand palm first up into the man's face, and even from where Jake ran at the two, a couple of yards away, the crunch of bone was loud and sickening. The dark giant tumbled to one side, and Enrique turned back to the circle with a snarl.

It was then that Jake registered the small form in the shadows. She had pressed off of the wall and was closing on Enrique from behind, moving silently. She had something in her hand, and Jake wasn't waiting to find out what. He lunged, and he cried out. She saw him from the corner of her eye, and cut to the side, forgetting whatever it was she'd planned to try on Enrique in favor of a quick retreat.

Enrique, meanwhile, turned his attention back to the circle. He didn't charge it again, but he stepped forward and placed both hands against the wall of smoke and air. He pushed, and Jake saw the veins stand out in the man's arm. He saw the exertion, but whatever force it was the prevented them from entering did not give.

"It's no good," Jake said. "We're going to have to get out of here. They aren't going to just ignore us, even if we can't get in."

Enrique frowned. He pressed his face against the barrier. Jake saw the flickers of blue sparks again. He wondered what it meant, wondered if it was the dragon on the jacket, or something that Martinez had done, or a little of both. He thought about the aerial maneuver his friend had just made, and the men they'd fought their way through to get to this point – the ease with which they'd fallen.

Then Enrique screamed again. This time it was sheer frustrated rage. Jake had never heard such a sound emit from a human throat. It was high-pitched and piercing. It cut through the music again and drove through the barrier. Jake saw, just for a moment, that Enrique was able to press himself inward. He crossed the threshold of that eerie circle, just for an instant, and then fell back.

"Enrique!" Jake cried. "Get off of there."

Enrique pulled back, just slightly.

"I can see them, Jake. I can see them right on the other side of this damned smoke. They're dancing past me like I wasn't even here."

"It doesn't matter," Jake said. "You have to get back. We'll try again – another day, some other way. This isn't working."

Jake scanned the outer circle and glanced back down the passageway the way they'd come. Whatever the girl he'd seen had planned, it wasn't happening yet. They had a clear path out, and he was ready to take it. He stepped forward and grabbed Enrique by the shoulder, pulling him back from the circle.

In that moment, a dark figure burst through the smoke from within. There was a sharp crack, like lightning striking a tree, or a gunshot going off too close to your ear. Jake reeled back, and Enrique stumbled after him. A second figure followed the first through the smoke, and suddenly it all began to drift and fall away.

"No!"

The cry rose from within the circle. It was a woman's voice. Jake had a momentary glimpse of a naked woman, her hands clutching her hair, staring at the broken circle in dismay. Then he had no time left to think at all.

The two who had broken the circle were *Escorpiones*, but they were nothing like those Jake had encountered in the tunnel leading inward. These two bent low to the ground. Their eyes were flat and dark, and they moved like greased lightning. His mind flashed on Santini Par, and the thunderstorm. He saw Vasquez going down under piles of small, powerful bodies, and he braced himself.

The first came at him low and hard. He had no weapon,

but bared his teeth and emitted a sound halfway between a low squeal and a hiss of escaping air. Jake felt a strange sense of detachment. What he saw approaching him was a Hispanic man in his early twenties wearing dark jeans and no shirt. His senses expanded though, and he felt something else – something powerful and dark – something frustrated and angry. Something trapped. The thing sprang, and Jake ducked to the side. Fingernails raked across his chest like claws, but the leather of his jacket protected him, and he spun, gripped the thin body of the thing and flung it at the wall with all the strength he could muster.

There was a wet splat. He started to turn away, but the creature peeled itself from that wall of broken metal and turned like a cat. It clung there, actually hanging off of the wall for a moment, and then, with a scream of its own, it scrambled to the top of the wall of ruined metal, looked back once, and disappeared.

Jake spun. Shadows flashed all around him. All of those who'd danced moments before in the circle were fighting to reach the exit. Anya Cabrera stood behind them, waving her arms and trying to be heard. Jake thought she might be chanting, but it was hard to tell. He ducked as another Escorpione took a swing at him in passing. They didn't seem bent on fighting, they were trying to get out of the circle – out of the junkyard. Apparently, though Enrique had not been able to break in, his scream had broken some spell, or disrupted the rhythm of the music, just long enough for one of those inside to break out.

Enrique held one of the *Escorpiones* by the throat, and they wrestled together, falling back. Jake saw his friend slam a fist hard into his attacker's head. The thing – that's all he could call them now – reared back, but it did not topple. Instead it fished a blade from beneath a heavy black belt and slashed out and down. Enrique saw it coming. He turned and released his hold, throwing the writhing bundle of hate he fought away, but it was too late. The thing was fast – far too fast to be human.

The blade slashed through the front of Enrique's jacket and buried itself in his flesh. He rolled, and the motion wrenched the blade form his attacker's grip, but it was buried deep in his chest, driven between ribs. Blood gushed out from the wound, and Jake cursed.

He went after the Escorpione, but it was too late. The thing followed the others up and over the wall, out into the yard and the streets beyond. Jake turned briefly to see that the circle where Anya Cabrera had stood was empty. There was no sign of the woman, or her followers.

There was more motion in the back of the circle, and Jake moved swiftly. He gripped the knife, pulled it from his fallen comrade's chest, and flung it in the direction of the sound he'd heard, Then, gripping Enrique under his arms, he pulled him aside into the shadows. The smoke was still thick enough to obscure sight, but still, he knew something was wrong.

He heard someone moving, and voices, but he saw nothing. He had the vague impression of something or someone passing through the exit, and then – as quickly as the sound and frantic motion had begun, it ended. He knelt alone by Enrique's side, pulled the jacket apart to get to the wound, and began to wonder how there could still be life when there was already so much blood. It coated his hands and soaked the ground beneath him. He knew he was going to have to do something, and quickly – but he couldn't think. He had never in his life felt more alone.

Chapter Twenty-Two

Donovan was running the second his feet touched the ground. Amethyst dropped down behind him and followed. There was no time to think about who or what they might encounter. There was a thin crack between two ruined vehicles that led into the main entrance tunnel. It opened into one of the small cul de sacs where Anya's guards had waited. The space was empty, and Donovan pulled up short as he slipped into it. Footsteps pounded by.

As Amethyst stepped in beside him something passed directly overhead. The metal wall thrummed with heavy footsteps. Whatever it was moved so quickly that it was impossible to see who, or what, had passed.

Donovan peered around the corner of the small alcove. The passage wasn't empty, but there were none of *Los Escorpiones* in site. One of Anya's followers stumbled past, and there were voices ahead, toward the center.

"We have to go," Donovan said. "The amulets should protect us; we just have to be careful not to actually run into anyone. They won't see us, but they'll know we are there."

Amethyst nodded. They stepped into the narrow trail and turned right, toward the interior of the yard. Ahead, lamps flickered. Voices whispered through the shadows and more footsteps approached. They pressed up against the right hand side of the tunnel and continued to move inward. In the light of the next group of lanterns they saw two *Escorpiones* stumbling along. The men looked as if they'd been through a fight, but there was nothing special about their speed, or the way they moved. Guards, then, just extra bodies. Donovan held

Amethyst close to him and pressed back to the wall, and the two passed without a sideways glance.

It had grown quieter, and they moved more quickly. There was no way to know what awaited them in the center court, but if they intended to be of any help to the two Dragons who'd run in like crazy men, they needed to get there as quickly as possible.

There was another bend in the tunnel ahead, and just before they reached it they found another of the small alcoves. Donovan ducked inside, and they were barely out of site before three more *Escorpiones* rounded the corner. These moved slowly and carefully. They didn't appear to be injured, but their eyes were wide, and they spoke to one another in hushed tones.

"What the hell was that, Hector?" one said. "Jesus, what happened? Where did they go? Raoul is my cousin man, what am I gonna tell his wife?"

"Shut the hell up," a second voice, obviously Hector, hissed. "You'd better worry about getting your own sorry ass out of here before you spend too much time planning speeches for someone else's widow. We have to get back to the others – we have to find out how bad this is, and what we're up against. We have to find Anya."

"Christ, Hector," the last chimed in. "That crazy old woman is the reason everything is messed up. We can't go to her."

"Maybe you're forgetting a couple of things," Hector said. His voice grew menacing. Donovan and Amethyst pressed deeper into their small alcove, listening carefully.

"Like what, man?" the third voice whined.

There was a sudden shuffle of feet, and then the sound of something slamming hard into metal. A man cried out in pain, and Hector's voice, now hard and brittle cut through the shadows.

"You're forgetting who you're talking to for one thing, motherfucker," he said. "You're forgetting that the only reason you aren't one of those crazy-assed dudes running over the top of cars is because that crazy old woman gave you something. That thing you're wearing, man – it protected you. *She* protected you. You might want to remember that before I yank that chain off your neck and give it to someone else. Maybe I break your leg and leave you here – see what comes back to get you."

"No man, Hector, no!"

There was a moment of silence, and then, apparently, Hector relented. The footsteps moved closer again, and then past. Donovan counted to three, and then stepped out, hurrying to the right. Amethyst followed.

"Hey!" a voice called out from behind them. "Who's there?"

They didn't turn, the hurried on toward the central court.

"They saw us," Amethyst pointed out.

"I know," Donovan said. "Did you hear what the one they called Hector said? They were wearing something for protection. What do you want to bet you just found out who the buyer was for the other figurines?"

"I should have thought of that," Amethyst said. "I can see you just fine, after all. It never occurred to me that others with the same charm could see us as well."

"I thought I saw something in the circle, but couldn't quite make it out," Donovan said. "I think now it must have been our three friends. I'm guessing that Hector is the Presidente of that group. With the binoculars, and with your crystal, they were shielded from us – but here? I have to say, they don't sound as if they are all on the same page about Anya. We might be able to use that to our advantage at some point."

Ahead the entrance opened onto the courtyard, and they hurried through. The smoke had pretty much cleared, and there was some light from the moon, as well as from scattered torches, now guttering in the night breeze. The fire pit glowed with coals, but wasn't much of a light source.

A man knelt to their left, and another lay back on the ground. The first spun like a cornered snake, rising to a crouch. Donovan held up his hand. Then, realizing the man couldn't see him, he reached up and pulled the talisman up and off over his head. Amethyst did the same.

"Who the fuck are you?"the man snarled.

"My name is Donovan DeChance. We saw what happened. Martinez told us there might be trouble. We're here to help. How is he?"

The man glared at them for a moment, sizing them up, and then turned to his fallen comrade.

"It's bad," he said. "I'm Jake, by the way – this is Enrique. They got him good. There's something – wrong about them. Too fast. The way he was moving..."

"That's something we can talk about once we're safely out of here," Donovan said. "I think it isn't going to take Anya Cabrera and her followers long to regroup and come back to see what happened. You two ruined something she's been planning for a long time. I don't think she's in a very good mood."

"I don't care about that old witch," Jake growled. "Enrique, I think he's dying," Jake said. "I don't think he's going to be able to move."

"Can you carry him?" Donovan asked. "I can help if I need to, but we have a better chance of getting out of here if my hands are free."

Jake nodded. "We have to stop this bleeding, then I can carry him."

Amethyst dropped down beside Enrique and gently pushed Jake aside. She pulled out a scarf from somewhere and ran her hand in under Enrique's jacket. She pulled back his jacket and started to remove it. Donovan stepped up and laid a hand on her shoulder.

"Leave it. Somehow I have the feeling that jacket might be the only reason he's still breathing."

Amethyst glanced up, then over at Jake. Jake nodded.

"He's right."

She worked the scarf in under the jacket and pulled it around his back gently. When it was in place, she tore a strip from the bottom of her skirt and packed it into the wound. A moment later it was tied in place snugly by the scarf, all of it soaking slowly in the man's blood.

"He doesn't have much time," she said. "We have to get him to somewhere he can get real care. I need light, and water. Even then..."

Jake nodded. As she rose, he stepped forward and lifted Enrique in his arms as if the man were a child. Donovan stared, just for a moment, and then let it go. This wasn't the time to ask about the jackets, or Martinez.

"Let's go," he said.

They followed the trail back out of the junkyard toward the street. They met no one along the way. There were no voices or footsteps. It was as if the entire ritual had never happened – as if no one had been there at all. They stepped out into the street cautiously, but there were no guards.

Then, to their right, they heard voices and tramping feet. Donovan reached into the folds of his jacket and braced himself, standing between Jake, Enrique, and whatever came next. A moment later, a group of maybe a dozen men appeared. They wore black leather, and they moved quickly and quietly. Donovan relaxed. They were Dragons, and moments later they were helping Jake carry Enrique's prone form back out of the darker half of the Barrio toward their clubhouse, Martinez, light, and answers.

Donovan and Amethyst followed quietly, and none questioned their presence. It was only a few hours until sunrise.

Chapter Twenty-Three

Martinez met them on the corner a few doors down from the Dragons' headquarters. Enrique was carried inside, but Martinez lingered. When the three of them were alone, Donovan filled him in quickly.

"So, when Jake tried to break into that circle, it held?" the old man asked.

"And when *Los Escorpiones* tried from the inside, it failed," Donovan said. "There is something here we aren't getting. Anya is no magician, as far as I know, but neither is she careless. What could she gain by letting the spirits out of the circle? We assumed that she placed wards to help bind them."

"That would make sense," Martinez said, "but the *Loa* aren't bound by the same powers as other spirits. I'm not certain their portal would be blocked by such a thing – not in the way you're suggesting."

"Then it has to be something else," Donovan said. "I have some research to do, I think. We need to go over this carefully and find what we've missed before it's too late – if it isn't already."

"You'll tell me what you find?" Martinez asked.

The two eyed one another for a moment.

"When are you going to tell me what you wanted the Rojo Fuego for?" Donovan asked. "Where did the dragons on those jackets come from?"

"Soon," Martinez said. "Give me a little time, and I will tell you everything. We owe you another debt, it seems, for bringing these two home."

"You'd better get in there," Amethyst cut in, "or there won't be two of them. It may already be too late. I didn't bring the proper things for a healing."

"I will do what I can," Martinez said.

He turned and disappeared into the well-lit interior of the Dragon's clubhouse.

Donovan watched until the old man was out of sight, then turned away.

"We may not have much time," he said.

They turned and left the Barrio. Donovan ducked into a narrow street. It was lined with curious old shops. Amethyst glanced around, then frowned.

"This isn't the way back to your place," she said. "I've never seen this street before."

Donovan stopped where a dusty stairway led down away from the street. It was deeper than made sense, and with a grin, he started down. He went down three steps, stopped, and Amethyst almost bumped into him as he took two back up.

"What are you..."

In the shadows at the bottom of the stairwell, a door appeared. It shimmered slightly. It was made of wood panels, and there was a dusty glass window near the center. Donovan descended the rest of the way, reached out with one finger, and etched a symbol in the dust. Then he opened the door and stepped through without a backward glance. Amethyst stared for a moment, shrugged, and followed him into the darkness beyond.

They stepped into a tunnel; stone walls stretched off into the distance. There were small alcoves to either side where candles burned. Donovan gestured ahead with a flourish.

"Where are we?" Amethyst asked. "This isn't a normal portal."

"It's older," Donovan said. "Not too many know it's here. I use it when I'm in a hurry, and when I don't want to be followed."

"Who would be following us?"

"I don't know," Donovan said, "but if anyone was, they aren't now. It took me ten years to locate the sigil to open this, and another two years to find the proper stairwells. There are half a dozen of them in San Valencez."

Amethyst shook her head.

"You're always keeping secrets," she said.

"I wouldn't want to lose all my mystery," he said.

He hurried down the tunnel, and as he went, he counted doorways on his right, carefully averting his eyes from those on the left. Finally, he stopped in front of one of the darkened entrances. He spun three times in place and stamped his foot, then stepped forward into shadow. This time Amethyst followed him without hesitation. They exited onto another stairway. Above them the night sky was dark, the stars blanked by the lights of the city. Traffic passed nearby, and a horn honked. Donovan led the way to the end of the street, and they turned into the alley behind his building.

"You know you're going to have to teach me," she said.

"Of course," he laughed. "There is more to that tunnel than meets the eye – more than I've been able to discover. Depending on how you use it, it can take you ... many places. I've been meaning to take you down there, because it's carved of stone – and because certain documents I've located seem to indicate that the original keys may have been formed of crystal."

"Now I'm intrigued," she said.

They climbed the back stairs and took the maintenance entrance. There was no one in sight, and moments later the elevator opened on the thirteenth floor.

"Let's hope we find something quickly," Donovan said, opening his door and holding it for her to enter. "A lot may be counting on it."

Martinez entered the room and went straight to where Enrique lay on a low couch. He still wore his leather jacket. Jake stood close beside him, as well as another man, slender and tall with very dark hair. As he approached, Martinez laid a hand on the tall man's shoulder.

"Let me through, Manuel," he said. "Give him room to breathe. I will do everything that I can for him, but you're going to have to give me room to work."

Manuel stepped aside, but only slightly. He had one hand on Enrique's shoulder, and he did not release his hold.

"You have to fix him," he said.

Martinez ignored this and knelt beside the fallen Dragon. Enrique was pale. His skin was clammy, and there was dried and clotted blood crusted on his shirt, and the inside of the jacket. Martinez peeled away the shirt. He drew a leather pouch from beneath his robes, detaching it from his belt with a quick tug. He opened the drawstrings and pulled out a long, thin blade. He gripped it and leaned over Enrique. Manuel reached down and caught him by the shoulder.

"What are you doing, old man?"

Martinez shook him off and glared.

"If you interrupt me again, I'll have you removed," he said. "You are here out of respect, offer me the same."

He turned back, lifted the soiled fabric of Enrique's shirt in one hand and began quickly cutting it away with the knife. He worked carefully until the wound was clear.

"Get me water," he said. "Clean rags."

Manuel turned abruptly and did as he was told. Martinez laid a hand on Enrique's forehead. He pressed his fingers to the man's throat. The pulse was there, but it was very, very weak.

Snake stepped out of the shadows. He stood by his fallen brother, watching over Martinez'ss shoulder as he worked. The Dragon's leader's eyes were deep pits. He obviously hadn't had enough sleep. Lines creased his forehead, and his hand was gripped into a fist.

"We shouldn't have sent them off like that," he said. "We should have sent more – all of us, maybe."

"It wouldn't have mattered," Martinez said. "More men would have died. This was the only way."

"That's what you say," Snake said. "It's not the way The Dragons live – not the way we die. I should have been there."

Martinez turned and stood suddenly, facing off with the taller, younger man, but not giving an inch.

"If this was a normal night, and you were facing a normal enemy, I would have watched you go and waved as you disappeared. You know better. You know this isn't like anything you've seen before – it's like nothing that *I* have ever seen. We are doing what we can. I know this isn't your way – it is mine

– and it is the only thing that has kept you alive this long."

Jake stepped forward.

"You should have seen him, Snake," he said quietly. "It was like watching some kind of crazy science fiction movie. Man, he ran up a wall of smoke. That thing that stabbed him – that creature – that was no Escorpione. They're fast, and they're bad news, but they're just men. You and me, we've been fighting them all our lives. The old man is right – and we should have been able to do more – but having the rest of you there wouldn't have stopped those things. They poured out of that smoke like demons."

Snake turned away. Martinez started to follow, but Jake shook his head. The old man nodded and turned back to Enrique instead. Manuel had returned with water. The wound was uglier even than Martinez had imagined. He cleaned it as well as he could, applied salve, and then, with a long, curved needle and coarse thread, he stitched the torn flesh carefully. When he was done, he packed a strip of cloth soaked in water and a small pinch of herbs from his bag over the wound. He bandaged the cloth in place, then laid his hand on top and closed his eyes.

He spoke very softly, and though there were several Dragons close enough to hear him, they could make out no words. Those watching carefully saw that where his hand met the bandage, flickers of bluish light rippled across the fallen man's skin. Martinez stayed like that for some time, and then suddenly, stood and staggered back.

He dropped to his knees, reached out to try and put his hand back on the wound, but he nearly fell. Jake leaned down and caught him, holding him up off the floor. After a moment, Martinez brushed his hands away gently, and stood. He was shaky, and his eyes were dark.

"There is nothing more I can do," he said.

Manuel dropped down beside his brother. The steady rise and fall of Enrique's chest had ceased. His face was still, but peaceful. All trace of the blue light was gone. Martinez stepped close again and brushed a fingertip across Enrique's throat. There was no pulse. He waited a long moment, and then stepped back, shaking his head.

"It was too deep," he said. "He should have died immediately. He was strong – very strong."

Tears rolled from Manuel's eyes and ran freely down his cheeks. He made no move to brush them away. He leaned in and laid his forehead on his brother's chest, as if trying to hear something being whispered to him, or to draw the man's soul up and into himself. To call him back. His shoulder's shook, but he did not release the cry of anguish building in his throat, or give in to the sobs that threatened to shake him apart.

He stood very slowly and left the room. The others stood in ranks and watched him leave in silence. Moments later the back door of the clubhouse slammed. Snake stepped in from the next room and walked to stand beside Martinez.

"This has to end," he said. "We can't live like this – I can't lose more of them. First Vasquez – now this. I understand the road. I understand the engine on my bike, and the wind in my hair. I understand that I have to fight, and that I might die. This…I don't understand any of it."

"We will stop her," Martinez said softly. "You have to trust me. I am doing what I can – and there are others."

"The two who helped us?" Jake asked.

Martinez nodded.

"They are powerful, and it is good that they fight at our side. What we are up against is more than any one of us could withstand. They will fight, and we have to help in any way we can. We have to take the war to Anya Cabrera and her demons, or we will be lost before we even know that the battle has begun."

Before Snake could reply, Manuel burst back into the room. He went straight to his brother's side, and he knelt again. He kissed Enrique lightly on the brow; his hands clenched so tightly the nails bit into the palms of his hands. Then, working slowly and very, very gently, he began to work the leather jacket off of his brother's arm. He pulled it free of one arm, and turned to Jake.

"Help me," he said. His voice cracked.

Jake hurried to do as Manuel asked. They gently rolled Enrique to the side, slid the blood-soaked jacket out from under him, and pulled it free. Manuel dropped it on the floor at his feet, then turned back to his brother. He carefully arranged Enrique's arms, crossed on his chest. He leaned closer and closed his brother's eyelids. Then, crossing himself, he leaned down and picked the jacket upheld it in his hands and stared at the dragon painted on the back.

It was still beautifully worked, but something had changed. It didn't have the luster it had possessed when Salvatore first painted it. The ice-blue seemed more like a dull gray. It might have been the light, but the jacket mirrored the death pallor of its owner.

Without a word, Manuel turned and headed for the door.

"Where you going, bro?" Jake called out.

"Don't follow me," Manuel said. "Don't. Fucking. Follow. I'm going for a ride."

"You should leave the jacket," Martinez said.

Manuel spun and locked his gaze on the old man. He held the jacket very tightly in his hands, and his arms shook from the tension of that grip.

"He was my brother, old man. This was his, and now it's mine. I will wear it in his honor, and when the time comes to take revenge – I will wrap it around the throat of the Escorpione bastard who killed him."

Before anyone could say another word, Manuel swung the jacket over his shoulders and slipped it on. He ignored the blood. Without a word he spun and left the room. Jake went to the door after him, but before he could even get onto the sidewalk the powerful growl of Manuel's bike ripped through the night.

With a squeal of rubber on pavement and a spray of gravel, the big chopper shot off down the street.

"Let him go," Snake said, stepping out beside Jake. "His brother is dead. *Our* brother is dead. Let him mourn. He'll be back. Let's do the right thing and take care of Enrique."

Jake nodded, and the two stepped back inside together. Martinez slipped past them to stand in the cool evening air. He stared off down the street after Manuel. His expression was troubled.

"Be safe," he said.

Then he turned and followed the others inside, closing the door on the night.

Manuel gunned the old Harley and skidded around the corner of Forty-Second, barely catching traction before he slammed into the curb on the far side of the street. There was no traffic, and he shot off toward the entrance to the freeway. He didn't know where he was going, but he knew he had to get out of town, get to somewhere he could cut loose without fear of being pulled over. The wind whipped through his hair, and he wanted it harder and faster. He wanted it to blow the world away behind him and erase the events of the night.

He turned onto the ramp without running into a cop and shot up the coast highway. He took the exit that led to the two-lane toward Lavender, and the mountains beyond. There were roads up there where he could be alone, where he and the bike and the road could mourn with one voice. He thought, maybe, if he reached the topmost peak of the mountain, up near the border of the sky, that he might catch a glimpse of his brother – of his spirit – his dragon.

The jacket felt heavy and wrong. It fit poorly, and he frowned. He and Enrique had always worn one another's clothing. They were nearly the same size, built the same, hard to tell apart after Manuel had shaved his beard. They had been inseparable, but now that word made no sense. It had no truth behind it. They were separated, and despite the fact that he somehow felt the outline of the dragon through the leather on his back – a dragon he could have sworn shared his brother's soul, he had never felt so alone. There was an ache in his chest – not where his heart was broken, but where the blade had sliced the jacket. He gritted his teeth and ignored it.

He flew down the highway and turned off on the mountain road, sliding up through shadows a little more slowly and then gunning the engine again. He raced upward, taking turns at crazy speeds and skidding into embankments.

At some point, a shadow rose to cover the moon. He could still see the pavement – the headlight of his bike sliced easily through the darkness. He glanced up, and nearly slid off the side of the road. Something soared overhead, something long and sleek, serpentine and powerful. He saw a flicker of blue light along its length, and heard the rustle of huge, leathery wings.

He roared around another corner. The road was narrow. The side of the mountain was steep, almost a cliff. He could not take his eyes off of the dragon. It was a dragon – it had to be a dragon. He drove straight at it, lifted his hand and reached out to it. He heard the impossibly loud scream as it called to him, and without hesitation, he launched the bike off into empty, open space.

"Enrique!" he screamed. "Brother!"

And then it was gone. Silvery clouds swam across the face of the moon, and he was falling, screaming, into tall trees and rocks. The bike struck first, bounced once, and flipped. Manuel's head slammed into the trunk of a tree. Branches broke and cut at his flesh, but he was already gone. He hit, finally, and slid for a very long time. The bike lay on its side, engine still idling. The headlight was smashed, but the taillight blinked through the shadows.

The jacket slid up and over the back of his head where he lay, covering him like a shroud.

Chapter Twenty-Four

The call came early the next morning. It did not come to the clubhouse, or to Snake, but to Manuel's mother. The dragon had never married, and though he didn't live at home, that was the address he listed when anything official had to be signed. Elena Delgado answered on the fourth ring. She'd been expecting a call like this one most of her adult life – since her husband Paco had died, and the boys had both taken up with Snake and The Dragons. They were good boys, for the most part, but it was a dangerous life they led. The Barrio was a dangerous place.

What Elena had not anticipated was getting two such calls in a single night. Snake had called, and then visited in person to tell her of Enrique's death. When she'd asked why Manuel had not come – where he had gone – Snake had shook his head. He didn't know. Men grieve in their own fashion, he said. Now Elena cradled the phone in her hand and brought it to her ear.

When the message had been delivered, she didn't hang up the phone. She let it drop from her hand, and she turned away. Tears unfocused the world, and she stumbled back, not really going anywhere, just unwilling to stand still and let reality grip her heart. She had to go somewhere, to do something.

Elena grabbed her jacket, and her purse. It was still dark out, and she knew that she couldn't' drive in her current state. She closed and locked her door, leaving the phone beeping it's off-the-hook busy signal to an empty home, and turned away. It was about a mile to The Dragons clubhouse. She pulled her jacket about her more tightly, bowed her head, and began walking.

It was not easy getting the police to release Enrique's jacket. Manuel had worn it when he died, and it was now stained with the blood of two men – two brothers – both dead. The deaths had to be explained. In the end, Elena's grief, and the tragic loss of two brothers in the prime of their lives softened even official hearts. Snake was allowed to carry off the jacket and a few other personal effects in an old cardboard box. Elena walked at his side, her back bent. She was silent, for the most part, and he left her to her grief.

At the clubhouse he found the others milling about on the street, awaiting his return. When they saw him walk into site, Elena at his side, they stood in ranks, three deep, on either side of the walk leading up to the door. Snake paid no attention to them at all.

He carried the box past them, looking neither right nor left, and entered the clubhouse. Once inside, he placed the box on a chair and pulled out the jacket. It was tattered now, torn where the blade has sliced through, scraped from crazed fall down the mountain. Snake turned it, held it up, and stared at the ice blue dragon.

There was no expression on his face. He studied the image carefully, as if imprinting it in his memory. The rest of the Dragons slowly trickled in behind him. None of them spoke. There was nothing that they could have said. Three of their number had now died in a very short span of time – more than they'd lost at one time since their formation.

Snake turned back to the box of Manuel's belongings. He reached in, and this time he pulled out a long, thin knife. With this in one hand, and the jacket in the other, he crossed the room toward an empty wall beside the fireplace. As he moved, he picked up speed, until at the last moment, he brought the jacket up, slammed the knife forward, and buried it through the leather into the plaster and wood beyond.

The impact was loud and it echoed through the room. Some of the Dragons took a step back. Others only flinched. Snake stood and stared at the dragon on the leather, now glaring back at him from the wall – trapped there. He turned, and he scanned the others. His eyes blazed with anger and pain.

"No one will touch that," he said. "Not now, not ever. I will personally kill the first who does. I have not liked these fancy painted dragons from the beginning. We have colors – they have always been enough. Martinez warned Manuel not to wear the dragon, and he took it anyway. He took it, and it took him in return. We have lost two brothers. It is time for this to be finished. Do you understand? Am I clear on this? That jacket will hang there until eternity comes for us all, and if it does not – it will not be the dragon on the jacket that you should fear. It will be me."

He stood in silence for what seemed a long time. When no one responded, he spoke again.

"Get the word out," he said. "Send notice to every chapter, every brother and sister you can reach. We will meet tonight, and we will decide what is to be done. *Los Escorpiones* have started this, and we need to find a way to end it. If that old witch Anya Cabrera is behind this – she will pay as well. We must stand, and we must fight. We cannot go on having our numbers whittled down a few at a time, cowering in the shadows."

They all stood very still, in case he wasn't finished.

"Go!" he said. "And someone send for Martinez."

Snake turned and left the room, and the others dispersed like mist, running for phones and bikes. Engines started and revved. In only a matter of moments, the clubhouse was as silent as a tomb. On the wall, impaled by the wickedly sharp, silvery blade, Enrique's dragon held court over the emptiness. It was just past noon.

Chapter Twenty-Five

Donovan bent over the keyboard of his computer, and Amethyst sat on the wooden arm of his chair, leaning on his shoulder and scanning the screen. The program he had open was the viewer he used to browse the documents he'd archived. He'd been working on the project so long that, when he's started, he'd needed a huge mainframe computer. As machines grew faster and programs grew more efficient, his system had evolved as well.

Now he had a small room off of the library, concealed behind several movable shelves, where arrays of water-cooled hard drives and blade servers maintained terabytes of data. He'd been scanning, recording, indexing and studying the manuscripts in his collection for decades, and unlike many of his peers, he embraced technology and all that it offered rather than denying it. One shelf in his den held stacks of recent technical publications and volumes on database design and administration. He liked to tell visitors that computer logic, programming, and magic weren't so far removed from one another.

There were exact sequences of numbers and precise patterns of syntax and data required for each operation. Taking a manuscript, converting it to tiny pixels on the screen, and then recording it on an array of data drives that could reproduce it in multiple formats, and even recover it if it became corrupted, was just magic of a different kind.

At the moment, he was very glad to have that particular magic at his fingertips. There must have been tens of thousands of references to Voodoo in his files, and those were only among the documents and volumes he'd recorded. He glanced over at the boxes and books piled along the wall and shook his head.

"Sometimes I wonder if I'll ever even begin to catch up," he said. "I have deposit boxes in the vaults beneath the bank downtown. You know Joel?"

Amethyst nodded.

"I've done business with them myself. Their security is top-notch."

"If I'm right," Donovan said, "what we need is going to be among the documents I've already recorded. I started with the oldest, the most dangerous, and those most difficult to handle without causing damage. In some cases I had to photograph them carefully because I couldn't pick them up, or touch them with my skin for fear of their crumbling away and being lost.

"A large number of those earliest and most fragile documents came out of Africa. Others were collected from the islands, Jamaica, and Haiti. I don't remember them all, there's no way that I could, but I've at least scanned everything once, and there's something I'm forgetting – something I've seen."

Cleo leaped from the floor to the desktop, walked to the edge nearest Amethyst, and arched her back, purring. Amethyst laughed, stood, and lifted the cat into her arms. She scratched Cleo's ears and pressed her face into the warm fur.

"I know," she said. "He gets like this around books. But what are we going to do? He's cute."

Donovan grunted, but didn't look up. He continued scanning documents and indexes. Amethyst carried Cleo over to the bar, set her down gently, and reached for a bottle of deep amber liquid. She poured two fingers each into two tumblers and carried one back to Donovan, who took it gratefully, but did not look up from the computer screen.

"What is it?" Amethyst asked.

"I'm not sure," he said. "I think I may have found something, but it's slow going. I scanned and archived these documents, but there was no way I could translate them all, so I'm having to wing it as I go. It's a little easier now – I have software that can perform OCR text recognition in nearly a thousand languages – but even computers take time for this sort of thing."

"You say OCR and I hear yada yada yada," Amethyst said. "Seriously, what is it you think you found?"

"This," Donovan said. He sat up so that she could see the screen better. What appeared was a very old document written in spidery, difficult script. It was even harder to make out because the paper it was written on was a dark shade of tan.

"Couldn't you whiten the paper in the image?" she asked. "I can't make out a word of it, but even if I knew that language, this would be hard."

"I did what I could," Donovan said. "It was darker before. That manuscript is written on human skin. It was a tattoo. When the original – owner – died, they preserved it. When I got the manuscript, it was rolled around a femur and sealed in a tube made of tree bark and sealed with sap. I'm not sure of the age, but it was brittle. I had to use special oils – a formula I got from the Egyptians, as a matter of fact – to work the skin so that it could be unrolled, and then it took another week to photograph it in parts and piece the images together."

Amethyst stared at the document a moment longer, and then turned to him.

"You have got to be kidding me? A spell so powerful – so important – that it was preserved on live human skin?"

"Apparently. I wouldn't have hit on this connection at all, but it cross-references to an entry I found to something resembling your amulets. I think they came from the same area of the world, and I think they are more connected even than Anya Cabrera knows. If I'm correct, the moment she set this plan of hers into motion, they were attracted – that they were meant to find their way here."

"The amulets, you mean? They are part of the spell?" Amethyst asked. Her face wrinkled in disgust.

"Not exactly," Donovan said. "What I've read seems to indicate that they are part of what was originally used to control, or combat it. I think they are here because they were attracted by need."

"What does it say?" Amethyst asked.

"I don't have all of it yet," Donovan said. "Translation programs are still pretty rudimentary, and as you can imagine,

those dealing with ancient languages are even worse. I know this much – Anya Cabrera is not summoning the *Loa* we are familiar with. She isn't hoping to see Papa Legba; it's something darker she's after. There are apparently levels of spirits that can be summoned and these are one of the lowest. They can possess worshippers just as the more powerful *Loa* can, but they don't assume control. They don't have the intelligence for it – they're elemental powers, and it's the summoner who retains control. In this case, that would be Anya."

"But the *Loa* don't remain beyond the ritual," Amethyst protested. "I've seen the ceremony."

"True," Donovan said, leaning forward as another bit of text spit out of the translator. "But this is a different ritual entirely. It's a matter of repetition and degree. These spirits linger for longer periods the more often they are summoned. If they return to the same hosts repeatedly, the forces binding them to the underworld weaken. Eventually they can be ripped free, snapping the bonds holding them in their own realm and remaining in their hosts."

"Like powerful slaves," Amethyst said.

"Exactly. They don't belong on this plane, and they are desperate to return, but they can't fight the summoning any more than those possessed can free themselves. Only the *Houngan* behind the spell controls their captivity, and by a series of rituals intended to promise a freedom that will never come, they are tricked into subservience and trapped in human form forever."

"There has to be a backlash," Amethyst said. "You can't just drag a power from one realm to another without repercussions."

"That's why the amulets exist," Donovan said. "This document explains how they were first created, from the residue of the bodies of those possessed. They exist in both realms, and when worn prevent those who have been displaced from seeing those who bear them. At the same time they apparently provide a conduit for spirits on the other side to assist. We didn't know about that little tidbit, or we might have made use of it."

"I don't know," Amethyst said. "You know how the things make your skin crawl, and feel – sort of unclean? That is probably the touch or influence of the powers you're talking about calling on. I'm not sure it's an improvement."

"Whoever wrote this believed it was."

The program finished its rough translation, and Donovan clicked the icon to print it.

"We need to get back to the Barrio," he said. "We have to find Martinez and show this to him, and we have to find out when Anya might be planning another ritual. If I understand this correctly, and it's entirely possible that I don't, since the translation is very weak, she hasn't performed the ritual enough times to make it permanent. There is time to stop her, but we have to find out if she's planning to repeat that ceremony, and if she does, we have to stop her. If she gets her army of spirit warriors in place, we're going to need a lot more horsepower than we have locally to put an end to it, and even with help we might be in over our heads."

"That powerful?"

"Powerful enough to tattoo the preventive ritual on a man's back, and to create amulets that are – at the most basic level – pacts with demons to prevent it from happening. I'd say it came close at least once in the past, and someone stopped it. Let's just hope that what they left us is enough that we can do it again."

He shut down the computer and rose, downing his cognac.

"Sorry, Cleo," Amethyst said, giving the cat a final scratch on the ears. "I guess you're on guard duty again. I'll try to bring him back in one piece."

Cleo meowed once, then curled up on Donovan's now warm and vacant chair and laid her head on her paws as if in resignation.

Moments later they were out the door and on their way, the printout rolled and tucked into a deep fold of Donovan's jacket. When they hit the street, the sun was low in the sky, dropping toward evening.

"I think we'd better split up for a while," Donovan said. "We need to know when Anya will hold that next ceremony, and where. You think you could track that down?"

"Of course," Amethyst said. "What are you doing?"

"I'm going to see Martinez. The more I think about this,

the more I believe he knows exactly what Anya is up to. You saw those jackets, and how the men wearing them moved. They were holding their own, maybe a little better. I noticed something about their dragons."

"What?"

"There was no red in either one. The paint was blue and green on Jake's jacket, and the dead man's was ice blue. The paint that Martinez wanted to create so badly – it was Rojo Fuego. Fire red. If his boy Salvatore could create the kind of power he did without that color...what's going to happen when he paints a red dragon?"

"Let's hope we never find out. I'll find you later, as soon as I know something.

They split, and Donovan disappeared down the side street behind his building. Amethyst stepped out onto the street and disappeared into the crowds.

Chapter Twenty-Six

Word had spread throughout the city. The Dragons had been founded in the Barrio, but there were other chapters. There was a group in Lavender, as well as groups as far off as Los Angeles and San Diego. Most of them weren't going to make it into San Valencez for the meeting, but there were more than the small clubhouse had seen in many years.

Snake set several of the younger members to work out in back. They had a large yard circled by a seven foot wooden fence. The center was a fire pit they used for barbecues. This night, it would just hold a fire. There were torches lined up around the outer edge of the yard as well.

"I don't want this to be cramped," Snake said. "I want plenty of room. The fresh air will be good."

Bikes rolled in all afternoon, and into the evening. There were a lot of questions, and not many answers. Those who came from outside the Barrio were filled in, but even those telling the tales knew how crazy they sounded. The only thing everyone understood was that *Los Escorpiones* were making a bid to rule the Barrio, and that there was a battle coming. There were also stories of the last confrontation. Vasquez had been well known, and the stories of his death were already reaching legendary status.

Snake stood in the doorway, drinking a beer and watching the preparations. He glanced over at the jacket on the wall. Even from where he stood, the bloodstains were visible. They haunted him. The dragon, limp and lifeless as the leather, seemed to accuse him. No matter where he stood in the room, he was certain those eyes followed.

Jake stepped up beside him.

"Did you find Martinez?" Snake asked.

"He'll be here. I'd swear he was standing on his front porch waiting for me, like he already knew I was coming."

Snake nodded. "Makes sense. If anyone knows what's going on, and how it's likely to end, it's that crazy old man."

"I've got scouts out," Jake said. "We're trying to locate *Los Escorpiones*. Delaporte is quiet, and there hasn't been a sign of Hector, or any of the others, since that night. Anya Cabrera's shop is closed. No one is out on the street, and the few people we've been able to find are either not talking, or they really don't know."

"She'll make her move soon enough," Snake said. "We just have to make sure we're ready. In about an hour, I want you to get the club organized and get them into that yard. Light a fire, hand out some beer, keep them quiet. Try to keep them from working themselves up too soon – try to keep them from getting scared.

"I'm going to meet with Martinez first. I want to be able to tell them all that we know, and I want to have some options to offer – some hope."

Jake nodded. "They'll follow you into hell, you know? All of them. I'll be right at the front."

"I know that, man," Snake said. "I only hope it's not misplaced trust, you know? I've never seen anything like this, and I don't know how we're going to face it."

"Yeah, you know," Jake said. His voice was rough with emotion, but he worked through it. "We'll face it like men. Like Dragons. What else is there?"

Snake turned and stared at him, and then – slowly – the old familiar smile slid over his face. He lifted his beer, saluted Jake with it, and drained the bottle.

"I might keep you around," he said.

Jake turned away then. Snake watched the big man walk out into the yard, then turned and dropped the empty bottle in the trash. He wanted another, but he knew he had to wait. There was a lot to do and maybe not enough time left to do it. The sun was low on the skyline. He turned, crossed the main room of the clubhouse, and walked into the back room – where he kept his things. Several of the Dragons lived at the clubhouse, and there were two rooms for those sleeping over when their old ladies kicked them to the curve, or they needed a place to crash and recover. Snake had the only private room. He closed the door and flopped back on his old leather couch. From where he sat he could watch the activities out back through a tinted window, mirrored on the outside. He ignored the Dragons and watched the growing, lapping flames as they danced.

Martinez arrived at the Dragons clubhouse just as the last of the sun's rays disappeared. Streetlights hummed to life around him. The street and the driveway were lined with motorcycles, Harleys, Indians, a few Triumphs and some others. They glittered in the dim light, their colors muted. The old man approached the doorway. Jake stepped out to greet him.

"Snake's been waiting for you," he said.

Martinez followed the big man inside. He saw that Jake still wore the leather jacket, and the dragon stared out at him from that dark surface. He felt its power, and its anger. He felt the coming storm so clearly in that instant that he nearly stopped in his tracks, turned, and disappeared. What he was doing was dangerous – not in the same way that what Anya Cabrera was doing, but it crossed lines he should not cross and brought danger to those he cared about.

Jake knocked on a door, opened it and stepped aside. Martinez entered a small, dimly lit room. The space was neat and organized. There was a small desk in one corner with a lamp and a laptop computer. The bed rested against the back wall, a cot like men used in the army. Snake sat on a low-slung couch directly across from the door. He rose when Martinez entered, and held out his hand.

"Thanks for coming," he said. "I guess I don't need to tell you why we're all gathered here."

"She is crazy, you know that?" Martinez said. "Anya Cabrera believes that she can control this – this darkness – that she is unleashing. It will eat her alive, and when it is done, it will come for the rest of us."

"I was afraid you'd say something like that," Snake said. "We have to fight them again, don't we?"

Martinez nodded. "Someone must stop her. We are here."

"How?" It was a simple, one word question, but it encompassed so much.

"It won't be easy," Martinez said. "You will have to trust me."

"Enrique trusted you," Snake said. There was bitterness in his tone, but not accusation.

"I did not send Enrique to Salvatore," Martinez said. "I sent Jake. If I had known another would come to the boy so quickly, I would have prevented it."

"You couldn't have prevented that with a steamroller," Snake sighed. "You didn't see the way Enrique's eyes lit up when Jake came in, flashing that dragon around and suddenly lit up with power like some kind of comic book superhero. Don't think I didn't see that. Most of the time, he just looks like Jake, but I know there's more to it. Hell, if there wasn't why would they do it at all?"

"You must call the boy," Martinez said. "You must call him to paint a final dragon. It is the only way. It is the only thing that I have to offer that can help – that can stand against this darkness. He has a gift – a power in his hands, and his dreams. He can bring your dragon."

"My club has colors," Snake said, turning away. "Every member wears them – exactly the same. They are a sign of strength, and brotherhood. They are a sign that though we ride many roads and live many separate lives, but we are equal.

"Those new dragons, the painted ones; I didn't like them from the start. I don't like the way they set us apart. I don't like the way they make one person stand out among many. Everything that I stand for, everything that I have worked to build here, is in danger. Some of that danger comes from *Los Escorpiones*, and from Anya Cabrera. Some of it, though, comes from closer to home. Some of it comes from a young man with chalk and pencils and paint . So what am I to do?"

"You must save them," Martinez said. "At all cost – at any cost – it is yours to do."

There was a knock on the door. Both men turned as Jake opened the door a crack.

"Martinez, there is someone here for you."

Snake turned and looked at Martinez curiously. The old man shrugged.

"Who is it?" Snake asked.

"That guy Donovan – the one who brought Enrique and I back. He's alone."

"I must speak with him," Martinez said. "He may have news of Anya Cabrera's plans. He is a good man – a strong ally. It is very good that he is on our side."

"You talk to him, and you find out what you can," Snake said. "I'm going to go out and speak to the others. I'm going to keep them busy for a while with what's happened already. Before I finish, come to me, and tell me what comes next. Tell me how we will beat this, and get our lives back. Tell me how we will win, and return to riding in the mountains, drinking beer and telling stories. Help me make this into one of those stories. That is what I want from you. If you give that to me, if you bring us peace, you will have my friendship for the rest of my life. I would say for the rest of yours – you are an old man – but I have the feeling that when I am dead and buried, you will be here, looking over those who come next."

Martinez nodded. There was nothing to say. He slipped out into the main room, and Snake watched him go. Then he stepped through with Jake and they headed for the yard in back, and the fire.

Donovan waited out front by the bikes. When Martinez stepped outside, he climbed the single step to the porch.

"We have to talk," Donovan said.

"There isn't much time," Martinez replied. "They will be calling for me shortly."

"You're right to say there isn't much time. We found out some things about Anya's ritual. She isn't finished, but she's close. If she manages to complete the binding again – to complete that ritual, it might be all that it takes to seal the spirits she's summoning into their hosts. If that happens…"

"I am aware of the consequences," Martinez said softly. "That is why I am doing everything in my power to prevent it."

"With the Dragons?"

Martinez hesitated, but didn't answer at first. Then he nodded, as if making some very difficult decision.

"Yes," he said at last. "Of course with the Dragons."

"Fighting the type of power Anya Cabrera is trying to unleash with another uncontrolled power is not a solution. You know that."

"I must do what I can," Martinez said. "I don't have the same resources available to me that you do – or that others do – but I have lived a very long life. There are things that I do know, and those are what I count on in times of danger. The boy has a gift – a gift that I discovered and nurtured. This is his time. It would be wrong to stop what I have started before it has run its course. There is danger in disruption, as well."

"One more ritual, and Anya will command an army of dark warriors. Can your artist paint so many so fast? Can he arm all of these and keep them safe?"

Donovan waved his arm in a wide arc that took in the clubhouse and all the bikes, the streets beyond and the Barrio, filled with innocent people uninvolved in the conflict raging in their streets. Martinez followed the motion of Donovan's arm, and then shook his head.

"You don't understand," he said. "There is not time for me to explain, but you must trust me when I tell you that the answer is yes. If he is allowed to, Salvatore will protect them all."

"And if you're wrong?" Donovan asked. "Or if he isn't given that chance? What's your fallback plan? Martinez, you came to me offering peace, but you walked in and out of my home without sharing the truth. Why did you need that formula, and the crystals? What are you planning to do with that paint?"

"I can't answer that," Martinez said. "I don't fully know. If I told you what I think, you might agree and help me, and you might try to stop me. If you chose the latter, we'd both end up losers because Anya would certainly have her way with the Barrio, and possibly the city itself if the two of us were out of the picture.

"I have my plans, and you have yours. I trust that you will do all that you can to stop Anya from completing her ritual. I intend to make sure that, should you fail, we aren't without protection."

"If you lose control," Donovan said, "who will protect us from you?"

They stood and stared at one another. For just a second, it seemed as if Martinez might look away, as if he might speak. Then the front door of the clubhouse opened, and Jake stood in silhouetted in the light from the room beyond.

"Snake wants you out there," the big man said softly.

"Tell him I'll be right there," Martinez said. He turned back to Donovan.

"You must do what you can," he said, " and I will do the same. We seek the same thing, I believe, but we follow different roads to our goals."

"When this is over," Donovan said, "if we are both standing … we will talk. If we cannot do that, there will be new problems."

Martinez held his gaze, and then nodded. "It is long overdue," he said. "Perhaps…you would like to meet my son…"

Without another word, or waiting to see that Donovan would answer, the old man turned and entered the Dragons' clubhouse. Donovan watched him go, cursed softly under his breath, and then turned away. He needed to find Amethyst, and they needed to get moving, or all of what they'd learned and done would be a waste of time.

Martinez walked slowly into the center of the yard, where Snake stood beside the fire pit. All around them faces stared out from shadows. They watched him approach with a combination of fear and awe. He knew they didn't understand him, or trust him. He also knew that they were frightened. Snake stood tall and silent, waiting. Jake had returned to stand beside him.

"I'm ready," Snake said, not wasting any time or words on preliminaries. "Bring your boy – your artist – to me. Bring his paints, and his magic. Bring him to me, and we will put an end to all of this once and for all."

Whispers sounded around the clearing. Words were spoken

too low to be heard. Hushed questions were stilled by nervous coughs. No one dared to voice opposition, or to question what Snake said. The time for debate had apparently passed.

"I will return within the hour," Martinez said.

Snake nodded, held his gaze for a moment, and then turned his back, staring off across the fence sealing them from the world. As solid as the wood seemed, the darkness encroached, and though the fire flickered and blazed, it seemed lost and empty in that greater void.

Martinez turned, and returned the way he'd come.

Snake turned to Jake and spoke softly.

"You'd better be right," he said. "For all our sakes...you'd better be fucking right."

Chapter Twenty-Seven

Donovan was halfway down the dark tunnel toward home when a shadow flickered across the floor. He froze. He'd never encountered another living thing in the tunnels. There might be things trapped inside. There might be others with the knowledge and power to walk those hidden roads. He hadn't survived by ignoring danger, and he had no time for confrontation. When a soft growl that rose to an almost inquisitive yowl floated from the shadows he could only stare in amazement. He hurried forward.

"Cleo?"

The cat stepped from the shadows, hunkered low, and then leaped. Donovan caught her and held her up, staring in consternation. The two were connected in ways that sometimes amazed him, but he hadn't dreamed that she could walk the portals.

"What is it?" he asked. "What are you doing out?"

Cleo emitted another low yowling sound. Donovan closed his eyes, concentrated on releasing his thoughts, and sought the link. If Cleo had something to tell him, they wouldn't be chatting about it. If she'd found her way out of his home and into this dark place to find him, something was very, very wrong.

His mind blanked, just for a moment, and then filled with a series of images that were hard to follow. He concentrated and made the shift from human to feline perception. Everything was larger, and his line of sight was very low to the ground. The world was a chiaroscuro wash of gray-scales and shadow. He gritted his teeth and focused.

After a moment, he recognized the Barrio, but not any of

the areas they'd visited recently. This was a park on the far side of Anya Cabrera's shop, several streets over and nearer to the city proper. He saw shadows moving, and at first thought it was just traffic on the street. It was difficult to interface with Cleo's thoughts. The world shifted, and he nearly broke the connection as she leaped to a fence, changing the perspective with sickening swiftness.

Donovan felt Cleo's anger grow, felt a shiver as the hairs on her back rose, and the world shimmered back into focus. He saw the entrance to a park. The park was drenched in heavy mist. Figures moved in and out along the edge of that mist. Then everything faded, and another image rose.

Donovan saw Amethyst's face. Her expression was a mixture of anger and fear. Mist swirled around her, and the connection broke. He staggered, and felt Cleo's claws drive into his arms, clinging tight. He caught his balance and cursed. Something had gone wrong. He didn't know exactly what had happened, but the message was clear. Someone had taken Amethyst, and she was in that park.

"Good girl, Cleo," he said.

He shifted her on his shoulder so that she rode more comfortably.

'There's no time to take you home," he said. "You're going to have to come with me. If she is already caught up in that mist we'll have to act very quickly."

Cleo hunkered, wrapped herself around his shoulder and clung to his jacket as he broke into a run. When he started to take a passage leading off to the right, she dug her claws in again, and he hesitated.

"What?" he asked.

Cleo leaped from his shoulder and dashed into another passage leading off to the left. Donovan shrugged and followed. If Cleo had found him in these tunnels, she very likely knew them better than he did himself. That was a curiosity to be looked into at a later time. He flashed on the image of Amethyst's face, and gritted his teeth. He fought to keep up as Cleo flashed ahead into the shadows, cursing under his breath.

They exited through a doorway Donovan had never tried. It

brought them into a very short alley between two buildings he didn't recognize. When they stepped onto the street, though, he saw that they were about two blocks from the park he'd seen through Cleo's memory. He kept close to the walls of the line of shops he passed, and moved carefully forward.

As he approached, he saw that there was a fire burning near the center. This park was very close to the line that bordered the Barrio and the city "proper." The police still patrolled it regularly, and Donovan frowned, trying to understand how there could be what amounted to a small bonfire in the center of a city park without drawing notice.

A mist had risen, turning to thick fog at its outer limits, and as he watched, it sifted across the ground and rose into the air. Within moments the park was nothing more than a low-hanging cloud bank from the streets. There were occasional flickers of light from within, where the flames licked higher for a moment, and then died down. Anya Cabrera had effectively erased the small area from the face of the city.

After a few moments, Donovan saw a young man in dark jeans walking down the road from deeper in the Barrio. He wore the colors of *Los Escorpiones*, and he glanced furtively from side to side. He was obviously not convinced of the privacy of the gathering in the park, or perhaps he feared that Anya Cabrera was as much a danger as an ally. He reached the park, glanced over his shoulder a final time, and then followed the young gang member into the mist.

"She's in there, isn't she, Cleo?" Donovan whispered.

The cat glanced up at him and let out a soft growl. She rubbed against his leg once. He leaned down and patted her head.

"It's time for you to get back," he said. "This is no place for you. I'll get her out of there, and I'll bring her home."

For a moment it seemed Cleo would ignore him. She glared up with feral intensity, and he feared she might dart off on her own through that dark mist. He didn't want to think about what might happen if Anya got control of Cleo. It would be bad for both of them.

Then, without warning, she turned and darted back into

the alley. Donovan watched her go. He thought about going in to be sure she got through the portal, then remembered where and how she'd found him, and shook his head. He turned back to the park and concentrated on the problem at hand.

His jacket was lined with pockets and hidden pouches. He never knew where he'd be caught, or in what kind of predicament. No one knew what he carried with him, and he varied his portable 'arsenal' as often as he could, adding new secrets and trying things he discovered in his research. It kept those who knew him off balance.

He still had the amulet Amethyst had given him, but that wasn't going to be enough. It would obscure him from the sight of most, but not all, of those in that park. It would keep any of the dark *Loa* from discovering him, but he thought it was likely that Anya herself possessed one of the amulets, and he knew for a fact that at least two of *Los Escorpiones* wore them. That meant he was going to have to find a way to 'disappear' that would work on them all, and even then he was going to have to be very careful. When he'd watched the previous ritual, those wearing the amulets had been vague – like pencil sketches mostly rubbed out, but lingering as gray shadows. That meant they would notice him if he made a wrong move, and if he got in and close to Amethyst, only to be discovered, or captured, they'd end up worse off than they already were.

He rummaged through his pockets and pulled out a small scroll. It was made of parchment, tied with a black ribbon, the knot sealed in wax. He broke the seal, untied the binding and unfurled the small slip of paper.

The spell was powerful, but short-lived. Once he used it, he would be racing against the clock. A quick mental inventory of the other things he had with him told him it was his only chance, so he took a deep breath, and began to read.

The words were in Latin, but not the Latin taught in schools. It was the Latin of a long ago world, pronounced just differently enough to bring the power behind the words to life. He enunciated carefully, reciting each word clearly. When he was done, the parchment burst into flames, but he didn't release it. Though it burned his hands, he held on until the words had drifted to the ground at his feet as ashes. He murmured a final incantation, stepped across those ashes, and disappeared in a wisp of smoke.

As he walked toward the park, he left no shadow. He moved carefully, making as little sound as possible, but at the same time he hurried his steps. The fire in the mist had grown larger and brighter. He had to get in, get Amethyst and get out, and he knew he had to do it quickly. The instructions for creating the scroll had been vague on only one point. They had said the effects did not last long, but the small segment of text that would have explained these limits had been smudged and indecipherable. It was a gamble, and Donovan hated gambling. With a softly mumbled curse, he stepped into the mist and disappeared.

Once in the park, Donovan noticed a lot of things at once. There was a fire blazing in the center, and a circle had been drawn around that fire. There was movement and activity everywhere, and he stood very still, taking it all in.

Central to it all was a sort of throne, a carved wooden chair with velvet cushions. It was heavily decorated, its arms carved snakes, and the legs those of some large jungle cat. It was a chair out of a nightmare, a museum quality nightmare. He'd heard of similar pieces, but never actually seen one. Anya Cabrera stood nearby, and he had no doubt that when things got into full swing, she'd be seated on that monstrosity overseeing it all.

Behind and to one side of the chair, another carved item had been added to the circle. Donovan's heart nearly stopped. A large stake, sculpted into scowling faces and strange creatures at the top, had been driven into the ground. The stake was nearly eight feet tall, and Amethyst had been bound to its base. Her arms were drawn around behind, and though she struggled, she was tied carefully and thoroughly.

There were five or six of *Los Escorpiones* prancing about the pole. They didn't move like men. There was something odd in their gait; their rhythm was erratic and too rapid. Apparently the previous ritual's effects were holding, at least for the moment. Donovan fingered the talisman beneath his jacket.

They wouldn't be able to see him, but if he made a mis-step and bumped into one of them, or the spell failed, and someone else was able to make him out, he was in real trouble.

Then he saw something that galvanized him into motion. The younger woman, Kim, was making her way around the circle again, as she had at the junkyard. She danced as she went, and he heard her voice chanting in an odd, rhythmic cadence. Scented smoke wafted up from a series of braziers in her wake. She was recreating the powerful outer protective circle from the junkyard, and if she completed that circle, there was no way for Donovan to be of any help.

Moving as quickly and quietly as possible, he rushed to where the circle was not yet complete and slipped inside. Kim stopped, just for a second, and raised her head. She looked as if she were sniffing the air – an animal with a scent to follow. Donovan stood very still, just inside the circle, and after a moment, she shook her head and moved on.

Donovan turned and circled back the way she'd just come. The only part of the circle that was free of activity was directly behind the stake. He hoped that if Amethyst noticed his presence she could keep it to herself. He had the feeling the element of surprise might be the only weapon left to them, and he had to figure out when, and how, to use it. As he hid himself behind the stake, Kim etched the final lines of the outer circle into the dirt, and the smoke swirled up and around them, blotting out the world.

Chapter Twenty-Eight

By evening, the clubhouse was alive with Dragons from all over the city and some from surrounding areas. There weren't as many as Snake had hoped for, but in the confines of the clubhouse and surrounding yard, they felt like an army. Snake stood aside, watching them, and knew that an army was exactly what he needed. Even that might not do the trick, if Martinez was wrong.

He sipped his beer and listened to the conversations around him. Nervous fear rippled through their words. Those who'd been in Santini Park remembered what they'd seen, and those who had not asked questions and listened to the stories, half-believing and half skeptical, of how Vasquez had been taken down. They knew why Snake had called them together, and they had come because the colors on their backs and the oaths they had made compelled them, but none of them wanted this fight. *Los Escorpiones* had always been their enemies – bringing darkness to the Barrio and the streets that was unsettling and somehow unclean. What Anya Cabrera had brought was much worse.

Just after sunset, Martinez reappeared. He had the boy, Salvatore, with him. The kid didn't look like much, but Snake had seen the dragons. He'd felt the energy, and he'd heard what Jake and Enrique had done. There was power here – power that was in some way connected to himself, to those who followed him, and to the ancient, powerful creatures they'd bonded with so long ago. How it could be true, he didn't understand, but Snake wasn't one to argue in the face of reality. It wasn't a question of whether or not the painted dragons were good, or powerful, it was a question of whether he would accept them, and how he would deal with them.

Snake walked over and laid his hand on Salvatore's shoulder. "So, we finally meet," he said. "My name is Snake."

Salvatore's eyes were wide, but he didn't drop his gaze. "I know you, Senor," he said. "You are El Presidente of the Dragons."

Snake studied the boy's face for a moment, and then turned to Martinez.

"How about you let me and Sal here talk for a few minutes. Alone?"

Martinez nodded. Snake slid his arm around the boy's slender shoulders and led him back toward the clubhouse. All around them, the Dragons watched, wondering what Snake was up to. Some of them knew Martinez, and they spread what they knew. Others knew of Salvatore, and the dragons he'd painted. They also knew what those dragons had brought – power, magic, and death.

Snake led Salvatore to where Enrique's jacket hung, pinioned to the wall by the blade of a dagger. He reached up and gently smoothed the leather so that the dragon was clearly visible. Though it had lost most of its original magic, the painting was still magnificent.

"You know, Sal," Snake began, "when you first came around and gave Jake that dragon, I thought you were trouble. The Dragons already had a patch, our colors. I was against your fancy dragons, because the dragon symbolizes our brotherhood, our unity. Yours are individuals, like the men who wear them. They send a different message."

Salvatore's knees quivered, but he didn't lower his gaze. He did not want this man to know how truly frightened he was.

"Then," Snake went on, almost as if he were talking to himself, "I saw how your dragons affected mine, and how they helped me. Your pictures make dragons into powerful, magnificent dreams. I've heard people talk about art all of my life, how it 'moves' them – I never gave it much thought. Somehow your paintings capture a part of the man who wears them and mirror him. You have seen this?"

Still uncertain of what Snake was getting at, Salvatore nodded. He knew that his dragons matched the men who wore them; that is how they came in the visions. He couldn't have painted them any other way.

"We have a battle coming soon," Snake said, turning his gaze to hold Salvatore's. "These are brave men, but we face *Los Escorpiones,* and this is a battle my dragons won't want to fight. It's not that they lack courage, but this is an old war, and their fire is dying. I want you to help me."

Salvatore's curiosity overcame his fear, giving him the courage to speak. "You wish me to fight?" He asked. "I am no fighter, Senor Snake, only a poor artist."

"No." Snake said quietly, and with conviction. "You are not poor; you are a genius, and I don't want you to fight. I want you to paint my dragon."

Salvatore's heart leaped. Again he was without speech. Such an honor! Almost instantly the dragon began to form in his mind.

"But your jacket," he blurted out, "it has upon it the patch of El Presidente! Where shall I paint the dragon?"

Snake looked at him, a warmth Salvatore had never seen in his eyes. "I don't want it on my jacket, Sal," he said. "These colors have ridden there far too long. I want a banner, a standard; let's call it a flag of honor. And when we go to fight these *Escorpiones,* I want you to carry that flag into the battle at my side."

Now Salvatore's heart took wings! This was beyond belief. He stuttered several times before the words finally broke free of his tongue. Snake didn't seem to notice.

"Such a dragon I will paint for you that it will seem a thing alive!" He cried. "Beyond my hopes have you honored me. I, Salvatore Domingo Sanchez, will make you proud!"

"I know that, Sal," Snake smiled. "You've got to do this fast, though. It is my men to whom you must bring the life, not my dragon. The battle will happen in tomorrow night, maybe sooner."

"Then I must go and start -- I will be ready!" Salvatore said.

There is no reason for you to go, Snake said softly. "I've had them clear a space for you. It's only a small room, but it's warm. There is light, and room to work. We'll make sure you have food. I've talked with Martinez, and with Jake. If you finish my dragon, and you fall, I'll be there to catch you before you hit the floor."

Salvatore stood very still. Despite all his efforts to appear calm and brave, this was too much.

"I...I'll need my paints. Martinez made them, and..."

"I'll send for them," Snake said. "I'll get you anything that you need to do this, and to do it quickly. You and I, we come from different worlds in many ways, but in others we are much the same. This fight – this battle I told you about. It will be for the safety of our homes, and our streets. It isn't just for the Dragons. If Anya Cabrera and her followers get their way, and *Los Escorpiones* own the streets, there will be nothing standing between them and the rest of the city. Do you know what a cancer is?"

Salvatore nodded.

"That's what they'll become. They'll creep across the city like Black Death, eating everything in their path. I think it's up to me, and to you, to stop them. I think that what we do in the next few hours will define us both. Are you ready for that Sal?"

Salvatore nodded again.

"I will do this thing," he said, "or I will die at your side."

Tears streamed down Salvatore's face, but he ignored them. No one had ever spoken to him as an equal except, on rare occasions, old Martinez. No one had offered him protection, or asked that he stand at their side. No one had ever acknowledged him at all. He met Snake's gaze, and the big man laid a hand on his shoulder and smiled.

Jake wandered over then, and stood on the other side of Salvatore.

"You ready to see your new digs, Sally?" he said. "I guess I sort of told everyone about your shack. Figured you might like a warmer place to crash and someone to talk to now and then. Hope you don't mind."

Salvatore didn't know whether to nod that yes, he wanted to see his new 'digs' or to shake his head that he didn't mind.

"One more thing," Snake said.

Salvatore turned back slowly, because the man's voice was

suddenly charged with emotion.

"This dragon you will paint," Snake said softly. "You have seen it? You already know what it will look like, the colors?"

Salvatore swallowed, and nodded.

"You've known you had to paint him all along, haven't you?" Snake asked.

"When they come into my dreams," Salvatore said, "I have no choice. I think if I don't draw them, or paint them, that I will go mad. They call out to me. They have been leading me to another place – a city by an ocean, but not the ocean that I know. I think one day the dragons will take me inside that city, and then I will know why they come to me, and why I must set them free."

"I've dreamed too," Snake said. "I didn't see a city, but in those dreams, I could fly. Give me my wings, Sal. Make it all real."

Then, without another word, Snake turned and left the room.

"Come on Sally," Jake said. "Martinez went to get your paints. We'd better get you set up."

Salvatore followed Jake down a hallway toward the other end of the building. Jake didn't look back, but as he opened a door at the end of that hall and ushered Salvatore inside, he spoke.

"That man isn't one you want to cross," he said. "If you give him everything you have, he'll stand by you through anything. You paint that dragon, Sally. You paint like you've never painted before. I have the feeling we're going to need all the help we can get."

He left then, and Salvatore stood alone in a small bedroom. There was a shelf on the wall, a small cot with clean sheets, a blanket, and a pillow, a table and two straight-backed chairs. There were no leaks in the walls; it was warm and dry. Salvatore stood still in the very center, and let his tears flow freely.

Then he sat at the table and waited for Martinez, already planning where he'd hang the flag while he worked.

The next time the door opened, Snake led Martinez and Jake

into the room. Jake had a bundle under one arm, and Martinez carried the paints and supplies from Salvatore's shack. They trooped solemnly into the small room, and Salvatore stood, eyes downcast. He wasn't sure what to say, or what to do. Luckily, Jake had no such problem.

"Hey, Sally," he said. "Help me hang this up, will you?"

Salvatore glanced up. Jake held what at first looked like an old sheet folded over his arm. When he shook it out, Salvatore saw that it was a piece of white canvas – the kind of canvas he'd seen in art shops from the street. The kind he'd dreamed of painting on one day.

"Over here," Snake said, stepping to a bit of wall where there was no furniture to impeded them. "We'll pull the table over for the paints."

Jake walked to the wall, and Salvatore followed. The big man turned, and held the bit of canvas up against the wall.

"How high is good?" he asked.

Salvatore took a step closer and held up his right arm, as if he had a brush in it. He let his finger fall against the center of the canvas.

"It is perfect," he said.

Jake nodded. He held one corner of the canvas to the wall. Snake stepped up and placed a nail against the canvas, then drove it home with shiny metal hammer. Jake moved to the other side and lifted the canvas until it lay flat against the wall, and Snake pounded in a second nail. Then he did the same for the two bottom corners. The canvas was nearly four feet wide and another three tall.

Salvatore stood in front of it and stared at the white empty space. He closed his eyes, and summoned that other place... that dark place with its impossibly tall walls, the ocean waves crashing, and the moon silver gray behind banks of clouds. The sound of the table's legs squeaking on the floor brought him back, but his mind remained in a fog.

"It's time," Martinez said.

"Time?" Salvatore answered. "Time for what?"

Martinez unrolled the tube of red paint. He turned to Salvatore.

"It will be red. Is that not true?"

Salvatore nodded.

"This is special paint," Martinez went on. "All of the colors that I mixed for you are special but this..."

He turned and stroked the tube of paint, gazing at it thoughtfully.

"This is something more," he said at last. "This is a very special hue, a color named for one of the elements. They call it the Rojo Fuego."

"Fire red," Jake said softly. "That means Fire Red."

Martinez nodded. "Exactly." He turned to Snake. "We should leave him now. There isn't much time left."

Salvatore was about to protest, to tell them that he had plenty of time, and that he didn't mind them being there, but he couldn't quite drag his mind out of that other, darker place. He heard a sound, like the steady beating of great wings. He thought, maybe, that Snake had said something more, or possibly Jake...but he could make out none of the words.

He turned back to the canvas, and a moment later he had a piece of charcoal in his hand. He made the first stroke of dark black outline on the pristine white, maybe the second, and then it faded. The walls stretched up before him, endless and unbroken, and the tide rushed in at his back. There were no stars.

Chapter Twenty-Nine

There were more dragons in the sky than Salvatore had ever seen at one time. They dipped in and out of the clouds, dove toward the water and soared over the walls of the dark city. He stepped across damp stones to the wall, and turned right, as he had on his previous visit. This time, something had changed.

Ahead he saw something jutting from the sand, turned perpendicular to the wall. At first he couldn't make it out, but as he approached, he saw that it was an easel. He'd never owned an easel, and he'd only seen them through the windows of art supply stores, but he knew what it was. He stepped closer, and saw that there was a small round-topped table beside it, it's legs embedded in the damp sand.

The moonlight was bright, and the canvas on the easel shone white in the silver light. Salvatore stepped closer. The shadow of something immense passed overhead, and he shivered. He glanced up, but was too slow. The very tip of a serpentine tail disappeared into the clouds above, just as they floated across the face of the moon.

He ran his fingers over the canvas. The charcoal outline he'd begun was there. The canvas was stretched tightly over a frame, not nailed to a wall as he'd first seen it, but there was no doubt the basic form was Snake's dragon.

On the table, Salvatore saw the palette, the three tubes of paint, and the small chunk of charcoal. He took the charcoal and turned to the canvas. The shadow returned overhead, but he ignored it. He drew a sweeping line, and the connection between his fingers and the chalk, the painting and the dragon snapped into place.

His hand flew across the canvas, only lightly touching as he filled in the outline and created the course his brush would follow. He heard waves crashing on the beach behind him. It felt and sounded closer than he remembered it. It seemed as if any moment salt spray would drop across his shoulders and dampen the ends of his hair where it brushed his collar in back. He thought it might splash the canvas as well, but that was the only thing he could see clearly, and there were no invading droplets.

Above him, the dragons continued their wild dance through the clouds, but he ignored them. He knew that any one of them could have dropped from the sky and smashed the easel, the canvas, and his small body to the ground. He felt that they would not – or that they could not – that they were in some way bound by the work itself. He also knew that if he pulled back, faltered, or allowed anything to truly distract him, he would forsake that bond, and that protection.

When the outline was complete, he set the charcoal aside. In that instant, just before he took up the brush, there was a violent rush of wind. He stood his ground and dipped the brush into the red paint. The silence was shattered by a scream of rage. The beat of leathery wings vibrated the air overhead, and the sand at Salvatore's feet shifted and sifted over his feet. He stood as still as possible, and pressed the brush to the canvas.

He did not look up to see, but he knew that, in that instant, the dragon soared back into the clouds, and was gone. There was something different about the red paint, something powerful. As he stroked it along the length of the dragon's curling body, heat emanated from the canvas. Sweat beaded on his brow. Even when it trickled into his eyes, burning and blurring his vision, his hand was steady.

He filled in the darker reds, moved through shades of coral and blended bright to dark as the dragon came to life. He knew that he could have stopped, looked up, and caught sight of his subject, but he already knew the dragon, and he sensed that it knew him as well. Something was different this time. Something had disrupted whatever thin cloud he passed through from one world to the next. Whatever it was, the dragons were restless, particularly the giant red one – the dragon he now painted.

As Salvatore worked, lights flickered to life and glowed in the highest windows of the city beyond the walls. The dragons soared in and out of the clouds, and though he felt them dive near again and again, they did not swoop down as they had in the past to lift him. Something prevented it. Something in the red of the paint, he thought. He had thought he would have to highlight with white paint to catch the way moonlight rippled over the great beast's scales, but it came easily. The air of this place lent power to the paint. He worked steadily up the body from the tail, moving toward the head and the eyes. Before he finished, he hesitated. He stepped back, just for an instant.

He studied his work. The dragon was so close...so nearly perfect. It would only take a single stroke of the brush to complete it. As he stared, the sky opened up with a roar of wind and sound that nearly crushed him to his knees. He threw back his head and saw the red dragon. It dove straight at him, dropping at impossible speed with a scream of rage and defiance. Salvatore still clutched the brush. He met that dark gaze, and held it. He reached up and dabbed the final bit of Rojo Fuego onto the canvas.

The action took no more than a second, but in that time Salvatore released himself to the dragon. He knew the dive was too steep. It would crash into him, crush him into the sand, and there would be an end to the visions. The brush dropped from numb fingers and he followed, dropping flat on the sand.

He closed his eyes and waited for the impact that never came. Somehow, as the painting came to life, the creature flattened its dive. It came so close that its wings raised a cloud of damp sand to choke Salvatore's breath and blind his eyes. As it passed, it gripped him tightly in massive talons and lifted him skyward. Its wings beat like huge tents in a high wind, and it screamed. Salvatore rubbed at the grit and sweat in his eyes and fought to regain his site.

He opened his eyes, and the city spread out beneath him. The towers rose so high their uppermost spires brushed the clouds. There were lights in the windows. They glowed, each a different hue. The streets, if there were streets between those massive structures, were lost in vast shadows near the ground. The clouds roiled, caught in the grip of a storm that raged and slashed at the city with wind and rain. The waves far below crashed against the rocky beach and pounded at the sand, as if trying to reach the stone walls.

Salvatore saw all of this in the few seconds it took the red dragon to rise and flatten out its flight beneath the lower edge of the clouds. He looked down from above at the uppermost spire of the city. Red light flickered in the windows. The dragon swept back its wings, and they stopped in the air, just for a second, directly above that tower.

Salvatore opened his mouth, as if he might speak, but in that instant, the dragon released him. His breath was sucked from his lungs by the speed of his fall. He tried to scream but couldn't force the air from his lungs. He approached the tower so quickly it grew from a tiny speck to a huge, stone edifice in the span of a heartbeat. For the second time in only a few minutes, he closed his eyes. Darkness enfolded him and he fell into it with a choked sob.

Snake stepped into the room as he saw Salvatore topple. He moved quickly, arms outstretched. He caught the boy just before he hit the floor and lifted him easily. He saw the brush on the floor and was oddly drawn to a splotch of red paint. Then he raised his gaze to the canvas, and stood very still. He rose, still holding Salvatore in his arms, and stared.

"My God," he said. "My God, Sal, look what you have done..."

He still stood there, staring, when Jake entered, took Salvatore from his arms, and carried the boy to his bed. Without another word, Jake slipped back out of the room. When he closed the door, Snake still stood, one hand outstretched toward the canvas. The air in the room felt uncomfortably warm, and the eyes of the painted dragon glowed like red hot coals.

Chapter Thirty

As the circle closed around them, the world beyond it became a murky haze of blurred images. The sky was clearly visible if Donovan stared straight up. It was like standing in a cylinder of smoke stretching toward the stars.

Amethyst struggled fiercely against her bonds, but she was tied tightly. They had gagged her to be certain she couldn't disrupt the ritual, and at least one of the tall, bald servants remained close by her side at all times. Anya Cabrera sat in her makeshift throne, overseeing the ritual. Donovan kept an eye on her, but she seemed not to have noticed him. He wasn't worried about the *Escorpiones* who were still possessed; he had the pendant Amethyst had given him tucked in beneath his shirt. His spell was holding, as well, though he had no way to know how long it would be effective.

He moved slowly toward the outer edge of the circle. To release Amethyst he knew he'd have to get around behind her; no easy feat with so many of Anya's followers milling about. A drumbeat rumbled to life, and what had been a somewhat disorganized mob coalesced into a sinuous, moving line of bodies. They spread out and formed a third concentric ring. Amethyst fell just outside that ring, and Donovan managed to slip beyond the dancers just as they closed the gaps. They danced in odd, disjointed steps that somehow fit the pounding on the drums. As they passed by Anya Cabrera, she handed each a bottle. They were identical this time, dark glass that seemed black in the firelight. Each man tipped his bottle up, took a long swig of the contents, and then continued around the circle.

Donovan watched his steps carefully as he moved toward the rear of the stake. Everyone else within the boundaries of the circle was involved in the dance except for Anya and Amethyst. The guardian who'd stood at Amethyst's side had been drawn into the dance with the others. All Donovan had to do was stay as close as possible to the outer ring without touching it.

Then the first of the dancers, one of the bald servants, drew forth a wickedly curved blade. He flicked it around his fingers and hands deftly, almost like a Japanese Hibachi chef getting ready to dice chicken. The silvery metal glittered in the firelight. Donovan held his breath. The big man was very close to Amethyst. The dancer drew back his arm and spun. The motion was sudden and graceful, and Donovan only bit back his scream with a desperate clench of his jaw. The blade spun down past Amethyst's chin and barely missed cutting her breast as it sliced cleanly through her jacket. The cut was clean, and as they passed, the others reached out, some flicking at her with fingernails, others gripping and tugging. The jacket was shredded in a matter of moments, and the man with the knife approached for a second time.

Amethyst wore a form fitting top and tight jeans. Her eyes glittered with anger, but she was tied securely, and there was nothing she could do as the drums pounded out their rhythm, and the dancers pranced and whirled past her in an ever faster, ever more violent circle of motion and color.

Donovan sped his pace, but there were only a scant few feet between himself, the outer circle, and the dancers. If one of them bumped into him, either the spell would break, or they'd find him. Then he'd end up tied on the far side of the pole if he couldn't fight his way out.

The key was getting Amethyst free. When *Los Escorpiones* had rushed the circle from the inside at the junk yard, it had broken like so much smoke. Donovan thought the same would be true here. The circle was meant to keep things out, not to keep them in. The ritual was essentially identical. He just had to make sure they were ready to make their break before that circle was broken. He had no intention of allowing the ritual to reach its conclusion, but given the choice between that and

Amethyst, he was ready to move quickly.

The dancers finished their circuit, and the big man with the knife drew closer. Donovan tensed. He had only seconds to make his decision. Move and try to get Amethyst free, or trust that the knife would not cut her throat, or worse. He had no illusions about her intended fate. Anya Cabrera intended to sacrifice Amethyst before she was done; the only question was – when?

Donovan held his breath The big man spun again. The blade slashed out with eerie precision. A tear appeared in Amethyst's blouse. Donovan heard her try to scream through her gag, but he hadn't cut her. The others followed along behind as before. Donovan slipped up close behind the stake, but didn't make a sound. He didn't breathe. The dancers passed, one after another, reaching out and tearing the shredded fabric of Amethyst's closing until it fell away to the sides.

Very carefully, Donovan slipped a thin blade from his pocket and began to saw on the ropes binding Amethyst's wrists to the stake. He leaned closer, took a deep breath, and spoke as softly as he could almost directly into her ear.

"If you scream or speak they will kill us both. I'm cutting your wrists free. Don't move them."

He continued to saw at the rope. He felt Anya stiffen, just for a second, and then, as if nothing had happened, she continued to struggle and fight to speak through the gag. He breathed a bit easier and worked harder at her binding. It was taking too long. He slipped the blade back into his pocket and fished out a small vial of white powder. He uncorked it and sprinkled a little onto the ropes, letting it sift into the knots. He squatted quickly and did the same for the rope binding her ankles. When he was satisfied, he corked the vial, slipped it back into his pocket, and waited.

There was a point at the end of the line of dancers, just before the big man made his next circuit, where there was a gap. The two ends of the line were like the head and tail of a writhing, whirling snake. One of the men on the far side of the circle suddenly flung his head back and screamed. He twitched crazily, his arms and legs moving in ways they were never meant to, and the line slowed. They didn't stop their dance, but as the spirit took one of their own, they accommodated the motion, making it part of the music and the ritual.

In that moment, Donovan moved. He slipped around to the front of the stake, standing scant inches in front of Amethyst. She knew he was there, but could not see him. He saw the fear in her eyes. He also noticed she was now naked from the waist up, and despite their circumstances, he smiled.

Then the line moved again, and the big man was dancing in slow, mincing steps straight at them.

Donovan closed his eyes. He imagined the white powder pouring into the knotted ropes. He imagined them slipping and sliding free. In a soft whisper, he spoke a single word.

"Libre."

Several things happened in a very short span of time. The ropes went suddenly slack. Amethyst, not expecting the sudden release, toppled forward. Donovan caught her in his arms, and without a word turned toward the outer circle.

Behind him he heard a disruption in the music. He heard Anya Cabrera screeching for someone to stop him. In that instant, his spell was broken, and they saw him, but it was too late. With a scream of his own, he dove through the smoke of the outer ring and broke the circle.

The effect was instantaneous. The smoke disappeared in thin wisps, leaving the circle, the dancers, and Anya Cabrera in plain view from the street beyond. Donovan didn't hesitate. He clutched Amethyst to his chest and ran for the alley. He had the element of surprise on his side, but that advantage lasted only seconds. Before he hit the alleyway where the portal lay, he heard heavy footsteps pounding behind him.

"Put me down," Amethyst hissed. "I can walk. We'll move faster."

Donovan clumsily lowered her to the sidewalk. She lurched forward, caught her balance, and then the two of them ducked off the street and out of sight.

"Wait," Donovan said.

He hit the short staircase, and concentrated. He took a step down, and then another, then one back up and three down.

The pattern was invariable, and it didn't matter if Hell itself was pouring in at their back, there was only one way he knew to open the door. It wasn't one of those he normally used, so he had to depend on the more generic key he'd first discovered. He stepped forward again, ignored all sound, and all thought but the pattern. One more down, four back up, and he reached back.

"Now!" he cried.

They dove down the stairs and into the shadowed alcove below. The doorway shimmered, then opened, and they stepped through. There was a horrible screeching sound behind them. Donovan ignored it and took Amethyst by the hand.

"Run," he said.

They rushed down the ancient passage, watching stairs and portals pass on either side, and ignoring them.

"Can't we take one?" Amethyst panted.

"Not unless you don't care where, or when, we arrive," Donovan said. "They aren't safe, and they aren't stable. I haven't had time to explore them."

He turned. Behind them, two very dark figures scurried down the passage after them. The figures didn't seem to hurry, but they moved with incredible speed, appearing in one place, and then another in quick succession. He saw that they were both members of *Los Escorpiones*, their dark vests covered in patches and glittering ornaments.

"We have to stop them from following," he said. "If we don't, we have to turn and fight."

"I'm not opposed to that," Amethyst said through gritted teeth. "I wouldn't mind a crack at the bastards."

"We don't have time," Donovan said. "We don't know how far she's gone, and we don't know if we broke the ritual."

"I can slow them," Amethyst said.

"Do it," Donovan said. "We're almost out."

Amethyst stumbled a little as she fished in the pockets of her jeans. Donovan noticed for the second time that she was topless. He tried not to smile, and failed. She caught his expression and glared at him as she spun.

Amethyst threw a handful of crystal dust into the center of

the passage. As it filled the air, she cried out a command that Donovan didn't recognize. Whatever she'd said, it solidified the crystals into a thick, glassy wall.

"It won't hold," she said.

Donovan grabbed her, darted to the right, yanked open one of the ancient doorways, and dragged her through. He slammed it behind them, even as they heard the glass wall shatter in an explosion that sent bits and pieces crashing into the far side of the now closed portal.

"Can they get out?" Amethyst asked?

"They can't open this door, because we just used it. They can get out, but there's no way to tell where they will end up – whether the spirits are permanently embedded in their souls, or if they are dark things that will never return to the light. It doesn't matter. We don't have much time.

They turned. Amethyst took a step, faltered, and nearly fell.

Without a word, Donovan scooped her back into his arms, pressing her nakedness into his chest to hide it from prying eyes, and hurried to the maintenance entrance of his building. He needed to find out what had happened, and he needed to check in on Martinez, but first he needed to get Amethyst to safety. There was a second crash against the inside of the ancient portal, but he ignored it. It was time to pull out all the stops and put an end to the craziness in the Barrio once and for all. He only hoped they weren't already too late.

Chapter Thirty-One

Donovan laid Amethyst back across the couch in his den and propped her head with a soft pillow. When he had her situated, he stepped to his bar and grabbed a wine glass. Behind the counter on the bar there was a wooden cabinet with a number of drawers. He opened the drawer on the upper right and pulled out a small leaf. With a quick pinch of thumb and forefinger, he crushed the leaf and dropped it into the wine glass. He closed the door, unstoppered a flask, and poured bright amber liquid over the leaf. After only a moment, he fished the remnant out with a spoon and carried the drink to the couch.

He sat on the edge and slipped an arm under Amethyst's shoulder, helping her to sit up straight.

"Drink this," he said. "It will get you back on your feet."

"You aren't drugging me, I hope?" she said.

Donovan laughed. "Hardly. It's brandy with Indian Pennywort leaf. There have long been rumors that the leaves bring energy and rejuvenation. Of course, as is almost always the case, there is more to it than that. Mine have been blessed by a Sri Lankan priest."

"Of course," she said.

She took the glass and sipped. Then she took a longer drink, closed her eyes, and frowned.

"Not good?"

"It's wonderful," she said. "I'm thinking that I'm an idiot. We shouldn't be here; we should be on the street."

"We should, but first you need to tell me what happened," Donovan said. "You're going to have to finish that, and you're going to need a little rest. We have to go to Martinez, but I'm going to need you healthy. We have time."

"There isn't that much to tell. I called some of my informants, trying to get a line on that ritual. I thought I'd gotten lucky; the second call got me through to a guy I've worked with off and on for about ten years. He said he had what I needed. I told him we didn't have much time, so we set up a meet, and he named his price. Now that I think about it, he settled pretty low.

"Anyway, I left immediately. We were set to meet in the alley behind the Buzz and Bean, that coffee shop over on Vine? I should have been more careful. I saw Benji at the end of the alley, and I went straight in. He wasn't alone. Before I'd gone three steps, that woman stepped out of the shadows – Kim? I had just enough time to see the silver caskets dangling from her braids – I heard them, like bells – and then she blew some kind of powder into my face. After that..."

"Everything went numb?" Donovan asked.

She glanced up at him and her frown deepened.

"How did you know that?"

"It's an old Voodoo trick. That powder is made in various potencies for different purposes. The most famous, when it's very strong, is the creation of 'zombies'. You're lucky they only hit you with a mild dose. It removes motor function."

"Tell me about it. I knew everything that was happening, but there was nothing I could do. Two of those big bald-headed goons came out of nowhere and caught me before I fell. They lifted me like a sack of grain and carried me to the park where you found me. We went by alleys and back roads, a few I didn't even recognize. All the while they talked about me as if I wasn't there at all, and there was nothing I could do about it."

Donovan saw her hand tighten on her glass. He reached out and squeezed her shoulder. After a moment's hesitation, she continued.

"When we reached that clearing, they were already making preparations. There was a girl tied to the post where you found me. She was young – Mexican, I think – and she'd obviously been treated with the same chemical they used on me. I caught her gaze. She was terrified.

"Anya was there, sitting in that chair like she was some sort of weird pagan queen. When they laid me on the ground at her feet like an offering, she hopped down and walked around me in a slow circle. I swear I felt as if I was being sized up at the market, like a prize farm animal.

"She knew me. I didn't hear exactly what she said, but within a few moments they had cut that girl down and carried her off and out of sight. It was only a few moments later I was lifted back to my feet and tied to the pole."

"I was afraid that was the plan," Donovan said. "You were her sacrifice. She intended to kill you and toss you into that fire. If she'd managed to do it, she could have closed the portal the *Loa* used to reach this dimension. They'd be trapped in the human vessels they possessed, and they'd remain under her control."

"How do you know she didn't complete the ritual?" Amethyst asked.

Donovan glanced down at her. He opened his mouth to speak, and then it hit him, and he sat up straight so quickly he almost made her spill the drink.

"You think they might have chosen another sacrifice?" he asked.

"They already had the other girl. I don't' know where she was taken, but we know that the circle was to keep things out, and not in. Once we broke it, they could have gone for the original sacrifice and then sealed themselves in again. We don't know if we stopped them or not."

They stared at one another in silence for a moment, then Amethyst downed the brandy, and then sat up. Donovan shifted so she could swing her legs off the couch.

"She also could have taken one of those already inside the circle, the dancers, as a sacrifice. If she closed that portal," Donovan said, "Then she has the equivalent of an army of demons. If she isn't stopped, there is nothing to prevent her doing it again, and again, until she has too much power to overcome. The Barrio is a small thing. She may gain control of that – all she has to do is to defeat the Dragons and drive Martinez into hiding. If she succeeded in her ritual, she might be able to pull it off.

"What about Martinez?" Amethyst asked. "What about the Dragons? You said he had something going on...can he pull it off?"

"We'd better make sure that he does," Donovan replied. "I don't know exactly what he's up to, but it's powerful. I can't say that it makes me feel any better if he controls dark forces than if Anya does."

"He didn't seem to be controlling them," Amethyst said. "He seemed to be unleashing them. There's a difference. Still, you have a point. I think it's about time we got back to the Barrio. There's a storm in the air – I can sense it – and after all we've seen, I don't want to miss the fireworks."

"You need to rest," Donovan said. "It's still early, and even if she continued the ritual, there's no way she can mount an attack tonight. It will be tomorrow. I think we both need to rest. A few hours, then head out for the Barrio."

Amethyst placed her empty glass on the table.

"If I didn't know better, I'd think you were trying to take advantage of me," she said.

"There are worse things to be accused of."

They both stood, and Donovan led her down the hall and out of the study. Cleo sat on the desk and watched them go. Her eyes were inscrutable, as always, but after a moment she leaned back on her haunches and began washing her back feet contentedly. Whatever was going through her mind, she obviously approved of the rest.

Chapter Thirty-Two

Salvatore slept all through the day after painting Snake's dragon. There were no dreams, and when he woke, he found clean, fresh clothing laid out beside his bed. The dragon was gone, but he didn't need to see it. It was embedded in his mind. Salvatore sat up, dressed quickly, and rose. He was hungrier than he could ever remember being, and parched with thirst, but he stood a long time looking at the wall where the dragon had hung. He felt it. He knew it was nearby; he also knew that Snake had taken it.

He turned and left the room, stepping into the clubhouse beyond. It was evening, and there were Dragons lounging all over the place. When they saw Salvatore, the room grew eerily silent. He lowered his gaze to the floor and walked through the main room, being careful not to bump into any of them. He knew the way to the kitchen, and though he didn't know what there might be to eat, or if it was okay for him to eat it, he was too hungry to care.

He was about halfway across the room when one of the Dragons peeled off and stepped out the back door into the yard. By the time Salvatore reached the kitchen, Jake was at his heels, clapping a huge, meaty hand on his shoulder.

"Morning, Sally," he said. "Thought maybe you'd sleep all day."

Salvatore glanced up.

"I did not mean to sleep so long, Senor Jake," he said.

"I'm just kidding, " Jake said. The big man ruffled his hair. "Let's find you something to eat. You were up almost all night."

"The dragon is gone," Salvatore said. "When I woke, it was gone."

"Snake has it," Jake said. "He wants to see you after you get some food and something to drink."

A few moments later, Salvatore sat at one of two old wooden kitchen tables with a sandwich, a glass of milk, and a chunk of cheese. He ate quickly and without talking. Jake slid into the chair on the far side of the table and watched him. Outside the window, night was falling. Through the windows they could see the flames of torches, candles, and the bonfire out back. Salvatore barely noticed. He could not remember ever having been so hungry. When the food was gone, he washed it down with the milk.

"Kind of takes it out of you, doesn't it?" Jake asked softly. "I know you ate a lot after you painted my jacket. Martinez told me."

Salvatore nodded. Now that he was done eating, he felt out of place and nervous. He glanced around the kitchen. The Dragons kept it clean and simple. There were a couple of old refrigerators along one wall, a stove, and the two tables. Despite its simplicity, it was almost overwhelming after the bare, drafty interior of his shack.

"Snake wants you outside in a bit," Jake said. "Martinez will be there too – and the dragon."

"You've seen it?" Salvatore asked. He watched the big man's face.

"No one but Snake has seen it. He said he came in, found you about to pass out on the floor, caught you, and then took it. He won't talk about it, but…you should have seen his eyes, Sally. I'd swear, if I didn't know it sounded crazy, that they glowed. They glowed red, and when he passed by me with that rolled up flag, I didn't recognize him at all."

"It is the same for you, Senor Jake," Salvatore said. "When you first saw your dragon – when you wore it – you changed. Do you not feel it?"

"Oh, I feel it, Sally," Jake said. "I feel stronger, faster – everything is clearer than it's ever been. With Snake, it was different. He's stronger, yeah…but a little scary. You know what I mean?"

Salvatore stared at the table for a moment and collected his thoughts. Then he raised his head and met Jake's gaze.

"His dragon is very powerful. It did not want me to finish the painting. There is another place – a city – I see it when I paint. I think his dragon is very important there. When I painted...it tried to take me. The paint – the red paint that Martinez made for me – it was different. I would very much like to see the dragon."

"I think we're all going to see it soon enough," Jake said. He studied Salvatore's face, as if there was something he knew, or saw, that he couldn't quite bring to the surface. "Martinez will be here soon. Snake is going to talk...and we're going to act. Most of the others don't want to go. They've heard what happened last time, in Santini Park. They've heard what *Los Escorpiones* did to Vasquez. They want to move on – find a new place. Snake wants them to fight."

"It will not be the same," Salvatore said, not sure why he spoke, or how he knew that his words were true. "You have changed. Snake..."

"I know," Jake said. "He's changed. The fight will be different. We might even have a chance at winning. The question is, what do we win? What's really at stake here? If it was just this clubhouse, and this town, I'd be with the others. I'd say, let's get the hell out of here and find a new place without a war in progress. It's more than that, though. I feel it, Snake feels it – I think Martinez knows it too. We're fighting against something that's not going to stop at taking over the Barrio, or Santini Park. We might be the only thing between some weird ancient darkness and the rest of the world. It's a screwed up feeling, but at the same time, it makes me want to fight. It makes me want to be a hero.

"You think that's crazy, Sally?"

Salvatore held the big man's gaze. What he saw took him far away, to that strange dark city on the coast of an ocean he knew did not touch any beach in California, or on Earth. He thought carefully about his words, and then he spoke.

"I do not believe you are crazy," he said. "I believe that you are a hero. I believe that Martinez has seen what might come, and that he brought all of us together to stop it. He's known me all of my life, but until now he paid very little attention. He gave me some food, and he listened when I had something to say. He brought me chalk and pencils when he found them. Now it is different. He saw something in my pictures and I am here. He saw something in you – and in Snake – and you are here. On our own, none of us could stand against *Los Escorpiones* – not with Anya Cabrera at their side. Together? Maybe we are all heroes."

Jake reached out and messed up Salvatore's hair. The big man smiled, and Salvatore could not help but return it. A knock at the door broke the silence, and Jake turned.

"That must be Martinez," he said. "I guess it's show time"

He rose and left the room. Salvatore carried his empty milk glass to the sink, rinsed it, and then stepped back into the main room. Martinez had entered, and the old man smiled and nodded at him. Without a word, Jake led the two of them out through the clubhouse and into the yard beyond, where Snake stood in the center of several rings of gathered Dragons.

As he stepped into the firelight and caught Snake's gaze, Salvatore felt a sudden heat on his cheeks. He had to fight the urge to shield his eyes.

Chapter Thirty-Three

The yard behind the clubhouse danced with shadows. Torches and candles flickered on poles planted in the ground and on every horizontal surface. In the center there was a larger fire; Snake stood alone beside it. He stared at the back door of the clubhouse, and as Salvatore stepped through, the two locked gazes, just for an instant.

All around that central fire, the Dragons stood in rows. There was a passage open from the back door of the clubhouse to the center, but it seemed as if every other square inch of ground was occupied. Where there were no men, there were shadows and flickering light. Salvatore tried to ignore them.

Jake had a hand on his shoulder, and the big man escorted him through the crowd toward the fire. Salvatore was glad for Jake's presence, but he wasn't frightened. Something in Snake's gaze drew him forward, and he felt a sense of purpose he'd never experienced – a sense of belonging. Martinez walked at his side. The old man said nothing. He looked neither to the right nor the left. He held his head high. This was Snake's moment, but it also belonged to Salvatore, and to Martinez. Salvatore felt a great many things converging, coming together in that clearing and binding them all.

They gathered by the fire. Snake stood very still. He barely acknowledged their arrival. Jake took his place behind Snake, and Salvatore stood beside Jake. Martinez stepped a little off to the side, but not so far as to seem separated from the group. The crowd drifted and covered the trail that led back to the clubhouse. Salvatore stared out into the flickering torches and candlelight. He saw shadowed faces. Eyes glittered, but he could not make out the features on their faces.

Snake began a slow circuit of the fire. He stared out into the gathered Dragons. He met their gazes, and, at last he came back to stand at Salvatore's side. Snake didn't move like he had the last time Salvatore had seen him. He seemed taller, quicker and stronger. His eyes glittered even when there was no light to cause it.

He stepped closer and took Salvatore by the arm. Salvatore detected no unity among those gathered, though they stood so closely packed it was difficult to tell where one ended, and the next began. There was fear in the air, some of it directed at Snake, and some of it beyond the yard and the clubhouse into the night. There was nothing holding them together but the iron will of the man they called Presidente and the presence of the crazy old man, Martinez, at his side.

Jake stepped forward and handed a long pole to Snake, who slammed the base of it into the ground at his feet. Salvatore saw that the canvas he'd painted on had been wound around the top of that pole. He stared at it, mesmerized. He knew what was to come, or thought he did, but he couldn't imagine the effect it might have on the gathered Dragons.

When he was certain that he had their attention, Snake reached up and untied the string at the top of the banner, letting the sheet uncurl from the pole. Opening it carefully so that the design remained concealed, he stood, tall and ominous, full of a strange energy that Salvatore felt rippling in the air.

"Tonight," Snake said, staring out into the darkness at some point beyond his followers, "I fight *Los Escorpiones*. Alone, or with you -- I fight." He swept his gaze over the gathering, catching the few that started guiltily at his words, boring through them mercilessly. "They have come to the very borders of our streets and homes. They have killed our brothers – they have dishonored our colors. If we allow this to pass, we are nothing."

He turned to Salvatore, and Salvatore felt the grip on his arm tighten. A part of him wanted very much to run, but he stood his ground.

"Here stands Salvatore Domingo Sanchez," Snake said. "In

his heart live dragons! There are those among you with whom he has shared their flame. He is what we should be. He is what we must become. I don't know when or where I lost the way, but he brought me back. He can bring us all back. Somehow he looked inside of us – of me – and found the Dragons. He found them, and he called them back."

Salvatore turned, ignoring those gathered, to stare at Snake. No one had ever said such things about him. No one had ever made him feel such honor.

"The old one," Snake gestured at Martinez, who stood still and silent, a knowing smile on his lips, "assures me that he knows what is to come. He has had a vision. He has seen the coming battle, and *Los Escorpiones* die tonight. They cease to exist. Who, among you, do you suppose will bring this about? The biggest? The strongest? No. It won't be me, and it won't be any of you, because we don't deserve it. We lost our way. We lost our power. It will be Sal who saves us; he bears our power. In his talent, and his art beats the heart of a Dragon!"

A wave of nervous energy rippled through the clearing. Salvatore picked up snippets of thought, though not clearly enough to tell which came from which man. He'd never been able to read minds, but somehow he knew that this was new... something different.

They were still scared, and now they thought Snake was crazy. They expected a fight, and they knew what they were up against – or thought that they did. This wasn't supposed to be a weird ritual like Anya Cabrera used against them – it was supposed to be a rally, and a battle. – the last act in a war. Nobody had quite the strength or the courage to voice their doubts. Snake was a dangerous man. If he was crazy now -- well, then he would just be more dangerous. They waited for him to make sense, and for the call to leave, a call they all dreaded.

Snake reached up and whipped the flag open. He almost yanked the pole from Salvatore's hands, but Salvatore clung to the pole with all his strength and dug his heels into the soft earth. Snake's dragon floated into the air on its background of white. The sheet rippled and whipped in the wind with a snap like thunder.

Salvatore stared up at the creature. He remembered it – knew it so well he could have traced its outline in the dirt with a stick and brought it to life – but he didn't remember the painting. His stomach lurched, and now he clung to the flagpole for support. He saw the city, rising up to meet him. He felt the air whistle past his years and saw the glowing towers below. He opened his mouth to scream, but no sound came. He felt the dragon's claws clutch him tightly. The sensation of falling became one of soaring – gliding flat just clear of the turreted towers and massive stone walls.

And then he stood, hands clutching the flagpole so tightly his fingers felt as though they would snap from the strain. Snake gripped his shoulders and held him upright, and that other world faded into a wall of faces reflecting firelight. His first thought was that they would think that he was crazy. Surely they hadn't seen that city – hadn't seen what he had seen. After a moment, he relaxed in Snake's grip. There was no laughter. They all stared up and over his head, where the flag and the dragon waved in the wind. Not a man among them spoke.

"It's time," Snake cried. "We ride...we fight."

He turned and yanked the flagpole from the dirt and Salvatore's hands. Salvatore fell in behind, and they passed through the crowd, who parted like a dark, brooding ocean. Martinez stayed by the fire. This would not be his fight, but Salvatore had been swept up in the moment. Snake didn't hesitate as he passed through the clubhouse and back out the front. He strode to his bike and Salvatore hurried at his heels.

Snake swirled the flagpole briskly, wrapping the dragon tightly. He handed the pole to Salvatore, who held it without question. Snake pulled a bit of rawhide from his pocket and tied it around the flag, securing it to the pole. When he was finished, he turned to Salvatore.

"You'll ride with me, Sal," he said. "When we get where we're going, you'll carry the flag. Whatever happens, you stay with me. No matter what you see, no matter what happens, you keep that dragon flying. Understand?"

Salvatore nodded. Snake climbed onto his bike, and Salvatore slipped in behind him, leaning on the tall sissy bar.

He clutched the flagpole like a lance, letting it rest on Snake's shoulder. He grabbed Snake's jacket with his free hand and held on for dear life as the big man kicked started the engine. All around them, the Dragons poured out of the clubhouse, mounted their bikes and started their engines. The roar of the powerful machines reminded Salvatore dimly of the far-off cries of those other dragons.

They pulled away from the curve and roared into the night. Martinez stood in the pool of light from the clubhouse doorway, watching as they disappeared into shadow.

Chapter Thirty-Four

Donovan and Amethyst returned to the park where Anya Cabrera's fires had burned only short hours before, but this time they traveled on foot. There was no way to know where the *Escorpiones* trapped in the portals might have gone, or if they'd gone anywhere at all. It seemed prudent to avoid that confrontation for the moment.

They stuck to the shadows, but there was no activity. Darkness had fallen, and though the street lights glimmered dimly, they weren't bright enough to provide more than small pools of illumination, surrounded by deep shadows.

The park was deserted. They stopped on the far side of the street and studied the scene of the ritual carefully. There were few trees in the park, and most of them were Palms. There was nowhere to hide. Nothing moved, and the only sign of the ritual that had taken place was a drift of smoke from the spot where the central bonfire had burned.

"They're gone," Donovan said. "But where?"

"That's not the only question," Amethyst added, stepping into the street and heading across toward the park. "I was the sacrifice for that ritual – but we don't know if they managed to complete it without me. We have to find them, but first we have to know what we're up against."

Donovan followed her, scanning the street a final time before stepping into the park. Whatever had happened here, it was over. Anya Cabrera and her minions had disappeared completely, taking *Los Escorpiones* with them. In fact, they'd taken everything with them, cleaning the area so thoroughly it was difficult to believe they'd been there at all.

Donovan moved to the remnant of the central fire. He grabbed a branch and dug around in the ashes. There were bits and pieces of wood and charcoal, but though he circled the entire pit, nothing else came to light.

"The ritual burned it out," Donovan said. "If there was anything in that fire that might have helped us, it's gone now."

Amethyst walked to the top of the circle, where the post had been driven into the ground. It was gone, and the hole where it had stood had been filled with soot and ashes. She leaned in and looked more closely.

"There's something here," she said.

Donovan stepped over and was about to poke the end of his stick into the hole, when she laid a hand on his arm and stopped him.

"Wait. I don't mean there's something you can find in the ashes. Something happened here – something…"

Amethyst pulled a thin, silver chain up over her head. A blood-red crystal dangled from the end of it. She held it cupped in her hands, breathed on it, and then let the chain slip through her grip until the crystal dangled from her fingers. She spun it in slow circle around the circumference of the posthole. At first, nothing happened. Then the ashes near the center of the hole shifted lifted and spun, as if caught in a wind, spreading out in a wider and wider circle as Amethyst widened the arc of the crystal's motion.

"What…" Donovan clamped his mouth shut as the ashes shimmered, and turned red.

Where the hole had been, a bright, wet circle had formed. It looked as if it was a puddle of fresh blood. Ripples began near the center, spreading outward. Then they cracked and broke like ice on a pond. The ridges and crevasses formed lines and then knit into an ever-sharpening image. Amethyst concentrated. Donovan stepped back for a better view. Before the image was complete, he knew the answer.

"My God," he said. "It's Anya Cabrera. She was the sacrifice."

Amethyst stood quickly. As she drew the crystal away, the bloody image shattered to ash and dust as if had never existed.

She dropped the necklace back over heard head and tucked the crystal out of sight.

"What does it mean?" she asked.

Donovan had already turned, and was headed back toward the street at a run.

"If she sacrificed herself, it means they completed the ritual. If that's true, then the *Loa* are trapped in this dimension in human form. That's what we feared. Now it's worse."

"Worse?"

"The worst that we feared was that Anya Cabrera would control an army of dark spirits and use them to take over the Barrio. Now those spirits are here, but there is no one to control them. I'm not sure what has happened, but we have to find Anya's followers, and we have to find *Los Escorpiones*, before it's too late, and not just for the Barrio. If those spirits get loose in the city, we may never track them down."

"Where are we going?"

"We have to try and find Martinez." Donovan said. "And I think we'll have to chance the portals. If whatever he's planning has already begun, they need to know what happened here. If not, it seems likely that Anya's people will act against the Dragons."

"They'll be slaughtered," Anya said.

"I don't know about that. Martinez has something up his sleeve. Whatever happens, it isn't going to be good for the Dragons, *Los Escorpiones*, or The Barrio."

They entered the alley at a run. Donovan leaped down onto the stone steps. This time, instead of carefully taking steps up and back, his feet moved so quickly it was like a dance. Within moments the portal opened, and they leaped through.

"This way," he cried.

They turned right and pounded down the corridor. They passed rows of doors to either side so quickly there was no time to take in details. Amethyst glanced over her shoulder several times, but whatever had become of the *Loa* they'd trapped in the passage earlier, neither they, nor their human hosts were in sight.

Donovan led her up a set of stairs on the left, and moments

later they stepped out onto the street. They stood outside an abandoned warehouse. There was nothing to indicate that this set of stairs had been used in the last fifty years. The building was run down with boards covering what remained of the windows. The bricks were painted in bright colors by graffiti artists. There was no one in sight.

"This way," Donovan said.

He hurried down the street and around a corner. Not too far in the distance, a single home was lit up. It looked as though a party was taking place in the back, but there was no sound.

"That's the Dragons' clubhouse," Donovan said. "There are lights; maybe we're not too late."

They ran the few blocks to the clubhouse, but before they arrived, Donovan's heart sank. There were no bikes out front. The door was closed, and though firelight flickered out in back, no shadows moved in that light, and there were no voices. As they reached the front door, Martinez stepped from the shadows.

"They are gone," he said. "They are heading back to Santini Park."

"We have to get over there," Donovan said. "Anya Cabrera completed her ritual, but she sacrificed herself in the process. I don't know what is waiting in that park, or if Anya's spirits will even answer the call with her dead, but if they are there, it's going to be bad. Much worse than last time."

"I sensed that something had shifted," Martinez said.

The old man looked exhausted. He seemed thinner, and older. His snow-white hair floated about his face like a gray cloud. His shoulders were stooped.

"I have done what I can," he said. "I gave them a chance. Salvatore is with them. He bears their standard into battle. You saw what the dragons he painted on their jackets could do. This one was painted with the Rojo Fuego. The boy is very powerful. He is connected to another place...a place where dragons are more than men. I cannot say that it will be enough, but I can say that I do not think Anya Cabrera's dark spirits will find it an easy battle to win."

"Can the boy control it?" Amethyst asked.

Martinez shrugged. "As well as it can *be* contained, he can. I can't help but think that if Anya gave her life for this battle, there is still something we're missing. I can't believe she would just perish and leave the world to its own devices. Her intention was to rule, not just to destroy."

"You could be right," Donovan said. "In any case, we have to get over there. I don't know what we can do to help, but we have to try."

"Go then," Martinez said. "It isn't far. I'm afraid I'm too old, and too weary, to make a good run of it. You'll have to tell me the story, when it's done."

"I hope there's someone left to tell it," Donovan said.

He turned, and ran down the street, his jacket trailing behind him. Amethyst followed. Martinez stood and watched them go until all there was to see was mist and shadow. Then, slowly, he turned back to the clubhouse, opened the door, and stepped inside. The empty street returned to shadows, and to silence.

Chapter Thirty-Five

Santini Park was awash in silent shadows. The Dragons arrived in a slow, winding string of bright headlight beams and rumbling engines. Snake pulled up first, as he had before the previous battle. He let the old bike roll to a stop against the curb, slid the kickstand into place, and sat very still. Salvatore sat behind him, clinging to Snake's jacket with one arm and holding onto the flagpole with the other. His shoulder ached from where the wind had fought to rip his burden from his arms. His eyes watered, and his eyes were wide.

It hadn't been a long ride, but Salvatore was unused to the precise balance and the whipping of the wind against his unprotected face. Snake had ridden without a helmet, his long hair flowing out behind him and tickling Salvatore's face. They had never gotten over twenty miles an hour, but it had reminded Salvatore of that other place, of flying in the grip of the great red dragon. When he closed his eyes, he could see the city below, and the glowing, colored towers.

Now the others pulled in behind them. They peeled off to either side, flowing out and parking like rows of dominoes, each bike tipping onto its kickstand a moment before the next in line. They followed Snake's lead and sat very still. Salvatore scanned the park, but nothing in that darkness moved. He allowed himself to hope, just for a moment, that no one else would come. There was no way to know for certain that *Los Escorpiones* would meet this challenge, though they certainly must know by now that the Dragons were on the move. Word in the Barrio traveled like smoke, or the wind. Nothing happened that did not eventually make its way to the most distant of ears.

When the last of the Dragons had cut his engine, and they sat in a long, glittering line, the chrome of their engines catching and recasting moonlight, their faces shadowed silhouettes. The night went so deathly silent that Salvatore thought they must all be able to hear the pounding of his heart. It wasn't so much the fear of *Los Escorpiones* as the fact he could not see them. He could not hear them. He felt them like prickles of ice walking on spider feet over his skin. He sensed them in the hairs at the nape of his neck. He tasted the fear of those surrounding him, and an answering…something…in the darkness.

Snake slid off the bike and stepped onto the sidewalk. He scanned the park slowly, but there was nothing to see. Salvatore climbed carefully off the bike and stood beside Snake. To the right and left, the others followed suit. They lined the sidewalk, and this time there were so many that the entire edge of the park became a wall of Dragons. They didn't speak, and they didn't move. Every man of them waited for a sign from Snake.

In the park, the shadows shifted and slid. Patches of darkness so black they stood out, even against the darkness of the unlit field spread out before them, moved and then disappeared. There were lights in the distance. At least, they seemed distant to Salvatore. He knew the park, though, and it wasn't that big. It wasn't that deep. Those lights looked too far away to exist, and they danced in and around the moving shadows like will-o-the-wisps.

At every movement, Salvatore felt a shiver of fear dance up his spine. His hands were cold and clammy where he held the flagpole, and he tightened his grip until it was painful. He had one purpose, one reason to stand where he stood. He had to hold the flag. He had to hold it no matter what happened. He had to hold it, or whatever was out there in the darkness would win, and he would be standing there unprotected.

As they waited, a fog rose. It shimmered up from the grass and licked at the bases of the swings and slides. It floated across the ground from the trees on the far side of the park, sifted through the metal tubes of the monkey bars and jungle gyms. There was no reason for the fog. There was no change in temperature, and when he glanced up, Salvatore saw a clear night sky.

As that mist obscured their view of the park, something laughed. The sound was dark and chilling. The laughter skittered along the sidewalks and shivered through the air. It was joined by an echoing voice, and then another, but Salvatore could not see where the sounds came from.

The Dragons shifted nervously. There were coughs and muttered words. Snake glanced right, and then left along the line. Whatever was happening in the park was getting to them, and they wavered.

Snake reached out quickly and grabbed hold of the flagpole. He didn't yank it from Salvatore's hands, but he shook it, and the motion loosened the ties. With a snap, as if caught in a wind Salvatore couldn't feel, the flag unfurled and flew above them. Snake released the pole and Salvatore stumbled, just for an instant. Then he stood tall. Snake turned toward the park. He slid a heavy dagger from its sheath on his belt. The fog had risen halfway to the lowest branches of the trees now, and nothing but flickering lights was visible in front of them.

With a scream of rage and defiance, Snake lunged forward. Caught up in the moment, Salvatore raised his own small voice, joining it to Snake's as he plunged after.

The Dragons, as though released from some common bond that had held them immobile, followed, slipping in behind in ranks of three or four, forming the long, serpentine shape of a serpent as they followed Snake into battle.

Where Salvatore and the flag moved, the fog dispersed. He saw Snake ahead of him. Shadows flowed in to meet them, and the Dragons surged up and around him. Then the darkness resolved itself into faces. They were men, though their eyes were far too dark, and their expressions held no humanity. Salvatore thought of that dark place, the city of the Dragons, and thought such men as these might slink around the base of the wall and hide in the alleys between buildings. They were fast, so fast they blurred, and Salvatore struggled to avoid the hundred small battles erupting around him.

Snake fought like a man possessed. He lashed out with his blade, and wherever he turned, shadow-figures fell. He seemed taller, and for every bit of the demon speed of *Los Escorpiones*, he was faster. To his right, Jake fought valiantly. The big man glowed with an odd, greenish light that emanated from the dragon on his back. Salvatore wished in that instant that he could have painted the dragons of every one of them, could have armored them for this battle.

He held the flag high, and when he saw a Dragon in trouble, he lunged closer. The presence of the standard rallied them, lent them strength, and drove *Los Escorpiones* back into the shadows. The battle raged around them, wild, surreal, and encased in a wall of heavy mist and fog. They fought on, but the enemy seemed endless, and Salvatore feared they might never stop coming. His hands were slick from sweat, but he clutched the flagpole with all his strength and prayed for more. He had never felt so alive.

Chapter Thirty-Six

By the time Donovan was close enough to see the park, the mist had risen to where it nearly brushed the clouds. Lights flickered deep within that mist, but it obscured any view of what was happening beyond the edge of the sidewalk. The street was lined with the Dragons' bikes; the glittering, polished chromed caught reflected shadows from the park itself, but they had no form.

As they drew closer, muffled sounds of a battle reached them, but it was impossible to make it out as more than the muted clash of metal and the distant echoes of screams. Donovan stopped and turned.

"What's happening?" Amethyst asked.

"I'm not sure," Donovan replied. "It could be *Los Escorpiones*, if they're still possessed. It could be something Martinez and the boy unleashed. We need to get in there."

Amethyst nodded. She reached up and unclasped a silver chain from her hair. When it unwound it was surprisingly long. There were crystal globes at either end, wrapped in coils of silver. She gripped it near the center and began spinning the globes with a deft flick of her wrist. After only a moment the chain was a blur of motion.

Donovan watched in fascination as she strode toward the mist. He followed, and as they made contact with that cloudy wall, it gave way before the whirling crystals. It didn't disperse, but the motion of the chain created a tunnel about twice the height of a man that stretched out slowly, cutting through the misty shroud toward the center of the park. Figures flashed in and out of that tunnel. Donovan saw a big man, one of the

Dragons, with his hands locked around the throat of a small, slender Escorpione. Before the two disappeared into the mist, the Dragon lifted his opponent and threw him like a rag doll.

Amethyst glanced over her shoulder at Donovan, her eyebrow raised. The Dragon was a big man, but what they'd just witnessed had been too effortless. A second later the man lunged out of sight with a cry of rage. As he turned, Donovan caught a flash of green, and knew it must be Jake.

Something cracked like a shot from a very large gun. The sound came from overhead, and Donovan glanced up. He didn't want to take his eyes off of Amethyst. While she spun the crystal she was unable to fend off any attack. Something very big and very dark soared overhead. The mist cleared, just for an instant, and Donovan saw vast wings stretching out to either side. He saw the passing of a long, serpentine tail, and before he could open his mouth to shout a warning, or even voice his surprise, a scream cut through the air that shook the ground and shivered through the mist like rippling waves on a pond.

At that moment, there was another cry. It wasn't as loud, but there was an echo of the dragon's scream buried deep in the sound. Donovan spun back to the park in time to see Snake leap into view. The Dragon leader had his head back and his face to the sky. He screamed in answer to the beast and spun, just in time, to catch one of Anya Cabrera's bald servants by the throat. The black man was much larger than Snake, but the Dragon gripped him with one hand and lifted him. A quick shake of that hand, and the big man's head lolled one way, and then the other. There was a horrible snapping sound, and Snake released him, turning again. This time he saw Amethyst and Donovan approaching.

For just a second it seemed he would come at them. Donovan braced himself. His hand went to the hilt of the slender dagger he wore on his hip. Then Salvatore stepped from the fog, the flagpole gripped so tightly in his hands that even from where he stood Donovan saw the boy's knuckles were white with strain. Salvatore's eyes had a glazed, far-away expression, so different from Snake's that Donovan's hand fell away from the handle of his blade in confusion. It was obvious the young artist saw nothing that happened around him. He stood very still, and a white light flickered up and down his arms. It shimmered on his hair and cast a brilliant glow on the ground at his feet.

Over head, the flag flapped and waved. As it moved, the dragon emblazoned across it swooped and dove. There was such a sense of motion and life, that Donovan found his gaze drawn to the sky above them once again. Somehow he knew that the dragons were connected. Salvatore was the key.

Two more *Escorpiones* leaped into sight. One came at Snake from the front, and the other literally climbed his back, clawing at his hair, scrambling to get higher and reach over to the Dragon president's eyes. Snake bellowed and rolled forward, flinging the attacker off his back. Donovan drew his blade and moved in. He had to step to the side to get around Amethyst without disturbing the spin of the crystal globes, and in that instant, everything changed.

There was a screech of rage from off to their left. A small form moving very quickly darted out of the mist. It was a young Hispanic woman. Her skin glowed a sickly yellow, and her hair spun out about her face madly. There was something familiar in the woman's gait, and in her voice. Donovan dove forward to try and intercept her course, but she was like a screeching bolt of lightning. As Donovan closed on her, he heard her chanting, and his heart glazed with ice.

"Anya!" he cried. "Snake! Look out!"

Snake spun. He saw the girl coming for him and he slipped to the side, narrowly avoiding the attack. He stepped back, but his motion was too swift, and Salvatore was lost in some vision the rest of them could not see. The two collided, and just for an instant, Snake was off balance. In that moment, the woman struck. She dove at him and drove a long, thin blade into his heart.

Snake reeled from the blow. Even as he lost his balance, he managed to grip the woman by the hair and toss her to the side. She spun with another screech of rage and came in low. Snake tried to dodge her again, but he was bleeding from the knife wound, and still tangled with Salvatore, who stumbled blindly back as if unaware of the encroaching danger.

"No!" Donovan cried. He flicked his wrist, and a rolled bit of parchment slipped into his hand. He raised it and began to speak, but even as the first words left his lips, Anya struck again. Snake screamed and clutched his chest where her blade bit deep. She drove it in again and again, and he toppled.

The moment lasted an eternity. Snake fell hard into Salvatore, driving him back and down. Even as they fell, the young artist clung to the flagpole. They struck the ground at the same moment and bounced once. Snake fell across the painted image of the dragon, his blood pouring freely from a wound directly over his heart and blended with the brilliant red paint – the Rojo Fuego. The mist faltered, and as Donovan stepped forward, holding the small parchment before him like a shield, the park grew deathly still.

Amethyst stepped up behind him. She stopped whirling the crystals and stood just behind his shoulder. Donovan felt her pressing close, and heard her mutter under her breath.

"My god," she said. "What have they done?"

Chapter Thirty-Seven

In the second that the world grew still and Donovan hesitated, Anya Cabrera regained her balance and spun on them like an enraged cat. The girl she possessed was lovely, but with Anya's spirit twisting her features she looked like a wild, feral animal. Donovan stood his ground. He held the bit of parchment before him and continued to read. His words were steady and measured. There was little or no variance in his tone. The sound was soothing, mesmerizing, and its effect was immediate.

Tendrils of light materialized from the air surrounding Anya. They began above her and out of her line of sight, but as she moved to attack they dropped over her in glowing ringlets and formed a net that stopped her in her tracks. She tried to break through, but it held against her assault; where her skin touched the links of light, sparks shot out in all directions. She screamed in rage and backed away, only to find that the net had dropped behind her as well. Donovan's voice grew in strength and volume and he took a step closer.

Anya grew very still. She watched him approaching, her eyes black pits of hatred, and then – without warning – she began to laugh. The sound grew from a low, crackle like waxed paper flapping in a breeze to the deep cracking of ice breaking in a river. It rose in volume, stretched out and increased in power until the web of light around her shimmered and wavered. She reached out with one hand, almost casually, and plucked at the net with a long nail. It shivered. One frail strand stretched, and though the sparks still flew, and there must have been incredible heat and pain, Anya continued to pull.

Donovan felt Amethyst move up behind him. She laid a

hand on his shoulder, and in the periphery of his vision he saw a golden glow emanate from something clutched in her fingers. She leaned in and read over his shoulder. The parchment contained only a single, two stanza charm. She whispered softly and carefully, and wound her voice in with his. The net around Anya Cabrera flared suddenly and grew strong. The old *Houngan* pulled her hand back with another screech of pain and rage.

"You will fail," she cried. "You will fail because your net is meant to cage a mortal, a human captive. I am no longer a part of your weak, puny race. I walk two planes. I share the power of the *Loa*. It flows through my blood and you have no power to bind it. There is no power in this world to bind it."

As she spoke, she stepped forward. She reached out and slid her fingers through the links of light, gripped tightly, and began to pull. Smoke rose from her fingers. Donovan heard the sizzle and pop of skin, but still she did not relent. She pulled, and the strands of light stretched. Amethyst gasped and leaned against him. The energy they were expending to create the web of light drained his strength, and he knew it was weakening her as well. They could only hold on for so long, but there was nothing else to do. She was too powerful.

"I can't hold it," Amethyst gasped. She clutched at him with her free hand, gripping so tightly he thought her nails might have pierced his shoulder. He used the pain and focused it. He drew power from deep within himself and funneled it through his lips. He pulled the words from the small paper, words he knew well, and flung them into the night. The web surged again, and then again, and once more Anya stepped back with a screech. Her smile didn't falter. She knew he couldn't keep it up. It was only a matter of time until the trap failed, and she was free. When that happened, he wasn't even certain the two of them would make it out of the park alive.

Beyond Anya, something moved. Donovan watched at the periphery of his sight, but he didn't lessen his concentration. Jake had knelt behind Anya and leaned over the flag. All Donovan could make out of the once magnificent painting was a spreading stain. It was dark, and there should have been nothing but shades of gray. Impossibly, the stain on that flag was brilliant, blood red. Snake's blood.

Donovan sensed that Snake still lived, but barely. A second figure rose beside Jake. Salvatore. He held something in his hands, and Donovan realized it was the tent pole. It had snapped in the fall, but Salvatore still clutched it. The boy stepped toward Anya, raising the broken stick like a club over his head.

"No!" Donovan cried. He spoke before he thought, and it cost him his control. The net abound Anya Cabrera shimmered and fell apart in a shower of sparks. She screamed in rage, turning in a circle as if uncertain which of them to attack first.

Salvatore struck. He swung the broken tent post in a quick, hard arc that slapped into Anya's head with a sickening crunch. She staggered. She did not go down, not exactly, but her legs seemed, just for a moment, to lose the ability to hold her erect. She took a lurching step toward Donovan, tried to turn, failed, and started to fall.

The night erupted in sound. The sky, which had taken on a silver glow as the mist cleared and the moon shone through, grew suddenly dark. A thunderous roar shook the ground, threatened to topple the trees, and drove Donovan back into Amethyst so hard they toppled. He fought for balance, failed, and did his best to land softly. He knew if he went down and stayed down, Anya would not hesitate to attack, and she was too strong to allow even a moment's advantage.

Then he was driven to the ground with such force the breath left him, and it was all he could do not to pass out. He gasped, clutched at the grass, and stared upward. The dragon dropped from the sky with stunning speed. It was like watching an eagle the size of an elephant dropping from incredible heights.

The only one who retained footing was Anya Cabrera. The old *Houngan* lifted her face to the sky, and she screamed in defiance. Donovan noted, as his pulse thundered in his ears and he fought desperately for consciousness, that Anya's voice could be heard, even over the scream of the dragon and the roar of wind that accompanied its descent. She actually reached up, as though she might catch it and drag it to the ground.

The two collided. There was a snap of sound and energy that blacked out all light. Once again the air was sucked out from around them, and then, as the dragon rose with another scream, it returned in a rush. The world swam before Donovan's eyes. He was lifted slightly by the returning rush of air and he spun, getting his hands beneath him and pressing up. He made it to his knees, and then to his feet. Dirt and dust and leaves swirled around him but he waved his arm, found his voice, and spoke. His single word stilled the air around him – a circle formed, about twenty feet in circumference, and he stood at its center.

He craned his neck and stared into the sky. The dragon was so high, even after only a few seconds, that it seemed no more than a large bird, flying into the face of the moon. Donovan heard a cry to his right and spun. Salvatore had crawled over to where Snake lay across the bloody sheet that had been a flag. The boy turned, his face awash in tears.

Jake knelt across from him. The big man turned to Donovan. "He's dead," Jake said.

There was a crackle of energy. Far up, thousands of feet, a tear in the darkness shot a bolt of pure energy to the earth. It struck with surgical precision, driving Salvatore and Jake back and slamming into Snake's body with the force of a lightning strike. The air filled with the scent of ozone, and the light blinded them all – just for a second. Then it was gone.

Donovan opened his eyes. The park was just a park again. Snake lay very still across the tattered remnant of what now appeared to be no more than an blank sheet of canvas. Salvatore lay to one side, and Jake was getting groggily to his feet. Amethyst sat in the dirt shaking her head, and in between them all, a young woman's body lay crumpled and silent.

Donovan stepped forward and knelt. He placed a hand on her throat. She was alive.

Far in the distance a siren rose.

All around them, men stood. They brushed branches, leaves, and dirt from hands, faces, and clothing. *Los Escorpiones* and Dragons alike seemed confused, lost and without purpose.

"You have to get them out of here," Donovan said, turning

to Jake. "Get your people back to the clubhouse. I'll help with Snake."

Jake stared at him for a moment, uncomprehending. Then the big man glanced around, took in the chaos, and nodded. He stared at one of *Los Escorpiones*, standing only a few feet away. The man met his gaze, but there was no animosity in that stare. Jake nodded once, and they turned their separate ways.

Jake gathered several of the Dragons nearest him and spoke to them in low tones. They spread out through the park, and in only moments, motors fired up and down the road. Headlights sliced the park, and the crossing beams of those brilliant lights, Salvatore, Jake, and Donovan lifted Snake on what had once been his flag, and carried the Dragon president's body from the park.

Amethyst had managed to revive the girl, and helped her along in their wake. They passed through the parked bikes and crossed the street, disappearing into a darkened alley. Santini Park stood dark and silent. Only Snake and Jake's bikes remained, tilted on their kickstands and watching, like silent sentinels. More sirens rose, but the park was bare. The moon shone bright and clear.

Chapter Thirty-Eight

Before they'd gone more than a block, Martinez stepped out of the shadows and fell in beside the make-shift stretcher. He reached out a hand, as if to touch Snake, or to check for life, and then pulled the hand back.

"It's over," Donovan said.

The old man turned, met Donovan's gaze, and then shook his head. He turned, spotted Salvatore, and went to the boy's side. Donovan saw him lean in close and whisper something, but he got no response. Martinez laid his hand on the young artist's shoulder and shook him gently, but again there was no reaction.

Salvatore's hair stuck out at crazed angles from his pale face. He still gripped the makeshift club that had once been a flagpole. Martinez tried to pry it gently from his hand as they walked, but Salvatore wasn't letting go, and again, the old man let it slide.

"We have to move fast," Jake said. "Those sirens are getting closer, and we have a ways to go. If they catch us before we get to the clubhouse, this is going to be hard to explain."

"They will not see us," Martinez said.

"I wish I shared your confidence," Jake said.

"I have taken care of it. They will not see us."

Jake stared at Martinez for a moment, and then nodded. He turned back and led the others through the darkened streets.

Donovan turned and glanced at where Amethyst supported the girl on her arm. He wanted to go to her, to talk to her and offer his help, but that would have to wait, at least until they got back to the clubhouse. He glanced up at the moon far above.

He thought he saw a shadow pass before his eyes, far above, and his heart chilled.   He flashed on Martinez shaking his head. If it wasn't over...

They turned the last corner and saw the lights of the clubhouse ahead. The bikes that had lined the park now covered the street, and the clubhouse yard. The fire in the back yard had been built up again, and light streamed from every window of the building. They hurried their steps. When they got within a couple of blocks, a contingent of quiet, silent Dragons took the makeshift stretcher from their hands gently and moved on ahead. Jake joined them, softly giving directions that Donovan noted were followed without question.

Relieved of his burden, Donovan hurried to Amethyst's side. "How is she?" he asked.

"She'll live," Amethyst said. "Salvatore gave her a good shot to the head, and she's confused. She hasn't been in control of her body for hours. Also, one thing we failed to consider when we brought her along with us ... she's one of the *Escorpiones'* women. The more her memory comes back to her, the more she's scared out of her mind. I've told her we'll watch out for her, but I think we need to get her away from here."

"Give me a few minutes," Donovan said, "And we'll go. We can drop her at the hospital and tell them where to find her people. I need to see what Martinez is up to."

"What do you mean?" Amethyst asked.

Just then, the shadow crossed the moon again. This time it seemed a bit lower, and a bit darker. They both glanced up. There was nothing in sight, but something hung in the air, something dark and angry. Something powerful and hungry.

"I think," Donovan said, "you have your answer."

He spun, and ran for the entrance to the clubhouse. He slipped in past the groups of Dragons, their heads hung and their voices low. They'd won a battle that night, but they'd lost their President, and they'd lost brothers, and for most of them, there were more questions than answers. They didn't prevent Donovan from passing, but he caught more than a few confused glances.

There were candles on every horizontal surface. Donovan

wound his way into the crowd and searched until he spotted the gray of Martinez'ss hair in the kitchen. He pushed through and found Salvatore seated at the table, staring at his hands. Martinez stood over him. The old man had a far-away expression. He seemed on the verge of saying something, and at the same time uncertain what it should be.

"Martinez," Donovan said, grabbing the old man's arm. "What have you done? They aren't gone. The dragons."

"They are not here either, my friend. They are ... between."

Donovan started to ask what that meant, and then he caught sight of Salvatore. The boy sat at the table, but there was little indication of whether or not he was aware of his surroundings. He seemed lost in some other place. Tears had streaked his cheeks and his eyes had dark bags beneath them, as though he'd been drained of energy...or hope.

"The painting," Donovan said softly.

"Yes," Martinez said. "It was the painting. It opened a portal – connected worlds. Now that painting is gone, but the portal...it never closed."

"No," Donovan said. "I understood that. The paint – the Rojo Fuego – is there more?"

Martinez blinked.

"Yes, a little. I don't know how much. There are other colors, as well. They aren't as powerful..."

"We need the red," Donovan said.

He dropped to one knee before Salvatore.

"Sal, can you hear me?" he asked.

The boy glanced up slowly. His eyes were glazed, but he nodded. He was aware.

"You have to paint," Donovan said. "You have to close the portal. The only one who can do it is you – you see the dragons. They are in your heart – your soul. You are the one who brought Snake and his dragon together. Now Snake is gone...you have to take his dragon home."

A light flickered in Salvatore's eyes. The corner of his mouth twitched.

"I don't know if I can do it," he said. His voice nearly broke. "Senor Snake...I did not know him for long, but...he was like a father...or a brother. He gave me strength, purpose. For the first time in my life, I felt as if I mattered. Now..."

"Now more than ever," Donovan said, "you matter. It's in your hands. Your gift – your talent – you can make it right. You can't bring him back, but ... you can make certain he didn't die in vain."

Jake walked into the room then. In his hand, he held a small square of fabric. Donovan looked at it more carefully and saw that it was part of the sheet that had held Snake's dragon. The big man held it almost reverently. He laid it on the table in front of Salvatore and stepped back.

Salvatore stared at the white cloth in silence. Martinez rose and left the room. When he came back, he held the remnant of the Rojo Fuego, still carefully wrapped. He also had a bag filled with the other colors, and Salvatore's brushes. He laid them on the table beside the cloth. Donovan nodded to the old man, and they turned. A moment later, everyone had left the room, and Salvatore sat alone.

"I'll return before morning," Donovan told Martinez. "I have to help Amethyst with the girl."

"Does she remember anything?" the old man asked.

Donovan shook his head.

"She's scared. The last thing she remembers is following her boyfriend to Anya Cabrera's circle. I don't think she'll go back there. Can't say that I blame her. If my boyfriend offered me up for a voodoo ritual sacrifice, I'd have some serious questions about the future of the relationship."

Martinez laughed drily.

"I'll watch over the boy," he said.

Donovan stepped to a window and glanced out into the night sky. "Can he turn them back?"

"I don't know," Martinez admitted. "It's what I feared all along. If Snake had lived, there would have been balance. Now the portal between this world and that other has grown thin. I have never been able to walk that road. The boy has been there many times. I wish I'd had the time to teach him more – but in this instance, he is the master."

Donovan glanced back through the doorway into the

kitchen. Salvatore had the paintbrush in one hand. He stared at the cloth intently. Dragons guarded the doorways, their backs turned to give the boy privacy.

"I hope he has the strength," Donovan said.

He turned to the doorway. Martinez faced him, and, tentatively held out his hand. Donovan took it without hesitation.

"We will have things to talk about," he said, "once things are settled. I will see you before the sun rises."

He turned and slipped out into the night. Amethyst waited impatiently by the side of the road. He slipped up on the opposite side of the girl and draped his arm around her back. They moved off into the shadowed streets without a word. Behind and above them, a huge shadow slid across the face of the moon.

Chapter Thirty-Nine

Salvatore stared at the cloth. He traced designs across the surface with the fingernail of one hand. At first the motion was random. His mind was far away. He tried to concentrate on the city, or the dragons, but something intruded. It was a pattern, a geometric shape. His finger began tracing that shape onto the white cloth, and he frowned. It was familiar, and at the same time he was certain he'd never seen it before – not exactly.

His paints were laid out beside him. There was also a worn piece of black charcoal. He picked it up almost absently and began to sketch. He continued to trace the pattern. There were six corners. He filled in circular shapes near the points, and in the center he drew a larger circle, with a concentric ring inside it.

He shaded the edges, and darkened the spaces between the circles. At some point he reached for one of his brushes, and the paint. He started with green. He shaded one of the circles carefully. He lightened the green and highlighted the edges, then switched to white until the sphere appeared to glow.

He worked more quickly now. He shifted colors and brushes. He worked with violet, and blue, red and yellow. His hand became a blur. He painted the spheres around the outer edge, but his mind – his concentration – was fixed on the center. It was plain and white, but in his mind, it pulsed and glowed. He reached for the last packet of paint, opened it reverently, and dipped his brush.

The shift was sudden and absolute. The second his brush dipped into the Rojo Fuego he felt the chair fall away. He was dropping through the air, and beneath him the city spread out in a wide, geometric panorama of color and shadow. He saw the towers, one for each color, and the pattern of his painting focused. Beneath him, the glowing read upper chamber of the central tower approached at sickening speed.

He gripped the brush, somehow it made the passage with him, and though it swirled in the open air and not across the surface of the white canvas, he knew he could not stop. If he let the pattern slip – if he failed to blend the colors in his mind, he was lost. As he fell, his eyes filled with tears. They slid across his cheeks and whipped off into the night sky of a world that could not be. It didn't matter. He didn't need to see what was in front of him. He knew what to do – what to paint.

An impossibly loud scream rose above and behind him. Even over the whistle of wind through his ears he heard the crashing boom as enormous wings flapped. The dragon screamed, but this time it was different. The sound echoed with sadness. There was pain in its voice, and loss. Salvatore's heart nearly stopped from a sudden, empathic sensation of immense sorrow.

Salvatore gripped the brush more tightly. The tower was very close. Red light glowed from windows on all sides of a circular parapet. The roof was smooth stone. As he grew nearer to it, he saw what appeared to be a network of fine, dark cracks rippling across the surface. They resolved into a pattern of scales. He couldn't tell if they were painted, or if the tower had actually been carefully assembled from thousands of separate pieces of stone.

He closed his eyes. The image in his mind was nearly complete. He'd filled in the red glow at the windows and now he willed the brush to shift colors. He painted the spider-web-thin cracks. Though he could no longer see the network of stone scales, he brought them to life in his mind.

There was a sickening shift that nearly cost his equilibrium. One moment he was falling, and the next he stood on solid ground. His first instinct was to open his eyes, but he fought it. He had a final line to draw. He bit his lip, steadied his wobbly knees, and drew the brush through the air.

Then he opened his eyes.

The chamber was circular. The walls were convex glass lenses. In the center of the room, too bright to look at directly, sat the largest ruby Salvatore had ever seen. Light shone up from beneath it, caught the carved facets of the jewel, and shot out in all directions. The very air was crimson, like walking through a froth of blood.

He was not alone. Facing one of the windows, seated in a very large, ornate throne, a tall man with long, wavy hair stared out across the city. He sat very still, arms resting on the chair and hands gripping the wood frame tightly.

Salvatore stood before a wrought-iron easel. The white cloth was stretched across it. The painting – the image of the city from above – was complete. Salvatore let his hand fall to his side.

"Is it finished, Sal?" the man asked.

Salvatore's heart nearly stopped. He knew the voice. Now, looking more closely, he saw that he knew the man, as well. It was Snake, and, at the same time, it was not. There were no tattoos on the muscled arms. There were flecks of gray in the dark hair. The man wore a dark red tunic and some sort of robes.

"Senor Snake?"

The man rose slowly and turned.

"No, Salvatore, I am not Snake. Not exactly. You know me, though. You know my brothers. We are connected."

Salvatore dropped to one knee. There was something in the man's expression, something in the tone of his voice that demanded respect. He felt as if he were in the presence of royalty, and he was frightened, but at the same time he was compelled to step forward.

"How…" he asked.

"It is not what you think," the man said. "We have met, you and I, but not like this. I have not spoken with one from your world in … centuries. I never thought to see the skies of that place again, though I have felt the pull. You opened a portal."

"I am an artist," Salvatore said. "The dragons … they haunted my dreams. I had to paint."

"I know," the man said. "I know."

He stepped closer, passed Salvatore, and stood behind the easel. The man stared long and hard at the painting. He reached out as if he would brush his fingers across the surface, but he did not. Instead he let his fingers flutter just above the paint. Salvatore thought, just for a second, that he saw the hint of a tear forming at the corner of the man's eyes. Then the moment passed.

"You must go," he said. "You are not safe here."

"You ... and Senor Snake..."

"Yes," the man said. "We were bound - connected. You and I are bound, as well, and that is the only thing holding the portal closed. My brothers and I...change. Generations pass in your world, and sometimes we bond with those on other planes. It isn't common...and this generation? I believe it is because of you. Once your dreams connected your Dragons with my own, the bonds formed too rapidly to count."

"You are...a dragon?" Salvatore asked.

"I am a dragon, and many other things, Sal. What happened tonight – that hurt me deeply. It's going to take a lot of time to heal. There is at least one of my brothers in the same state – in the blue tower."

"Enrique," Salvatore said softly.

"Yes, but it is different for him. In your world, his spark is gone. In ours, he transferred. They are twins here, now. It has caused an imbalance, but I believe that it will pass. The man you knew as Snake was too far gone to be brought through, but I took the dark one."

"Anya Cabrera?"

"Yes, that is the name she went by on your plane. Here she has bonded, as well, though not with one of us. There are lower things, in the seas, and in the ground. I am certain I have not seen the last of her, but she poses little threat in her current state. In the same manner that drawing us through to your plane increases the energy and power of those we are bonded with, drawing your kind through to us weakens what is here. Having your Anya Cabrera on my plane for the span of her days is a blessing, of sorts."

"But," Salvatore frowned. "I am here. I have not bonded with a dragon."

"You are different. Surely you see? You are bonded with this place. There will always be a connection. It makes you dangerous to us. It makes you dangerous in your own world, as well."

Salvatore took a step back, and the man let loose a thunderous laugh.

"I will not harm you. I only want you to understand – the gift you have is rare and wonderful. Most men – and dragons – never come to understand a single world. You have seen two, and your mind – your art – keeps them alive for you. In my lifetime, there has never been another *Worldwalker*, though I've heard stories."

"That is what I am?" Salvatore asked softly. "A *Worldwalker*?"

"It is your gift. This may not be the only world you will visit. For now, you must go. And you must do something for me."

Salvatore nodded.

The man stepped over to the easel and glanced down at the painting.

"It is a remarkable likeness...exactly as I see it from above. As you have seen it. You must take this back with you, and you must guard it well. Without this, you cannot return – in the wrong hands, another might open the portal. If it is open for too long, it will break. As long as the history of my people stretches, I cannot tell you what might happen if you were to allow this to happen."

"Can't you keep it here?" Salvatore asked. "Safe?"

The man shook his head. "It is of your world. It belongs with you...or your kind. Find a safe place for it. It would be best if its existence were forgotten."

"Can it just be destroyed," Salvatore asked, though he believed he already knew the answer.

"No, it is bonded to this place. I am not certain exactly what might happen if you destroyed it, but it is a likeness of my city..."

The man's voice trailed off for a moment, then he turned to Salvatore with some urgency.

"Roll it up carefully. You must go."

Salvatore carefully rolled the painting and tucked it into his pocket. Somehow, the paint had dried completely in the short time he'd stood in the dragon tower.

"I do not know how to go back," he said.

The man winked at him. Before Salvatore could move to protect himself, he was lifted, carried. One of the windows was not a lens. It stood open to the night, and without another word, the man / dragon tossed Salvatore over the edge. He fell away into the blackness below with a high-pitched, keening wail. Sometime before he struck the ground, his mind went blank. The last thing he saw, winking and strobing in the back of his mind, was the red tower.

Chapter Forty

When Salvatore slumped over the table, Jake slid his hands under him just in time to protect the painting. He lifted the boy as easily as if he'd been an infant, cradled him in his arms, and carried him from the room. Martinez stepped forward and stared down at the tabletop.

"What is it?" Jake asked, returning to stand by his side.

"I'm not sure," Martinez replied.

Jake reached out and ran his finger along the edge of the cloth. He stayed clear of the paint, and the design, though when the tip of his finger neared the green circle, he hesitated, and his expression grew vague. The longer he stared at it, the more certain he became that there was something obvious in the design, something ready to leap to life. The perspective was strange – alien even – but he thought if he stared a little longer, it would all come into focus.

The room wavered slightly as he stared, and he stepped back. The air in the room, which had grown heavy with potential, cleared. Martinez shook his head and stepped back as well.

"It has power," he said. "Like the dragons."

"We can't just leave it here," Jake said. "I don't know what it can do, but if the dragons he painted are any indication..."

Martinez nodded.

"Leave it tonight. I will care for it, and when Salvatore awakens, I will talk to him about what he knows, and what he has seen. When I have learned what I can, I will take him to see Donovan. We will take the painting, as well. If it is safe anywhere, it is safe with Mr. DeChance. He has the finest and most comprehensive collection of magical books and documents in the world. He will protect it."

Jake nodded.

"I guess we owe Sal that," he said. "I don't know what would have happened back in that park without him – or the dragons. I do know that what he did felt at least as dangerous as *Los Escorpiones*, demons or not. It will have to be controlled."

"I think it is time," Martinez said, "that I take on an apprentice. I am an old man, and I have a lot to pass on."

"I hope that we'll see a lot of you," Jake said. His voice nearly broke, but he fought back the emotion. "A lot has happened. I don't know if you heard, or noticed, but I've ended up in charge here. It's a mess."

"You're a good man, Jake," Martinez said. "Snake would have chosen you himself, given the chance. You know that."

"Doesn't make it any easier. And Sally? I don't know much about apprentices, but your place is pretty small. Helen and I... we'd love to have him stay with us..."

"I believe that the boy would love that more than almost anything in this world," Martinez said. "I also believe that, of all of us, he is the only one to see into another. It's a big responsibility. I won't make any more of the paint he used... it's too dangerous...but his gift is what it is. We will have to watch him, you and I. We will have to raise him to be the man he needs to be to wield such responsibility."

Jake laid a hand on Martinez'ss shoulder.

"I hope that you will not be a stranger," he said. "There is a lot of work ahead of me. There are a lot of things that I don't know. Snake was a very strong leader – I'm a little different. I'm going to need advice."

"I will be here when you need me," Martinez said. He smiled. "I'll have to be certain the boy is receiving the proper care and education, after all."

Jake glanced over his shoulder

"Speaking of that, I'd better get back in there. I'm going to sit up with him. I'll catch some sleep in the chair, but I want to be there if he wakes up. I don't think he should be alone."

"Agreed. I will return after sunrise. He'll need to rest, and he'll need to eat. We'll want to start for DeChance's home as soon as possible. I believe he trusts me, but he has good reasons not to. I want this to end as quickly as possible."

"What about *Los Escorpiones*?" Jake asked.

"I don't think we'll hear much from them for a while. I also believe that, if any of Anya Cabrera's people remain, they will remain quiet as well. There is no trace of what she summoned left in The Barrio. I would sense it. Now will be a time of healing on all sides. We must work to make that happen as quickly, and as completely, as possible."

"You can count on it," Jake said, turning. "I've had enough battles and losses for a lifetime."

Martinez watched the big man until he was out of sight. When he was alone, he rolled the painting up carefully and tucked it into a pocket in his jacket. When he was sure it was safely stowed, he returned to the main room of the clubhouse, found an old, leather armchair, and sank back into it – exhausted.

When he closed his eyes, the colored spheres strobed softly, just once. He slept immediately, and deeply. He did not dream.

Chapter Forty-One

Martinez rang the buzzer and was admitted to Donovan's building the next morning around ten. Donovan had been cataloguing a small pile of new manuscripts, preparing them for storage. Amethyst had left about an hour earlier, after staying the night to recuperate. She had her own affairs to sort out, and the past several days had left her with a lot of catching up.

Donovan ushered the old man inside. Salvatore followed more slowly. The boy didn't drop his eyes, as he had during earlier encounters. He met Donovan's gaze levelly and gravely, and he took the offered handshake with a firm grip.

"Good morning, Sal," Donovan said. "You all right this morning?"

"Yes, Sir," he replied. "I am a little tired."

"That was a brave thing you did in the park yesterday," Donovan said. "Most men would have run, given the chance. I'm pretty sure you saved all our lives. I won't forget that."

"I only did what I thought was right. I have always tried to do that. Sometimes, it is hard."

Donovan chuckled.

"You couldn't be more right about that."

He offered the two a seat on the dark brown leather sofa. He brought Martinez strong black coffee, and a glass of sweet iced tea for Salvatore, who took it gratefully. The boy still looked pale, and Donovan saw that his hand shook when he took the drink.

"What happened after I left?" he asked, sitting across from them in a wing-back chair. "Did you paint?"

Salvatore nodded. It took him a moment to form the words in his mind, and he didn't speak in haste. Whatever he was about to say, or explain, it was very important to him.

"I painted the city of the dragons," he said finally. "It is another place – a place I have visited when I paint. It is where I found Senor Snake's dragon, and Jake's."

Donovan didn't reply, but his heart raced. He'd read similar stories in a few of the oldest of his books, but the information was spotty. He wanted to be certain he understood what Salvatore was telling him.

"You mean you had visions of another world?" he asked.

"No, Senor Donovan, I was there. When I painted Senor Snake's dragon, I stood on a beach. There is a city there with walls that stretch to the sky. There was no gate in the wall, at least not that I could find, and there were towers."

"My God," Donovan said.

"It happened more than once," Martinez cut in. "Last night, he spoke with...well, I'd better let Salvatore tell the story. He painted this."

Martinez pulled the rolled painting from his pocket and handed it to Donovan, who unrolled it carefully and flattened it out on his lap. He stared at the colored spheres and the perfectly symmetrical walls for a long time. The image gave him a strange sense of vertigo. Though it was easy to see what Salvatore had painted – the details were eerily clear – it was impossible to reconcile the scene to his understanding of the universe.

There would be no way to enter such towers except from the air. If there were streets, it was impossible to make them out in the deep shadows, and somehow Donovan knew they weren't there. They weren't necessary. What kind of creature didn't need the ground? What would it be like if your entire world existed in, and just beneath, the clouds and the storms?

He rolled the painting carefully and glanced over at Salvatore. The boy watched him carefully, and Donovan got the distinct impression he was being measured in some way. Once the painting was rolled, Donovan rose and carried it carefully to his desk. He grabbed a bit of ribbon, held it up, and breathed on it. He spoke a couple of words so softly they were barely perceptible. He wrapped the ribbon carefully around the painting and tied it in an intricate knot. When he was satisfied it would hold, he turned back to Martinez and Salvatore.

"This is very powerful," he said. "I suspect you know that. Do you know what it is, Sal?"

"The man – the dragon – told me it could be a portal," Salvatore said slowly. "I did not understand everything that he said, but he told me that it must be kept safe. He said that if we destroyed it – it was bound to his city. He did not know what might happen. He told me that I am bound to the painting, and to his world."

Salvatore fell silent for a moment. Donovan was about to break the silence, when the boy spoke again.

"He called me a *Worldwalker.*"

Donovan grew very still. Martinez didn't react, but Donovan suspected that he'd already heard this story, and was better prepared.

"*Worldwalker,*" Donovan said softly. "So it's true."

Salvatore looked confused. Donovan walked over and squatted, so that the two of them were eye to eye.

"I have documents here," he said, "that speak of *Worldwalkers.* The references are very rare, and the information that remains reads more like legend than fact. To my knowledge, there have been three *Worldwalkers* in the history of our world. You would be the fourth. It is an awesome responsibility…and an amazing gift. Do you understand that?"

Salvatore nodded. "The dragon, he told me there might be other worlds. That I might paint other portals."

"If you do," Donovan said, "you must promise me that you will not do so alone, and that you will prepare properly. There are ways to protect yourself, and those around you. There are ways to seal such a portal. Martinez can help you – and I will be honored to help, as well, if I am needed.

"I don't know if Martinez has explained what I do. I have been gathering books and manuscripts, documents and secrets – and archiving them. When I began, I had books and shelves and paper. Now I use computers, and technology, which are a kind of magic themselves. It is important to know as much as we can about things of power. Much has been learned, forgotten, and relearned over the years. I am trying to provide …stability."

"I told him you'd be the one to hold the painting," Martinez said. "If there is a place in this world where such a thing could be considered safe, it is in your hands."

Donovan stood up and nodded.

"I don't know if I deserve such confidence," he said, "but I will do my best to store this safely. I will hold it…for you, Salvatore. I can sense it's power, but I believe that it is your gift to make connections. You made the connections between Snake, and his dragon, and it allowed you to open a portal between worlds. Your art is an extension of your ability to take something from the world – or from your mind – and bind it to whatever surface you work on. It is a rare gift.

"Some famous artists have shared it in a weaker version. They could trap images and amaze the world, but it never went beyond that. A few went mad from the visions their work brought them."

At that moment, Cleo, tired of being ignored, scampered across the floor and hopped up onto Salvatore's lap. The cat rubbed its head against the boys chest. After the momentary shock of the animal's sudden appearance had passed, he reached down and scratched Cleo's ears.

Energy shifted in the air. Salvatore turned his gaze on Donovan, and it seemed as if he saw something far away – something beyond Donovan in the distance. Cleo let out a plaintive meow, arched her back, and head butted Salvatore gently, breaking the boy's concentration.

"You – and the cat – you are connected," Salvatore said. "I would not paint a dragon for you – it would be a cat. And…a crow?"

Donovan stared down at his familiar, and the young artist, and then glanced over at Martinez.

"No cats," he said. "Promise me he will paint no cats. And I don't even want to know about crows."

Martinez laughed then, and the sound broke the tension in the room.

"I think it will be a long time before I paint again," Salvatore said. "I will stick to drawing with charcoal and chalk. I slept well last night for the first time since the dragons invaded my dreams. I am very tired, and I have a lot to learn. Also, Senor Jake and his lady, Helen, want me to start in school."

The boy's smile was bright, and innocent, and Donovan reached out to ruffle his hair.

"I'm sure you'll do very well in school," he said. "Jake is a good man. You tell him Amethyst and I will stop by to visit soon."

Martinez rose, and Salvatore, after he managed to get Cleo to step off onto the sofa, did the same.

"It has been ... interesting," Martinez said. He offered Donovan his hand.

As they shook, Donovan nodded.

"I will check in on Anya Cabrera's people," he said. "When I know what the situation is, we'll talk again."

"I look forward to it," Martinez said.

Salvatore was saying goodbye to Cleo, scratching gently behind her ears. The two men watched him for a moment, then Donovan lowered his voice.

"Take good care of him, Martinez. That one...he may be the most powerful of us all one day."

Martinez nodded. "I think you are right. One thing Snake said was true. That one has the heart of a dragon – and he has walked in their world. There is no telling what he might do."

Salvatore glanced up, as if he knew they were talking about him, and smiled. Donovan shook his hand as well, and then he showed the two of them out. When the door had closed behind them, he went to his desk and pulled out a metal tube. He tucked the painting into it carefully, then sealed the end with a black cap. Once it was secure, he breathed on the cap and repeated the incantation he'd used on the ribbon.

He walked to the left hand shelf of the center cabinet of his library and gripped the fourth book from the right on the bottom shelf. The entire unit slid out. Behind it was a safe door. He carefully worked the combinations on the three locks securing it, and the door swung open. Inside was a solid block of black stone – obsidian – with round holes drilled into it. He tucked the tube into one of the slots. About half of them were already filled with similar tubes. The painting slid in easily. Donovan closed and sealed the door and swung the shelf back into place.

With a sigh, he turned away. The image of the city and it's colored spheres pulsed in the back of his mind. He shook his head to clear it, walked to his bar, and poured two fingers of strong brandy, which he carried back to his desk. Cleo jumped up beside the pile of documents he'd been cataloguing.

Donovan ruffled the cats fur and gazed into her eyes.

"You know, don't you?" he asked. "You know what he would paint, and what he would see."

Cleo didn't answer. She sat back on her haunches and began washing her forepaw as if bored.

Donovan chuckled and went back to work. He knew he'd have to start researching soon. He had to gather all the references on *Worldwalkers* he could find and get them to Martinez. Something told him he had not heard the last of Salvatore Domingo Sanchez.

He wondered what it would be like to talk to a dragon.

About the Author

David Niall Wilson has been writing and publishing horror, dark fantasy, and science fiction since the mid-eighties. An ordained minister, once President of the Horror Writers Association and multiple recipient of the Bram Stoker Award, his novels include Maelstrom, *The Mote in Andrea's Eye, Deep Blue,* the Grails Covenant Trilogy, *Star Trek Voyager: Chrysalis, Except You Go Through Shadow, This is My Blood, Ancient Eyes, On the Third Day, The Orffyreus Wheel,* The DeChance Chronicles, including *Heart of a Dragon, Vintage Soul, My Soul to Keep, Kali's Tale* and the stand-alone spinoff *Nevermore – A Novel of Love, Loss & Edgar Allan Poe.* His novels in the O.C.L.T. series include *The Parting, Crockatiel,* and the novella *The Temple of Camazotz* .He is also the author of the memoir / cookbook *American Pies: Baking with Dave the Pie Guy.* David can be found at: www.davidniallwilson.com and can be reached by e-mail at david@davidniallwilson.com .

Curious about other Crossroad Press books?
Stop by our site:
http://store.crossroadpress.com
We offer quality writing
in digital, audio, and print formats.

Enter the code FIRSTBOOK
to get 20% off your first order from our store!
Stop by today!